C0-AWA-400

Padrec stood as if frozen when Anii walked toward him, her red garments sliding from her as she cast them aside. What was she doing? No . . . she was alien . . . she could not be thinking of *that*! It wasn't human, the very thought unnatural . . . but he felt it begin, now within himself as well, as though her naked, glowing beauty had robbed him of all will and his body betrayed him, his knees going weak and not obeying the screaming voice in his mind that urged him to flee. *Oh, no, this can't be happening, isn't happening* . . . But in his nostrils he caught a faint trace of the sweet musky scent that had followed him in the forests . . . *Oh, God, no*—he shook his head and tried to back away from her. But it was too late, had been too late from the first moment she had touched him.

LINDA STEELE writes of this, her first novel:

"*Ibis* is a science-fiction romance, a love story between a human man from a crashed Terran research vessel and a female from the native, and very different, human species. The humans are stranded and the native society at first sees no need to absorb them—until they discover that human males, unlike their own, do not die upon mating. This leads to a direct confrontation between a human society struggling to preserve its own integrity and survival, and the native society which has found a use for the Strangers in their midst, embodied in two characters who learn to love each other despite, and perhaps because of, their differences."

LINDA STEELE

IBIS

DAW BOOKS, INC.
DONALD A. WOLLHEIM, PUBLISHER
1633 Broadway, New York, NY 10019

Copyright © 1985, by Linda Steele Uzquiano

All Rights Reserved.

Cover art by J. Chiodo.

DAW Collectors' Book No. 644

DEDICATION
To my husband Jorge—who made it possible.

First Printing, September 1985

1 2 3 4 5 6 7 8 9

Printed in U.S.A.

Anii told herself that it was silly and perhaps dangerous to spy upon the Strangers, but she could not help herself. The strong call of mating sand in her blood and the urge to repeat what she had seen before burned with an almost physical pain within her. More and more of late she had stolen away from her companions to catch a glimpse of their strange tall bodies mysteriously concealed by layers of shining cloth which her active mind had taken to stripping away. Shining cloth like their vessel which had fallen from the sky, white and shining and clean. Pressing herself flat in the long cool grass that brushed her long limbs with a folding caress, Anii crept over the lip of the ridge to get a clear view of the place where the newcomers had fallen.

As ever on a clear day with much sun, they stood many about their strange habitation, working, talking, organizing. In many respects, they appeared to serve a nom. As she became more familiar with their habits through observation, she discerned a definite, well-organized social behavior in which every individual served a defined function. For some she had not yet discovered the nature of the function, but she had come to recognize many by the jobs they performed. There was the tall gray-haired male who appeared to command the others, although this she did not understand; and the dark-haired male who liked plants; and an older female who might be a healer, for she had been seen bandaging an injured limb for one of her fellows, a female with the short hair of a worker, who had not gone on any of the expeditions beyond the clearing, but had stayed with the ship, in the company of several males, whom she directed in the tending of the great grounded thing Anii had begun to think had never flown, or at least would never fly again. That female alone had shown any true leadership. For some reason, buried among their other strangeness, males were often dominant among the Strangers. Never had she seen such a thing.

What a shame we are going to destroy them, Anii thought briefly, but they are too different. They could not live here with us, they depart from the natural order. D'nia is wise; she foresees a conflict. And yet, look how they work—.

A pair she had watched for weeks moved away from the others, the female touching the male to lead him away from the nom that had flown and into the forest edge beyond. Drawn by them as before, Anii crept back down the rise and returned to the protective overshadowing of the forest, making her way to follow. There was not much to explore on that side of the alien nom, a densely forested low valley and a little lake, the tall mountains beyond; the plain and the lands ruled by the noms lay in the other direction, and it was there the Strangers were most inclined to travel. Her keen olfactory sense picked up their scent near the forest edge where the odor upon the known path was alien and strong. The smell of the female was faintly musky, that of the male more rank. She followed that spoor as far as the little lake, where she halted, hearing their laughter. This, too, was strange to her, a sound so unreal she had at first thought the maker to be in distress, until others of the female's kind had joined in and it had become clear that the exchange was not threatening. Not distress, then, but something else—and it was not yet clear to her what that might be. Otherwise, their speech followed a pleasing, even melodious, tonality.

She found them on the shore of the lake, where they had shed their garments into twin piles of white on the sand and now stood upon the rocky beach, both wet and dripping after having come from the water. Creeping under the lowest, densest branches nearest the shore, Anii watched the unfolding dance, rapt

with barely suppressed wonder. The female moved
slowly and gracefully, twining her pale limbs about
the male, pressing their bodies together. The darker
male, eager for her, took her to him. This was the
second time she had seen the Strangers unclothed,
clasped in the mating rites. How strange, she thought,
they resemble the nomari! Her own people looked so
in the female and male forms, the female curved and
supple, the male equally equipped when aroused, in
every part like a drone. . . . Heat flooded her mating
parts, her color heightened as the male pulled the
female to him and gently laid his mouth over hers,
made motions with his tongue as she submitted. This,
Anii could not understand. How could she let him do
that? No queen would ever submit to a drone—! And
why did she court him so if she did not intend to draw
him down? Or was it that she had not yet come into
her nuptial phase and wished to save him until her
circumstances were more sure?

Voices hailed from the surrounding forest, calling,
coming nearer. The mating pair broke apart, the male
flushed with agitation as they quickly retrieved their
garments, jerking them on in great hurry. Retreating
back into the shadows, Anii hid herself in the undergrowth. To come so near the Strangers was forbidden.
They had readily captured the first warriors who came
to spy on them.

Other humans came from the forest surrounding
the blue lake, two females and three males, making
the strange noises upon discovering their companions'
disorder. All was done with much baring of teeth, a
gesture her observations led her to believe indicated
nonaggression. Among them was another she had
watched for many weeks, the graceful dark-haired
male she had followed in the forests, watching from
behind the trees as he gathered rza'li blossoms from
the high branches where one misstep could have sent
him falling, broken, to the forest floor. But he was
nimble and strong, and he had returned with the
misty flowers, and had stroked their delicate petals

with wonder, his face softly musing while she watched unseen, her own skin quivering like that of the flower surely must. She had wanted to go to him and show him where the nectar was. But he, too, would die when the warriors swarmed upon the fallen ones.

Reluctantly, for the shadows were growing long-toothed with sun, she left them and, keeping hidden until she was well beyond the ridges and the Strangers' detection, circled back across the glowering plain to the nom.

The nom stood in the midst of the plain, a great ziggurat of concentric circles, terraces upon terraces, commanding all around it. Within the deep, inner circle lived the Queen, secure, surrounded by her warriors, organizing and overseeing the lives of her nom. For the nom was also a social unit, with many subordinate reproductive females and subservients, and a worker hierarchy of exquisite complexity. In all, many tens of thousands of warriors and workers lived in the nom, with a great many more if the outlying colonies were included. And D'nia's nom was the largest and most dominant on Mi. Anii was one of D'nia's ranking daughters, a young queen but yet virgin. During the last mating, she had been mature but had not found a drone to mate with. Drones were valuable breeding stock, closely held and hard to come by. D'nia occasionally allowed her ranking daughters to mate with drones from the home nom, after which the newly pregnant queens were allowed to leave the nom to found colonies which added to the number and prestige of D'nia's domains. Anii could hardly hope for this. The other alternative, and one with scant chance for success, was to raid another, hostile nom for one or more of its drones. This could only be done during the nuptial phase, when the pheromones of the fertile female would draw the males willingly to her; only then was there any chance of a drone being willing or able to leave his sedentary, almost parasitic existence. The chief danger was that warriors guarding the nom would be alert to the theft, with the result that the thieving queen would then be swarmed to death. Anii had lost two birthing-sisters to that fate.

As Anii approached the nom, the bronze-skinned, guarding warriors parted to let her pass. She was a ranking female, second in status only to the Queen, different in form and feature from the elegant warriors or stocky workers who moved about the nom in perpetual, perfect hurry. She made her way through endless upward corridors to her quarters, only to be met there by Hli.

"You avoided your companions again," Hli reprimanded, following her into her many-chambered living quarters. "Have you lost your mind? Do you wish to be captured by the warriors of a queenless nom from across the mountains, forced to bear but not to delegate?"

Anii shuddered. It was the one fate that had kept her from going more often to observe the Strangers, the chance that she might be captured by the renegade warriors of a nom that had lost its queen. A secondary female, capable only of reproducing workers, usually ran such a nom, and the new queen would only serve as receptacle to whatever drone was presented her—if one even was. It was possible, though uncommon and not preferred, for a queen to reproduce without a male. The resulting offspring were female and inferior and for that reason a queen usually left the making of workers to such females. Only a true queen could give birth to both male and female offspring, and warriors as well.

"My apologies, that I have caused you concern, Hli," she said sincerely, for the older subservient's attention had always been directed to her best interests. "But it is not to be helped. I find them interesting."

"The Strangers?" Hli's lined forehead fairly furrowed with disapproval.

"I enjoy watching them work. They are much like us."

"They are not much like us. D'nia has seen them, we are told; she watched them when the warriors showed them the nom. She has spied upon their place. They are very different."

"Not to look at them. She should have received them herself, not left them to the warriors. They look very like us—their drones are bigger, sturdier, of course, and they seem to lack subordinate classes in their females. Even their hierarchy lacks distinction. But to look at them—Hli, would there be any way we could use them? Perhaps we are too quick to destroy them."

Hli wrinkled her nose in disgust. "Use them for what? They are ruled by drones too ugly to mate, though it seems they are intelligent. It has occurred to me we could use a little of that in our own males." The sad fact was that Misian drones were as stupid as they were necessary and, as they were good for nothing, it was just as well they died with the mating. "And D'nia has judged their females too intelligent to serve as workers, and too independent to make good warriors."

"But the things they must have seen, the things they must know—the nom that fell from the daytime sky, it is said—surely there is much that they could teach us."

"This has been discussed. They will not. But they will disrupt our lives, our social order, as they seek to advance themselves. D'nia is right."

Deep in her heart, Anii had the impertinence to doubt this.

After allowing Hli to groom her and drape her and anoint her silken skin with scent, Anii reclined before her mirror to consider her plans. She was near mating. It was imperative that she find a male to mate with. She could not bear the thought of another mating season like the last, rather would she have thirst without water than lust without surcease. Already she was taking on the heightened color of the nuptial stage; soon she would become aggressive, ready to kill to procure a mate. D'nia, of course, would relinquish none of her own. The nom had undergone a reduction the season before, giving up a third of its population to queens D'nia had allowed to emigrate. She would not do so again this season. That meant Anii would have to seek out a drone from some other nom if she hoped to satisfy the mating heat.

Or be satisfied with no drone at all. No drone of her own, to die in her arms in the sweet bliss of mating. For she had heard it was bliss, that her body's formless urgings were but a prelude to that which the queens called the highest of bodily pleasures. There had been a queen once, many ages ago, it was told, who had used her drones solely for the pleasure of it, one every night, and each night one died in her arms— but she had destroyed her nom by doing so, for in her madness she was left with no drones for the mating. And so the nom, droneless and unable to procur another, was left queenless when she died. Such a thing still happened from time to time, and occasionally in war some captive drones were used for pleasure, if there were many of them, but using the drones of one's own nom for pleasure was forbidden by all noms which hoped to prosper.

Anii rose and stood, clothed in queenly gossamer before her golden mirror, feeling again those vague yet strong urgings that had wakened while she had watched the Strangers in their twinings. *They are much like us*, she thought again. *They, too, are not as the other creatures of Mi. Our bodies are the same.* She too had breasts for the nurturing of her young, those glands which produced the special food that nourished the immature form into a young queen. Her two legs were also long, her body also slim waisted and shapely. The Strangers had indicated to the captured warriors that they were of the same ancestral race, that some ancient race had seeded many places with the ancestors of the Strangers and the nomari. As great as the differences between these species might be, the similarities could not be avoided. She cupped her breasts and stroked the taut smooth curve of her hip, wondering if it was possible. . . .

Padrec Morrissey had never seen Earth, except in travelogues and still transparencies filed in the ship's library banks. But he thought that Ibis 2 must have been spun from the same barrelling glob of space debris. The chemical structure was very similar, the gravity almost identical, the atmosphere rich in oxygen and more or less the same, the plant life less so but as lush and abundant as that he liked to think old Terra had once harbored. Botany had been his passion ever since he had first wandered into the greenhouse of the colony ship carrying him and his parents from Ferro 4V to Cygna 7. His father, a hygroculturalist who specialized in setting up new installations among the colonies, had hoped for his son to go into the study of agriculture, a looming field in the rapidly expanding space program. But Padrec had opted for exotic botany, loving plants as he did for their miraculous structure and myriad forms, both practical and extravagant; an orchid thrilled him as much as a corn plant, and where a colonial horticulturalist would have for the most part dealt in the latter, he had wanted to keep in touch with the former as well. So he had transferred into the Planetary Exploration Service and taken his training in xeno-botany. Not for a moment had he regretted it. This was his third planet, but only his first crash landing.

No one knew for certain what had happened. That great brooding sun, deep gold and glowering, was Ibis, which was where they were *supposed* to be. But upon approaching the distant star cluster, just coming out of hyperdrive, something had gone wrong. The huge interstellar research vessel, with its many scientific crews and support personnel, had encountered a maelstrom of distortion, a shattering of light and sound

and senses, an instant without life or breath or anything. No one knew how many had died as parts of the
ship had buckled under the strain—very few even
remembered landing. One of the navigators, Padrec
later learned, had taken a reading confirming Ibis
before the crash. Captain Leveso thought they had
encountered an uncharted energy warp, one of those
strange ripples in space only now becoming known as
actual entities. There were hopes that in the future
such warps would help give starships a boost across
even vaster areas than they had already explored, but
that was theory at best. And the crash of the research
ship was fact, because whatever it was had killed the
drives and nearly all other ship's systems, and structural damage had cost the lives of fully half the several hundred personnel. At least the planet on which
they had landed had been listed by earlier probe spec-
trometry as Class M, suitable for human life. And
other life as well.

"The natives are restless," observed Samuro Toroya,
setting down his dinner tray, wedging himself between Padrec and Communications Officer Lara Brown.
"More than the usual activity at the hive."

They called it that, the "hive," mostly because it
looked like one, but also because its denizens showed
a highly organized societal behavior very like that of
certain Terran insects. Especially sexually, the local
sentient race had demonstrated a gross deviation from
the mammalian norm. And the Ibisians were not only
sentient, but strangely human. A few had been captured, and tests run upon them, proving that they had
evolved from the same human prototype that had pep-
pered the galaxy in eons past, leaving behind popula-
tions that were essentially, even disappointingly,
human. After a few brief contacts, however, the Ibisians
had become elusive, going about their own business
and staying far clear of the landing site, but surveillance equipment aboard the ship kept track of any
large-scale comings and goings, just to be safe.

"There've been a few lurking around here lately, I

know," said Penny Carmeyez, the ship's chief engineer, voicing what most already knew. "I spotted some of them on the ridge the other day."

"Spies," said Padrec offhandedly, "they're as curious about us as we are about them."

Carmeyez frowned at him. "I shouldn't wonder. Wandering around the planet the way you do, I'm surprised they haven't picked you up for vivisection."

"Lay off him, Pen, it's his job," Toroya said. "You have the nasty habit of falling into the same mood as your screwed up drives."

"They were damaged, Sam, and I'm doing the best I can. But pardon me if I find it next to impossible to work on grav drives and pod hulls when there are hostile life forms looking over my shoulder!"

"If they were hostile, they'd have let us know it before now," said Lara Brown, folding her tray and rising from her place. She smiled brightly at the others. "Excuse me," she said, "Time to retrieve the signal. I keep hoping that one of these turns I'll get an answer."

They watched her walk away. "I wish to hell someone would answer," one of the technicians said.

"Exploratory Service motto," intoned Toroya, "If you run into trouble, you're on your own."

"Then why the hell give us the beacon—"

"If you've got a long shot, take it?" Padrec suggested. He did not yet consider their situation hopeless.

"I'll give you a long shot," snapped Penny Carmeyez, glaring at him. The young man's constant optimism had long since gotten on her nerves. "How long do you think it will take before the Ibisians try to run us off this godforsaken planet?"

It was the same conversation the crew fell into at every meal, every gathering, although lately there had been breaks in that pattern, a sort of unconscious acceptance of their situation. They had been lucky to land with as little loss of life as they had, lucky to find a flat place, lucky to have plowed into soft earth instead of the side of some mountain. At the speed they had been coming ... the two Research shuttles with geo-laboratories and marine divisions had been jettisoned within the planet's gravity and their smaller drives, inactive at the time the warp had been encountered, had enabled them to land safely on one of the sub-continents. But the main body of the ship had slammed into the plain. . . .

That had been six standard weeks ago. The crash had decimated the survivors, claiming Padrec's senior officer and a good many of the bridge and engineering crews. Many more had been injured, but the synthesizer had been spared, as had the core facilities, the hospital and most of the labs. All in all, chances of getting off the planet looked excellent. Even if they could not get off again on their own, PES would send a rescue expedition after them ... wouldn't they? Why hadn't they responded?

Maybe the satellite was damaged ... maybe they aren't getting the signals ... Those were the thoughts plaguing every mind, crushing them under, not knowing for sure if there was to be any rescue.

Folding his mostly uneaten meal into his tray, Patrick carried it back to the synthesizer, which would recycle the remains and add them to his next meal, fresh on his tray when the rations were served. It was a neat system, and efficient, but recently he had taken to supplementing his diet with edible fruits from his forays into the surrounding forests, choosing only those species which exhaustive analysis had found perfectly safe for human consumption. Often, just before biting into the sweet pulpy flesh of a fruit, he would wonder about the Ibisian diet, whether it was supplemented by plant protein or animal, fruit or meat. He had ventured as far as the northern fringe of the desert abutting the inhabited plain without finding signs of cultivation. But that meant little, since the natives seemed to live in concentrated enclaves and he seldom strayed near their habitations. Samuro Toroya, with his advanced training in xeno-biology, was in a better position to discover the answer to any questions he might have about the Ibisians.

"Since they are basically human, they are likely to be omnivorous, although variations along several extremes have been discovered in numerous other subspecies," the slender scientist had told him during an exchange session, when the two had matched notes on the planet's myriad life forms, sorting out those best suited for further study. Edible plants had been high on the list, for practical reasons. "But Ibis 2, as you have pointed out, is a botantist's garden of specimens—and, in many ways, it is a zoological desert."

"Not if you're an entomologist," Padrec had offered. Insects abounded on Ibis and he had had ample opportunity to fall astray of a vast variety of the creatures, several times returning to base with nasty bites and specimens in hand in case an antidote was needed.

"Well, yes—and we have found a few aquatic forms. Crustaceans, mollusks and the like. But no vertebrates. Except for the Ibisians."

"So they probably eat vegetable protein and insects?"

"It sounds good. The ones we first captured refused to eat anything. Analysis of stomach and bowel contents was inconclusive. We have yet to witness actual feeding. But, unless they're cannibals, I do not think we need to fear that they will develop an urge to sample us. Warm meat is beyond their experience. Care to try some of my insect parts? This blue arachnid might be tasty—"

"*You* perfect the recipe, I'll dish up the other courses." Padrec was not at all sure if Toroya was serious behind that inscrutable smile. Some Ibisian insects grew to be very large, even meaty after a fashion, and were being investigated no less intensely than the plants for edibility when the synthesizer could no longer function.

"You know," Toroya had said a short while later as they compiled the necessary data onto slides for field reference, "The Ibisians are an interesting society."

"Human?"

"Yes, and no. I wish we could get closer to them, study them more. Did you notice the ones we captured? They were neuter."

"Neuter?" Padrec had looked up, intrigued, though he had heard rumor of it. He had seen the Ibisians, out of curiousity, the day they had been captured. He remembered them as humanoid, bronzed and pale-eyed, small beside the taller humans.

"No gender," Toroya explained, "Or rather, they were chromosonal mosaics, females lacking sex organs. Absolutely incapable of reproduction. But I suspect that when we know them better, we will find that they have a few true females for reproduction—and perhaps males as well."

Padrec had returned to his botanical files. "That doesn't sound very human to me."

"It isn't. But they are. Human genotype: tissue analysis proved it. *Homo sapiens ibisian*—human genes all the way down the line except for certain sexual and endocrine mutations. Human skin, human blood chemistry, human nervous system. The only mammals on the planet. They certainly did not evolve here. Fascinating."

"Scary, if you ask me."

"The prototype appears to have had a penchant for such things," the xenobiologist had mused with a crooked smile, "Some planets are veritable experiments in human variation. This could be one of them."

Padrec had looked at him then, astonished. "You don't want to stay, do you?"

"Oh, not under these circumstances. But I might want to come back."

That was when Padrec had whispered, for the first time and half to himself, "So might I." For him to classify the planetary phytology would be a life's work. He could see that Toroya understood.

"You've never run into any Ibisians in the field, have you?" the older scientist had asked, looking hopeful.

"No." Padrec had hated to disappoint him, but it

was nothing less than the truth. "Sometimes on the plain I see a few in the distance, those giant insects they herd. But when they see me they keep their distance. And I don't go near that place of theirs."

"The nom." Toroya had smiled, then, with a sort of remembered triumph. It was the dream of every xenobiologist to be the first to contact another race, an alien society, to discover the key that would unlock its secrets. Soon after the crash landing, Toroya and an assistant had attempted to make contact with the Ibisians, and they had been taken to and shown the hive. The Ibisians had been disturbed by their study of them, however, and soon thereafter had isolated the Terrans and shown themselves to be uninterested in further contact. "That's their word for it. The *nom*."

"What's this?" Padrec had laughed a bit uneasily. "Are we going to try speaking to them next?" It was something he found quite foreign, since plant intelligence rarely lent itself to conversation.

The scientist had answered quietly. "That all depends, doesn't it, on whether or not they have anything to say to us."

So far it had not happened. And Padrec had not sat in on most of the discussions which followed, preferring his own work in the botanical section, where talk of aliens did not detract from his own discoveries and dismembered corpses did not litter the tables. Zoological dissection struck him as rather more gruesome than botanical mounting. He was more at home with his plants, surrounded by species charts and specimen screens, and a rare whole specimen, a huge blossom he had mounted in a support substrate, its wonderful purple shadings alternately velvety and diaphanous as the beautifully ruffled petals cupped a flowing head of nodding anthers aglow with a soft silver sheen in the overhead light. It was an epiphyte he had seen growing high in the trees, dangling from the tallest branches in floral clusters, draping the trees with color. It had nearly cost him his life to gather one by the roots so that he could have it to look at while he

did his work. A lingering perfume, indescribable, filled
the room, deepening as one drew near. Ibis, he thought,
gently touching those petals as he was so often compelled to do, what a beautiful planet. So full of life. If
only they could get off, he would feel so much better
about it. Tomorrow, perhaps, he would avoid the plains,
the Ibisian problem, and instead take a jog to the high
meadows . . .

There was something about the air of this place.
Every so often he would catch a fleeting scent of something that would bring his head up, compelling him to
heed, to search, but not yet had he discovered what he
was searching for.

"The strangers are to be destroyed," Hli told her as the sun filled her chamber with light, bathed its lovely golden objects with beauty. "D'nia has decided."

Anii had expected to hear nothing less, but the verdict displeased her. It was too soon. "We are mistaken to destroy them so quickly. There is much we do not know."

"Do you doubt D'nia's wisdom in this?"

Was that not the reason a reproductive female was gifted with intelligence, to lead the nom for which she reproduced? The offspring she had engendered? And did not the most intelligent, the most aggressive, triumph over her challengers to become Queen? D'nia must be obeyed by those who would not overthrow her.

"D'nia will prevail," Anii told her chaperone, "I but mourn the necessity. These Strangers have not harmed us. The warriors they captured they set free. And they have not trespassed near the nom since the passing of the third moon, nor have they threatened our herd grounds."

"I do not think they have found them. They will ruin us. They are too strange."

"And aren't you even curious?"

"No." Hli's orange eyes narrowed. "You are too near to mating. The nuptial heat muddles your brain. D'nia agrees. Soon you must leave the nom."

It was nothing more than the standard rule. Only the ruling queen could mate within the nom, and a young female in full nuptial heat, whose presence could unsettle the queen and entice the drones, was not to be endured. It was therefore the custom for a young female to be absent from the nom during the height of her sexual phase. Since this was also the phase in which she was most likely to be waylaid by the warriors of a hostile nom, her seclusion was imperative. For this reason, Anii, like all young queens, had constructed her nuptial lodge in preparation. But the urge to seek out a possible mate often overpowered the known danger of wandering afield. Anii could feel in herself the mating call that would soon rule all that she did or thought or attempted. Last time had been but a pale foreshadowing of the taut swirl that seized her now. Soon she must be allowed to mate, or be driven from the nom in search of one, or possibly, as was often done, killed by a ruling queen who knew which aggressive young queens posed a threat to her power.

"I will obey," Anii said, gesturing submission.

"Large numbers are leaving the hive," the systems operator told a worried, gray-haired Captain Leveso. "It looks like a swarm." He indicated the movement on the sensor screen. A readout of actual numbers ran into the tens of thousands.

"My God—!"

"Just like damned insects."

"Get Toroya. Brown, have you contacted the geo-team?"

Communications Officer Brown turned her pale eyes on him, but her voice was crisp and sure. This man had brought them to safety from space. Surely he could do as much again. "They are due to contact us in three solar days to feed data through the main banks. They have only limited fuel for their sleds but say they can sabotage the shuttles for more if needed. Should I contact them, Sir?"

"No." Leveso made that painful decision. "If I know that madman Rubinsky, he would try to reach us. At least they will be safe where they are." His brow furrowed and he asked, more evenly, "Any others out there?"

Calling up the records, Lara Brown nodded. "A few field teams. Meeno Ree and a meteorology team on the south plain. Sal Lonnaghan has two people out plotting possible settlement options. And Padrec Morrissey took out a sled this morning."

"Another of his plant gathering forays?"

"I think so. He said he was going to the mountains for a few days."

"Good, did he take anyone with him?" Though he had never openly said as much, Leveso had taken a liking to the young botanist. Not only was he hard-working and eminently likable, but Morrissey's boundless activity had often seemed to belie the trouble they were in.

"A scanner technician, let's see . . . Ranwood Hayes."

"Okay, leave them alone, monitor their communications for signs they want to come back and then warn them away. Call the others in, they may get caught and we may need the sleds." Leveso turned back to the systems operator. "How long do you estimate we have?" When the man had told him, the Captain sighed and uttered a muffled curse, "With those numbers it won't make a hell of a lot of difference what we do."

They saw the smoke from afar, a billowing thick cloud of burning polyplastics, a lower layer of gray-blue chemical haze, none of the dark smokes usually thrown up by burning fossil fuels or wood. On a backward planet it was all terribly wrong.

"The ship!" Hayes, the scanner technician, shouted.

Padrec took over the controls as the sled swerved dangerously beneath the stunned technician's unsteady hands. He guided to a stop on the crest of a spur ridge of the mountains overlooking the broad sweep of plain where the ship had crash-landed. Across the golden haze of grassland, the smoke stood forth like a beacon. For a long moment, the two of them simply stood mutely on the sled, gaping. Then Padrec said, in a tight, thin voice, "If it's the ship, we'd better get back."

They had kept in touch. Lara Brown had received each call at sunset, the appointed hour for routine daily field communications, had answered easily, had not indicated that anything was amiss. But now that he thought back, the conversation had been stilted and short. At the time, he had thought nothing of it. *They were having trouble, and they wanted us to stay away*! His first thought was that the ship had taken a system short and caught fire, but in the back of his mind he could still hear Penny Carmeyez calling the Ibisians hostile. His heart pounded with a growing, sickening fear.

The sled was fast, but not fast enough. It skimmed surfaces and had to be guided carefully where the land sloped sharply as it did on these mountain spurs and ridges; the sled was strictly a terrain vehicle—they could not simply shoot it off the edge and hope it would function as a glider. Only when they reached the plain did they make good speed. It was late afternoon, the swollen dark gold sun of Ibis hanging upon the jagged landscape by a thread as they came to the landing site. The ship lay before them, vast and sprawling, its white hull cracked open, Ibisians crawling over and into it. The clearing surrounding the landing site was piled with the thousands of corpses that it had taken to overload the defense shield. Within that circle, some of the corpses were regulation grays. "Oh, God! Oh, God!" Hayes cried, unable to stand the sight as he slumped to the floor of the sled, shrieking uselessly, while Padrec, knowing that the greater danger was to stay, sharply turned the vehicle aside and powered it to maximum altitude to avoid the trees, fleeing the swarming carnage below. It could have been ants devouring a beetle carcass, swarming it—. The fighting was long done; what they had come upon was plainly the aftermath. A sudden barrage of boulders, some nearly as big as the sled, hurled by ground-based catapults, shot past the sled's nose and Padrec dodged the machine lower, barely skimming the treetops, but too late. Another barrage catapulted after the first slammed into the underside of the sled, hurling him from the controls and hard against the side railing as the vehicle got away from him and careened with a sickening rush to the forest floor.

Padrec awoke some time later, vaguely aware of noises puncturing his hazy consciousness. Blood from a cut matted his hair and dripped in sticky rivulets to earth. He was sprawled in a thicket, damp moldering leaves clinging to his hands, and clothing, indicating that he had rolled down the matted incline that reared above him. Umbrels of leaves hung down, stems snapped, dangling after having broken his fall and, quite possibly, saved his life. The sled, or its remains, were nowhere in sight, but memory of the crash, and the reasons for it, tore at his mind. He must have been thrown from the sled as it spiraled out of control—he had heard it crashing, breaking up. Like something out of the nightmare from which he had just awakened, a horrible thin wail rose from the trees surrounding him, a mad cacophony of hoots and shrill whistles following in its wake. Taking great pains to be quiet, Padrec pulled his bruised body through the dense undergrowth and peeked out over the edge of the hollow he had fallen into. The sun splashed its last blood-amber rays of day through the trees, touching the jerking movements of a man. It was Hayes. The scanner tech was stumbling, dragging a leg as he limped from tree to tree, crying out wildly in pain and mindless terror. Several humanoid figures pursued him, slender, sexless figures, their bronze skins shining in the last sunlight, jabbing at their prey with the long curved metal tips of their spears, sawing at his limbs. Hayes shrieked in agony as one of the spears caught his hand and severed fingers dropped uselessly to the forest floor in thin spurts of blood. Blindly, Padrec reached for his belt, seeking the laser weapon he sometimes carried, only to remember that he had left his weapon in the sled. And he could see that Hayes' belt was also empty. Neither of them had expected what they found. And the man could not run from what had found him; his leg was broken through, and his hands were half severed, his throat pierced. He simply had not died yet.

Padrec choked and buried his face in the decaying plant matter, unable to watch. He knew that there was no use in trying to save Hayes, even if he had had the training, the skill. But his heart was sick that he did not dare try, that his own life, until now held so lightly, suddenly was not a thing to be lost. As if it mattered. He only knew that it did. And he did not want to hear it, couldn't bear to see, couldn't . . . *I'm a coward, a craven coward. I don't want to die* . . . A single scream punctuated the silence behind him as the Ibisians, tiring of their sport, swarmed upon Hayes, piercing him through with their spears, thus ending the tortured life.

Padrec remained where he was, burrowed into the soft, yielding earth, frozen in perfect stillness, barely breathing but still weeping with fear, pure mindless terror. The ground beneath him was damp and crawling with tiny life that did not fear to trail upon his hands, make tracks upon his face, his closed eyelids, as other senses keyed to the sounds of the forests, wondering if now they were searching for him. Or didn't they know that the sled had held not one occupant, but two? Was it possible they did not know to look for another survivor? Hidden in his hollow, surrounded by a host of plants he had not yet classified or given names but which hovered in thick ranks to conceal him from hostile eyes, Padrec dared to hope that he, at least, would survive. He needed only to wait, to wait until the Ibisians, certain that their work was done, had gone, returned to their horrible hive, and would leave him alone with what was left of his life.

It was the gray light before dawn when Anii stole from the nom to the dying strains of the victory celebration, the last of the oahod drunk, the last tambourine sounded. The dawn was chill and heavy with the smell of smoke. The warriors had suffered terrible losses. The Strangers had not defended themselves at first, offering the ranking members of their nom as captives in a most civil manner until the warriors had undertaken to slay the remainder. Then, as suddenly, the Strangers had refused to accept the customary terms of defeat and had retaliated savagely, hurling lightnings and death. Beyond all imaginings they had proven to be deadly prey. Just as the Strangers had not expected to be killed for surrendering their leaders, the warriors had not expected their enemy to turn on them—and though the Strangers had ultimately perished as planned, they had taken many of the nom's warriors with them, much to the nom's detriment. D'nia had been greatly distressed by the loss, for it weakened her nom's strength.

It was dangerous for a young female to leave the safety of the nom uncompanioned, especially one who had entered her nuptial phase, but Anii could not wait to know the fate of the Strangers she had watched so often from afar. Her interest in them had not died with their perishing. And perhaps there was something left by which she might learn something of this strange race destroyed too soon. So it was that Anii crept to the edge of the ridge overlooking the Strangers' encampment, and peered down upon it. A sudden splinter of sadness, remote and unexplained, pierced her. The shining nom that once had flown was now a blackened husk, a hulking, ruined shadow on the floor of the plain. Certainly now it would never fly again.

Debris lay scattered far and wide across the clearing, torn from the bowels of the nom that had flown, reduced to useless metallic glintings. All else was silence and emptiness and the smell of charred flesh. Nearly all of the thousands of scattered bodies belonged to the nomari.

The Strangers died as easily as we, without their weapons. And now they are gone. D'nia was wrong.

She stole down through the grasses to the place of carnage, prodding carcasses as she went, looking for a body belonging to the Strangers. The Strangers had not been many in number, fewer than two hundred, and some had escaped into the hills before the nomari had reached the nom that had flown. Of the thousands dead, only a handful would be Strangers—the power of their weapons had increased the slain only by the number of their dead enemies.

A movement on the fringe of the forest caught her wary eye, a shadow in the tall grasses. Anii's hand fled to her knife, her search forgotten, alerted to the possibility that smokes from the fires and smells of battle had drawn the warriors from other noms. If so, she was in danger here. But the figure was not alert to her. It continued to move, slowly, oblivious to the presence of another; another of the nomari would have noticed her intrusion. Her curiosity aroused, Anii approached across the wide field of wind-rushed grasses, her lower garment brushing at her long golden legs as she crossed. She came to a place where the ground had been disturbed, twice-twelve mounds of fresh earth, and a sole survivor of the Strangers, on its knees, felled by exhaustion, striving still to create another. It was the young, dark-haired male she had seen in the forests, gathering plants. Only after she had stood there, watching him, for many minutes, did he see her, his shoulders suddenly dropping with hopelessness as his eyes looked back at her, accepting what he thought would be his death at her hands.

First seeing her with the golden sun rising behind her, Padrec knew that this Ibisian was female. No age-old wisdom told him this, only the vision that met his savaged eyes and imprinted itself forever on his brain. The alien stood above him, tall, long-legged, beautiful even through the dull haze of his loss. To look at her, he would have thought her human, this Ibisian life-form who watched him without understanding of what he was or had been, who probably would kill him once her curiousity was satisfied. Never before had one stood so near to him. In the first light of dawn, her rich golden hair tumbled like molten flame, her eyes reflecting back at him that image of an idol clothed in garments of red, more skin to meet the eye than shimmering cloth. The Ibisians who had killed Hayes in the forest had not been so tall, so obviously female, nor had their skin been so delicately colored, so warm even though the light was cold. And the dead ones, the dead ones he had found in the dark, grinning in death, had not been like her. . . . He shuddered in the icy cold grip of morning, remembering how he had stumbled back to the ship under cover of darkness, looking for other survivors, and had found his friends already the prey of insect scavengers. He had been forced to claim the bodies just to bury them . . . Through the exhaustion of a night spent finding and burying the remains of his fellow crewmates, as if in some way he could defeat the human horror of being eaten, Padrec no longer had the strength to flee.

"Look what you've done," he said to her, choking on his own voice. "Do you know what you've done?"

She understood not a word of what it said, only that the Stranger was speaking to her. It was defeated, accepting, weaponless. She removed her hand from her knife.

He took the gesture for what it was worth and looked away from her. He pushed more dirt onto the shallow grave. "The Captain," he said, more meaningless speech. "He was a good man. He tried."

Even as she watched, tears formed in his eyes and wetted his dirt-streaked cheeks as he brushed at them dully, too confused, too exhausted to know what he was doing. Almost absently, his hands placed more earth onto the mound. Anii noted a carcass of one of its kind half-hidden in the tall growth, not far from them; to judge by the signs, it had been dragged there. *A ritual,* she realized, astounded, *it is burying its dead!* The significance of that discovery could not be comprehended all at once. She looked again at the row of mounds, seeing in them a night spent in honoring the dead, its companions ... as might the nomari burn their fallen warriors to send their spirits heavenward, back to the Goddess. What strange Goddess must the Strangers have, that they put them in the earth?

Her heightened hearing first told her of the approach of the workers, come to clean the field of carcasses and usable salvage. There would be warriors with them, warriors who would kill the Stranger if they found him. But the sight of the Stranger, grieving and exhausted, mindlessly placing handfuls of dirt upon the carcasses of its kind, moved her unexplainably. Why should she allow them to slay him? He was certainly intelligent, capable of independent action despite his present state; she had often studied his comings and goings, taken note of his habits, and now she knew him to feel emotion. And for all his differences, in body he looked nomari, one of her own kind in the male form ... *Animals do not cry. Nor do animals speak. He is too like us to slay without reason. He is not dangerous in himself. And knowledge of him might prove useful when we come upon the others.* For there were others, and now they must stay here, since their nom would never leave.

And again she thought, *D'nia was wrong.*

"Come," she said to the kneeling Stranger. But he only stared at her, uncomprehending. They could not communicate by speech. And while she could probably subdue him, persuasion would better serve her purposes. "Come," she said again, kneeling before him, within reach if he chose to attack, but she did not think he would. Anii tried to keep her movements non-threatening, thinking that if he was human as she was, he would understand somewhat of her intention. Very carefully, she put her hand upon his, closing her six fingers over his five. Yes, that, at least, was different. And yet the same: it was a hand, a very definite hand; not a claw or a tentacle, but a hand with bones beneath the pale, dirtied skin. The touch of him was warm, nomari. . . .

The sounds of the approaching scavengers drew closer. Soon they would come over the ridge and the sharp-eyed warriors would certainly spot them—warriors who obeyed D'nia's wishes, not Anii's. Her pleadings would not sway them, or save him.

"Come!" she urged more forcefully, but he turned his head from her, now able to hear for himself the sounds of others coming. "Come!" Rising suddenly to her feet, with no more time to spare on persuasion, Anii grasped his arm and forced him to follow, half-dragging him, struggling through the grass until somehow the message that she was trying to get him away sank in and he stopped fighting her and began to stumble after willingly. Released from the burden of dragging him, Anii led the way into the shadowed safety of the forest where they would not be seen. Only when they came to a hidden glade she knew, a place carpeted by stardangle moss at the foot of gray rocks, shaded and silent and cool, did she pull him down and allow him a reprieve—and herself a chance to think of what she was to do with him. As he sat on the mossy bank beside her, his head cradled in his arms, huddled in misery, she studied him, the dark-haired one she had often watched, pleased that it was he. Perhaps for another she would not have behaved in so foolhardy a manner, for what was she to do with this Stranger now that she had him? He was not a usual captive, good for some known purpose. Indeed, what had prompted her to spare him but that he was unique— and male. She did not make little of the mating heat's part in her decision, the stir of eagerness she had felt upon touching him, the helpless look in his eyes that, for a moment, had permitted her to think of him almost as a drone. Her captive. . . .

He was male, and his nom was lost, destroyed, there would be no angry warriors coming after . . . and it was ever the fate of captive males to be mated . . . Even as she watched him the heat grew in her loins, as if some chemistry within her found this idea compatible with its needs. *He is not so very ugly*, she found herself thinking, *And he is very like a male of my kind.*

The Stranger, too, had been watching her, uneasy, aware of her awareness, her golden eyes flaming at him across the clearing. Backing away from her, his back to the rocks, he slowly rose to his feet, prepared as if for flight. Beneath his soiled clothes he was well-made for a male, taller than she had at first thought, graceful of his kind but coarser than a nomari drone, harder, tougher; his dark hair was strange to her, as were his eyes, as alien as they were blue, but these things were not unpleasing and there were suggestions of a pleasant appearance beneath the dirt and blood of his ordeal. In her present state she could hardly ignore him. Nor did she try. In all things he was shaped like the nomari, in all things . . . even the smell of him was male, inflaming her senses. And the need for a male was upon her, more now that he was near. She smiled, the answer dawning to her. *Why not? He is nothing—none will ever know what I have done here this day.*

"Lovely one," she spoke gently so as not to frighten him, "It does not matter if you die."

Padrec stood as if frozen when she walked toward him, her red garments sliding from her as she cast them aside. What was she doing? No . . . she was alien . . . she could not be thinking of *that*! It wasn't human, the very thought unnatural . . . but he felt it begin, now within himself as well, as though her naked, glowing beauty had robbed him of all will and his body betrayed him, his knees going weak and not obeying the screaming voice in his mind that urged

him to flee. *Oh, no, this can't be happening, isn't
happening* ... But in his nostrils he caught a faint
trace of the sweet musky scent that had followed him
in the forests ... *Oh, God, no*—he shook his head and
tried to back away from her. But it was too late, had
been too late from the first moment she had touched
him.

Anii knew him hers, her captive now in truth. That
the pheromones had affected him, she could see from
the stricken expression on his face, the sudden harshness of his breathing as she brushed her hand upon
his cheek. He was even as a drone would be when the
scent and touch of the female's mating lust affected
him and rendered him helpless, pliant. Like one dazed
he allowed her to touch him, to loosen his garments,
to stroke his flesh to hardness. Wanting to please him,
if only to sweeten his last moments and heighten his
eagerness to enter the sweet death she had prepared
for him, she followed the custom of his kind that she
had witnessed by the lake. Pressing her body to his
slightly taller one, Anii pulled his head down and his
mouth to hers, parting his lips that were like those of
the nomari and probing the dark warmth of his mouth
with her tongue, tasting his willingness with breathless wonder. By his allowing this, accepting the perversion, she knew herself dominant, his alien maleness
submissive.

And he was. He wanted her. He lowered his mouth
to her tongue's invasion and his body pulsed to the
heat of hers. Though his mind knew the horror of
what she was doing, yet he was powerless to stop her,
to stop himself, and he gave himself willingly to the
embrace, shattering, all willpower gone, wanting the
the unholy possession. ...

Gently, ever so gently, she drew him down to the
mossy floor, into the sexual embrace for which she
had preserved him, taking him in a coupling that
surpassed even the imaginings of her body for sweetness and sheer urgency. His alien body, so hard and
strong, yet human and male, awakened her to the

meaning of the mating call. At the height of her
passion, and his, she felt it, the tender shuddering of
his final gift . . . dying, softly dying, in her arms.
*Stranger, you are mine now forever. I found you among
the dead, and now you too shall die.* Aching at the
depth of that loss beyond imaginings, she clasped him
to her, grateful for his gift, the pleasure he had given
her, the release . . .

It took her many minutes to realize that he was still
breathing, that he was not dead. That, in fact, he was
in no worse shape than she as the price of her rapture.
He gave a strangled sound like a dying thing as he
pulled away from her, but he was definitely alive, and
undamaged, as aghast as she at what had occurred.
The effect of the pheromones had worn off.

He lives. Anii could hardly believe it. *But drones do
not survive mating!* Then the full impact of that statement struck her with an impossible possibility. *Drones
do not survive mating—but the Strangers do!*

The nomari had many sexless offspring, with only a
few males and fewer females. The Strangers were
obviously different; they were always either male or
female, many of each—and the males did not die upon
mating. If they are capable of reproduction as we are,
she thought, they shall soon overrun the noms!

I shall kill him now—

Stealthily, Anii reached across the moss, seeking
her garments, the belt which held her knife. But the
Stranger, shocked out of his apathy by the use to
which he had been put, noted her movement and moved
as quickly to stop her. Her hand closed about the haft
of the blade as he grabbed for her wrist and strove to
take the weapon from her or at least prevent her from
using it against him. But in the struggle his lean body
strained against hers, reawakening memories of their
mating, the heated lust of her nuptial phase, and from
the depths of that hormone intoxicated state another
thought pushed to the fore, seducing her astray of her
intention: *remember how he felt when he was in you*

. . . you can use him again, and again . . . as many times as you want him. . . .

She did not have the strength of a worker, or a warrior's quickness and agility, but she was not weak from hunger and thirst, suffering from the loss of her people and the effects of a night spent digging shallow graves in the ground. The poison which tipped her knife was not deadly; it merely incapacitated the victim, leaving her free to kill or not kill the one she had infected. It was an understandable precaution, since an accidental cut therefore could not rob the nom of a potential breeder. Nor would it rob her of this male. One twist of the blade was all it took, a tiny nick that pierced the tough fabric of his garment at the upper arm, and the male weakened so that she could thrust him from her.

Padrec fell back from the armed Ibisian, the drug quickly paralyzing him, his hands relaxing to earth. He could feel himself breathing, the world crowding in as she stood over him and all he could see were her ankles, the golden strands of whatever she wore on her feet. *My God,* he thought when she bent over him and the world slipped away, *she's killing me—*

Although she didn't, he often wished she had.

Padrec awoke to a dimly lighted haze. He was naked, wrapped in silk, his body strangely reluctant, wanting only more sleep. Yet somehow he was certain that he had already slept overlong. Why then did he feel so tired, and yet so well cared for? His skin had that faintly raw feeling that came from being scrubbed clean . . . His eyes shot open to the pure amber light pouring in from an opening at the apex of the tall, cone-shaped ceiling, illuminating what appeared to be a circular chamber. *It looks like a hive.* He swallowed, realizing what he was thinking. With an effort, he sat up . . . and found himself staring into the golden eyes of the Ibisian who sat on the foot of his bed.

He was in her room . . . her lair. . . .

It all came back to him, the ship, the bodies, the encounter. . . . The memory chilled the blood in his brain and pulled it from his face, a sick sinking dragging at the core of his soul. She had not killed him, the alien who had found him and taken him on wild impulse, a half-remembered, half-dreamed coupling in the forest . . . she had kept him, alive. . . . Or was this a continuation of some nightmare, an extension of the madness that he had fallen into when he had come upon his companions in the night only to be attacked by the beetles which fed on them? There had been so many, human and nonhuman, all dead, the flesh stripped from their bones . . . the smoke had hung over them, the drifting veils of another world's final shroud. . . . He had fallen to his knees upon an earth made muddy with blood and looked into dead eyes where there were eyes, hearing dead laughter and hopes and intelligences scattered to the alien winds by a sudden horror that had ripped the life from them. But not from him. For some strange reason, she wanted *him* alive. . . .

Those alien lips, rose-tinged and lovely, parted slightly at seeing him awake. Not a smile, but a gesture of awareness, invitation, intent, and her golden eyes, warmly waiting upon him with a predator's impatience, accepted the answering awareness in his own. Dully, moving away from her, Padrec knew again the horror of being drawn against his will, her scent filling his nostrils, his lungs, his very blood, her six-fingered hands claiming him without consent, as the Ibisian, victorious, murmured her approval. Captive and helpless, he could not even struggle when she pulled him to her and, in a brief quick heat of lust that stole every vestige of his manhood, devoured him with a softly deliberate delight.

Only in the aftermath did he fully realize what he had done, again, for the second time. He had mated with an alien, pleasured something not human. That was the true horror of it. Not the coupling itself, though the thought of his body being used in such a way tore at his stomach, but the deep sensual plea-sure the Ibisian took in the act she compelled him to perform. Even now, sated, she seemed to wear the afterglow like a glistening of fruit upon the lips of a one whose hunger would soon demand another. And if she wanted him again—he knew, he could sense deep in his lingering awareness of her, that again he would respond. She was different from the others, the ones who had killed Hayes, destroyed the ship—something about her was different, provocative, deadly. . . . He watched her walk away from him, graceful and shapely in her extraordinary nakedness, nearly but not quite human. She returned with a tall vessel filled with a strange colored liquid, which she held out to him. Not taking his eyes from those golden orbs which ordered his actions, he accepted it. *Drug me or poison me,* he thought, *it is no worse than what you have already done. You have stolen everything from me, even my dignity.*

The liquid refreshed him. When he indicated that he desired more, the Ibisian handed him the scaled flask which contained it. Then she turned to put on her shimmering garments. For his part, Padrec pulled himself to the edge of the bed, sitting there so that his bare feet touched the soft carpets which completely covered the floor, turning the flask in his hands and studying its making. What substance gave it such jewel-like color and texture? It did not seem to be enamel, and it could not be reptilian leather, which it resembled: there were no reptiles on Ibis. Insect skin, maybe? He looked up at her, but there was no way he could ask her a question of that sort. Such complex communication was beyond them. Yet he deduced that she was interested in his survival and even his well-being. *Of course,* he decided then, bitterly, *I am her plaything now. She can do whatever she wants with me.*

He pulled the sheeting across his lap as she ap-proached him again. One thing he dearly wanted to know was what she had done with his clothes. She set a tray laden with strange foods on the bed, with gestures indicating that he should eat. He turned his head from the food, refusing it. But he noticed her hesitation at his refusal, the trace of concern. Why didn't she go?

After a few minutes during which he would not meet her eyes, she did go. A circular door led from the chamber; he could hear the sounds of metal bolts falling into place. *That's right, make sure I don't escape.* But once she was gone, he sprang from the bed and searched the room. No windows, and only the one door. The door was of wood, very thick, and he did not know that there were not guards on the other side. He did not know where he was—for all he knew, he was inside the hive, the nom. As the walls of this solid chamber were of stone, the only other possible way out was up, the circular opening in the center of the high, conical ceiling, which provided the room with both light and ventilation. In all likelihood it provided a way of escape. But how to reach it. . . . The rods and pulleys which were used to operate a protective flap were too flimsy to support his weight. Other fabrics in the room seemed stronger, usable, but he had no sure way to anchor them. . . .

While thinking through his dilemma, Padrec sampled the food, greedily satisfying his gnawing hunger now that the Ibisian no longer stood over him, waiting to see if her captive would entertain her with his eating habits. Whatever the food was, some admixture of plant or animal or even insect parts, it was good, a tasty and filling meal to someone who had gone two days without any. He could almost think she had cared for his liking of it. Indeed, the variety hinted that she had attempted to please him by offering a selection. Her treatment of him so far had been benign, if strangely dominated by her sexual use of him. It was this aspect of his situation that he found difficult to understand or accept. Among sentient races, engaging in sexual behavior with a member of a species not one's own was exceedingly rare, an almost universal taboo. Even related sub-species only occasionally made allowances for it, usually among highly intellectual, outwardly directed species which found it easier to overlook fundamental physical and cultural differences. The Ibisians did not fall in that category; as a culture they were primitive, if highly organized, and inwardly directed. And they had made it known that they thought Terrans nearly as physically and sexually aberrant as Terrans had thought them. But this Ibisian, with her golden, exquisite, female form and apparent intelligence, did not appear to follow that line of thought, to judge by her behavior. He had met female members of other human sub-species on several other occasions, and not once had he felt so much as a stir of sexual interest beyond ordinary curiosity. Until yesterday, and today. By all usual standards, the Ibisian should not have acted upon her interest, even if she had felt any.

But she had, and he had. Why?

"You were overlong from the nom."

Anii met Hli's inquiring gaze evenly, determined not to betray her secret, the excitement she was feeling, thinking to get rid of the subservient by letting her know that she was nearly at the height of her nuptial phase. Thus she could also explain her absence.

"I had to prepare my lodge, Hli. Tonight I shall go there, to be away from the nom."

"You are almost eager," observed Hli.

"I am near mating," Anii reminded her. Though outwardly casual, she chose her garments carefully, with an eye for those that were light and of bright color, iridescent veils of gossamer as airy as nightgosset wings. Yes, she thought, studying her reflection in the polish of her mirror, just thinking of it brings the heat to your eyes. Carefully, she said to Hli, "The destruction of the Strangers has attracted much attention from other noms."

The subservient frowned, the observation apt. "It is not a good time to be outside the nom."

"Tell D'nia that."

"Do not be impertinent. You know well the reason."

Young females in heat, stealing away the queen's drones . . . yes, she knew well the reason. A queen who could not keep her drones would not long rule.

"Perhaps it is well you go now," Hli concurred, continuing to watch her. "Your color, your eyes, you have the look of one very near the height of her phase. How came you by it so quickly, I would know? Have you been putting yourself near the drones?"

"No," said Anii. That would have been foolish; D'nia would never have tolerated it. Restless with the sensations of her phase, she wandered to the opening of her chamber where it overlooked the plain. The puckered surface shifted between grassland and mounding hills, one of which she called her own. After subduing the Stranger, she had lured a worker to carry him to the only hiding place she had known would allow her to keep him in secret, her nuptial lodge. Once there, she had killed the worker to be sure of the secret. Her possessiveness was but an expression of the nuptial phase, during which even the gentlest female would kill to gain or keep a male—. Last night, knowing that the Stranger would almost surely sleep the night, she had returned to the nom, and as soon as the nom had awakened for the day, Anii had escaped surveillance to return to the lodge, to see to her tenant and to experience again the heady physical release that came with the mating. For that alone, she would fight to keep him.

And he did not die upon mating. Still she could hardly believe the events which had led to her discovery. It had occurred to her to think it perverse, to mate with the Stranger as if he were one of the nomari, but he had been so like in form, his attraction a strange thing but undeniable, the mating need within her too strong not to succumb to the lure of a male so near, so readily available to her. And now that she had enjoyed him twice, she no longer questioned the propriety of wanting him again. *If the Stranger were not a suitable mate, I would not have attracted him in the first place! He must be very like the nomari to respond to our lures—.*

That the Stranger more than superficially resembled the nomari she had discovered immediately upon examining him. When the worker had washed him, she could see that his skin, though pale, had the texture and structure of human skin, even down to the tiny pores and little hairs; that his fingers, though there were but five of them, ended in shell-like nails instead of animal claws; that his bones could be similarly counted, were similarly shaped and positioned. And, like the nomari, he was warm-blooded. Yes, she had thought, sensing a profound and enduring truth, we are of a kind, somehow. These Strangers are our kin from afar, from the times before the High Ones vanished and the Goddess turned her eyes on Mi.

But his lack of interest in the food disturbed her. Captives taken from other noms would sometimes refuse to eat, even to the point of perishing. She wondered if his distress was such that he did not wish to live. If so, for all that she had gained, she would lose him. Sensing her mistress's pensive mood, Hli sought to entertain her. "D'nia keeps one of the Strangers," she said casually.

"What?"

The subservient had not expected Anii to react so strongly, to see her golden eyes suddenly become wide and staring, her color pale beneath the glow of her phase. But Hli attributed the reaction to the young female's oft-voiced desire to spare the strange race that had descended upon them like an infection that would not be removed.

"There is one the Queen in her wisdom chose to spare. He is of no use, but she hopes that by studying him we may better know how to deal with any others that come. Already he tries to speak with us, but he does poorly."

"One of their males—?" Had D'nia somehow had her followed, stolen the Stranger from her? In the struggle between a young queen and an old, nothing was impossible.

But Hli only snorted. "One who was too ugly to mate and therefore has lived to be old," she said, setting that fear to rest, never knowing Anii's relief.

"Bring him to me."

"I thought you would say that." Since the Stranger was not one of the Queen's drones, his presence could be requested. Not many minutes later, a short male old enough to be losing the dark hair on his head, but clean and apparently handling his situation well, was pushed into her antechamber. Hli placed herself between her mistress and the Stranger, guarding the young queen protectively, and issued a warning to the ugly one that he must be properly respectful. The Stranger made a rather elegant bow, even though Anii could see that he did not understand; but his eyes as he looked upon her were curious. Like those of her Stranger sometimes were.

I cannot talk with him. But Hli has said that he is attempting to learn. I can see that this is not because we are attempting to teach him.

She did not attempt to come near to him; it was possible that even at his age, being a Stranger and able to mate often, her pheromones could arouse him. His eyes were dark, intensely alert, and he studied her openly, as if to satisfy himself as to certain questions he had formed. For her part, Anii could discern little that was new, except that this male was much older than her Stranger, with less potential as a mate, and that he looked less lost and less vulnerable. Less afraid. He had not seen the massacre, Hli had informed her, having been one of the captives taken beforehand. He might not even know that his nom had been destroyed.

"Toroya," the Stranger said quietly, placing his hand upon his breast and bowing again deeply.

Was that a greeting? Anii saw that he did it differently the second time, repeating the same syllables as he made the pointing gesture, turning it upon himself. "Toroya."

Anii spoke in an aside to Hli, who then went to the Stranger, pointing at him and saying, "To—ro—ya—"

The Stranger bared his teeth. Only Anii's sharp command prevented Hli from drawing her knife. The gesture of baring teeth had been one of non-aggression, of friendliness, among the Strangers. Not once had her Stranger used it with her, though she had seen him use it among his companions.

"To-roya," she said to him, and the male, having noted his earlier error, simply nodded, repeating the word and gesture again upon himself. So, she thought, that is how he tells us his name. Since it would be improper for so lowly a captive to address a young queen by her name, or at all, Anii pointed to Hli, who might protest but must accept her decision. "Hli."

The Stranger bowed to the subservient. "Hli," he said.

She called in a warrior. As the elegant, bronze-skinned creature stood dispassionately before them, she said, as simply as she could, "Hli, eh?"

Toroya hesitated. Then his lips curved but did not bare. He pointed to the subservient. "Hli."

He had grasped the distinction. They understood each other. And the discovery would serve her well, if with it she could teach the other Stranger to understand her.

For hours, Padrec had been twisting the sheeting from the bed, and other pieces of fabric from the room, into a lightweight rope. He had turned the chamber upside down looking for suitable fabrics and a pole that was long enough and yet would not break with his full weight. He had finally found both, along with his clothes, which, though they were filthy, he had decided to put back on. But the rope had proved difficult to work, and by the time afternoon had died, he knew he did not have enough to make good his plan. He had replaced the pole and was preparing to conceal the rope when the Ibisian returned. Although he hurriedly attempted to hide the rope beneath some cushions, she noticed. Striding toward him like a tigress, she shoved him aside and ripped the makeshift cord from its hiding, staring at it and then at him in mingled disbelief and unconcealed rage.

How dare he! He had clothed himself, had twisted her drapings into a rope—! He wanted to leave her! Without thinking, lashing out at him as she would have an impertinent subservient or stupid drone, Anii struck him across the face with the full strength of her hand, reminding him that he was nothing before her need of him.

Padrec stumbled back, stunned, his face stinging from her blow. The pain of it barely registered. She had struck him, and perhaps just to start. Wiping at the blood on his lip, he glanced around the room for a weapon, any weapon, any chance of escape. . . . The door, she had not closed it behind her. But even as he moved toward the dark mouth of the open portal, the Ibisian detected his intention and, drawing her knife, caught him short. He stopped, the glinting metal of her blade held before his eyes with shining warning.

Anii secured the portal, never taking her eyes from him. Just when she thought she could rely upon his passivity, this changed Stranger, his determination still to be seen in his eyes, surprised her. Though he respected the power of her knife to kill him, the door to keep him, she could see in him the intelligence, the resolve, that would make holding him more of a challenge than she had at first thought. In his eyes she saw tears of frustration, and defiance.

"Lovely one," she said softly, addressing him, "I do not mean to hurt you. But I will not let you leave me." She lowered her knife and gestured him back. Though he backed away from the door, his alien blue eyes never left her face. The angry red mark of her blow stained his cheek like blood. When she reached for him, however, thinking to gentle the force of her reprimand, he pulled away. Her pheromones, though at their peak, were not affecting him. *He is too angry,* she realized, seeing the consequences of her blow, *his anger surpasses my effect on him!*

How remarkable he was, she found herself thinking, watching him as he left her and sat himself in a corner of the chamber, far from the bed and far from her. No simple drone would have had the intelligence to conceive of a rope, far less attempt to make one. And his anger necessitated a change in tactics on her part. Though nomari drones were too passive for anger, often the extreme fear of capture negated the pheromones or greatly reduced their response, making it necessary to court and reassure them before they could be mated. This Stranger's anger must be soothed, or at the least distracted, or he would not respond to her—and at the height of her phase she would require his response, else in her frustration she might harm him in earnest. And more and more she did not wish to harm him, or see him harmed. *But you cannot leave me,* the thought echoed in her heated mind. *I will not allow you to leave me.*

Always with one eye to him, Anii restored the chamber and set the tapers to light, noting as she did that

he had eaten his meal. That discovery restored somewhat her temper, meaning as it did that he was not
given to self-destruction. The food that she had brought
with her, then, would also please him. If she could get
him to eat it . . . but she did not know his ways, what
could be done to win away his anger.

She went to where he sat against the cold stone
wall and knelt on the carpeted floor before him. She
gestured with her hands the way the Stranger at the
nom had. "Anii," she said, indicating herself. It occurred to her that she should teach him to address her
as "royal one" in the manner of subservients; but
some part of her wanted him to answer to her name.

Stubbornly, Padrec refused to look at her. She might
be able to hold him against his will, use him or abuse
him as she chose, she could as easily kill him as
others of her kind had killed his companions. She had
already, and with jarring brutality, demonstrated their
relationship. Her hand on his face could as easily
have been a knife cutting off his hand, or a whip to be
brought down on his naked back until he was dead.
He could feel his heart trying to expand in his chest, a
dull cold pain like something screaming, as the meaning of that blow took hold of him and would not let go.
The thing had sunk its teeth and all that was left was
the dying. He was hers, to do with as she wanted, a
stranger with nowhere to go, whose fate was of no
consequence. If that was the case, then what did it
matter if he refused her? Another blow would not hurt
more than the first.

Anii rocked back on her heels, contemplating his
refusal to acknowledge her, to heed her attempts at
communication. He kept his face turned away, his
eyes closed or staring blankly elsewhere, his expression strained. Something was gravely wrong. And it
had started when she had struck him.

Was it possible that in striking him she had injured
him? The red mark had almost entirely disappeared,
but those places where it showed would darken to
bruises by morning. She had not intended to hit him

so strongly, but her fury at his attempt at escape, and
the possible loss of him, had caught her by surprise. It
had been the violence of an enraged queen, fully in
her nuptial phase, seeing her drone being taken from
her, that had lashed out at him. The blow had been
meant to enforce a lesson, not to injure. But the damage appeared slight. The injury, then, had not been to
his flesh, but to his feelings. He was angry, not at
being thwarted only, but at being struck—

*He has never been struck by one in authority! He is
not accustomed to submission, to having lessons enforced by blows—*

*It is not the way of his kind. I forget that he is not
one of ours.*

There had to be some way of getting his attention.
A moment later she had it. "To-roya," she said, using
the name of the Stranger she had seen in the nom.

His eyes swung to her, startled blue, comprehending. "Toroya," he whispered, pale-lipped.

"To-roya." Yes, she could see he understood. She
pointed to herself. "Anii," she said.

For a moment Padrec stared at her and said nothing, not sure how to proceed, or even whether he
should. She had used Toroya's name. How did she
know it? Was the xenobiologist still alive, then, even
as he was, a captive in some alien hole? Were there
others? Even if the Ibisian knew and was trying to
tell him, he could not be sure he understood her. But
she was trying to establish a grounds for communication. By most patterns, the word used when pointing
to an object or person was its name. She was telling
him her name.

But her name did not interest him. "Toroya," he
said again, insistently. "Tell me about Toroya—"

Anii understood that he wanted to know about the
other, but that was not what she wanted to teach him.
He must first learn who he answered to. "Anii," she
repeated sternly, her eyes staring into his, denying
his request for any knowledge of the other Stranger.
"Anii."

She understood. He could see that she knew what it was he wanted to know. And she wasn't going to tell him. She wanted him to say her name, and would tell him nothing more until he did. "An-yi," he said. It was not perfect, he knew, the vowel sounds were strange to him, but the Ibisian appeared pleased with his attempt. Accepting that he must take the necessary second step, he pointed to himself, saying, "Padrec."

So that was his name! His voice was pleasing saying it, deeper than that of a queen, richer than a warrior's moderate voice, not at all like that of a drone. But then drones rarely spoke, they were so stupid.

"Pa-dric." It was close enough. She saw his cheeks color at the sound of his name on her lips. Was it important to him, then, that she could say it? Or was it the pheromones, working their magic through his disarmed anger?

Turning, Anii picked a vessel from a nearby tray. "Drink," she said, making the drinking motion.

Realizing her intention, Padrec allowed scientific curiosity to get the better of his misgivings, his interest in her returning with the establishment of communication. As alien as he knew her to be, her humanity was becoming more and more pronounced with contact. She was attempting to teach him her language. Which could only mean that she thought him capable of learning it. And her own intelligence, as it became more apparent, lent intriguing possibilities to their association. It was becoming less a matter of what he knew about Ibisians than what he was in a position to learn.

He could no longer deny the effect she had on him, this golden-haired, golden-eyed creature he could now know as Anii, the pure physical response she aroused—while angry he had not felt it, even though she had been near, but now that his anger had diminished . . . sweet mercy, but he wanted her again. As hard as he found it to explain, he felt his body fine tuned to a fevered pitch, her mere presence enough to awaken a lust so primal in its unbridled sensuality that it was frightening, unnatural, because he could not fight it.

Didn't she notice, or care, that he was not willing, that he was not even one of her own kind? Or was he some strange perversion she enjoyed . . .

Taking note of his state, his distraction that to her was the gentle proof of her success, Anii put aside her game for another more urgent, all words forgotten. As if to draw forth what he still sought to deny, she touched his lips with her fingers, trembling as he gently kissed them, and then her lips, little by little submitting to her overtures, until at last there was no turning back from her. She drew him to her then, his sadness inspiring her to be gentle. *He is not one of ours,* she reminded herself again, *This is strange to him. . . .*

He could not help himself. And neither could she. She only knew that if she did not take him, she would surely go mad with wanting a male to pierce the heated aching of her nuptial need. And if he refused, she would force him—.

But you will live.

From the moment that she touched her lips to his, Padrec forget himself completely, lost in the siren song of her golden desire as she pulled him to her, never knowing when or how she took his garments from him, how she led him to the bed. It did not matter why this goddess wanted him, he existed only to serve that softly curved body glimmering with candlelight and the filmy perspiration of their lovemaking, golden and serene upon red sheets as her hands upon his flesh brought forth a molten passion that commanded him to give himself to her again and again, a pathway without love or end. He was but the slave of a desire that consumed him without mercy, her lover not once, but several times that heated night, unable to believe in or escape his own compulsion, until at last both collapsed from their exertions, drained of the last drop of that heady nuptial sweetness Ibisian

tales exalted: two bodies, one golden, one pale, entwined upon the red silk sheets of the nuptial bed.

Anii awakened first, the male at her side still deep
in the sprawling sleep of exhaustion. She had used
him to excess, she knew. But, stretching her own
sated body, she did not regret having done so. Yes, she
had done well to keep him. Even his alien features
had become acceptable to her, so that in the vacant
expression of sleep she found him pleasing to her eyes
in ways she had not thought him before. The length of
his nose, his eyelashes, shadowing the pillows, were
part of that same strange, non-nomari beauty that
had given her the blackness of his hair beneath her
fingers, his hard sinewy strength beneath her hands.
Even his five-fingered hands were gracefully made,
long fingers cupped upon the covers in sleep.

What was he? she wondered as she studied him. Not
simply a male to be mated, he accepted his role with too
little liking or grace. And the males who led his nom
had not lived to be old only because they were not
mated, this she could now understand. Among his
kind, the males, too, had led—.

She stole from the bed and picked up the rope she
had caught him making earlier, remembering how
she had struck him and his reaction to her discipline.
His intelligence, and the gentle sensitivity that accompanied it, was rapidly showing itself greater than
she had at first thought. And intelligent creatures
suffered most in captivity. Among the nomari, warriors, possessing limited intelligence, relied primarily
on an overwhelming instinct to defend their queen
and nom and would soon die from starvation if captured. Workers suffered even less, since their intelligence was too low to make distinctions of service, and
a nom's workers lived only to serve. Even drones lived
only to eat and ate only that one day they might
mate, and a drone did not care who owned him. Only
queens greatly suffered in captivity; they wasted away
from loss of companionship, from loss of authority,
choice, control over their own lives and reproduction.

That was why capture by a hostile nom was a fate to be abhorred beyond death: it delivered the captive into a lifetime of living servitude without reward.

Is that what I have done to you, my captive, my Stranger? Are you being mated like some captured queen in a hostile nom? You do not know that when this nuptial phase has passed, I will not have this need for you. Poor exhausted thing—.

But until then. . . .

"**D**on't you have anything else to do?"

Anii had just finished making love to him for the third time that morning. Padrec had resigned himself to an almost continual state of copulation, and her capacity no longer amazed him: for three days and as many nights she had been insatiable. Her golden eyes drew heat from his words, but she had finished, and left him, this time differently than before—she was putting her clothes on.

Thank God. He lay back in bed, anticipating the unparalleled luxury of her absence.

The expansiveness of his gesture did not go unnoticed by Anii. He did not know that most of what glowed in her eyes was amusement. Pretty thing, she thought, you have earned your rest. Almost she could feel sadness that this nuptial phase was passing, that only lingering desire, pale beside its former glory, moved her: her pheromones, past their peak, no longer incited him for hours, lessening her use of him, but not her enjoyment. And now she must return to the nom, to reassure Hli and make it unnecessary for any to be sent in search of her. She wanted no others to come upon her trysting place.

Once cleaned and dressed, Anii gestured to the food and drink, repeating the words she had been teaching to him between matings, implying that he should see to his needs. He repeated them after, imperfectly but with understanding; she no longer questioned that he would one day learn to speak as the nomari. But how impatiently she must wait! There was another word that she must teach him.

"Stay." Anii enforced the command by forcing him down on the bed, and again when he attempted to rise.

The Ibisian stood above him, her shining hair bright about her face, the harsh golden authority in her eyes. "Stay, pretty one, and I will return to you."

He understood only part of it. Stay. That was clear enough. And the words she used when speaking to him. He did not know what they meant, only that they were not his name.

Even though she thought he understood, she removed his garments and all strong fabrics to the outer chamber before taking up her travel garments and knife, securing the portal behind her as she left.

With her gone Padrec gave in to the aching urge of his abused body to rest from days and nights of repeated, unrelenting use. He ached in places that had never ached before, and parts of him were painfully tender—he had barely been capable of performing this last time, leaving Anii dissatisfied but surprisingly patient. Alone now, feeling only physical exhaustion, he dropped off into deep, much deserved sleep. But a few hours later when the sun passed over the high opening in the ceiling, he awoke. Glancing up at the light-filled hole which poured its shimmer into his eyes, Padrec was reminded of his only avenue of escape. It would be the easier course to stay, of course. The food was good, though he had begun to guess what was in it, and he was almost certain that Anii had no intention of killing him, even eventually. She would not be making an effort to teach him her language unless she was planning on keeping him. But what was she keeping him for? For amusement? Even so, her treatment of him was not deliberate abuse; she had taken extraordinary pains to be patient with him, even gentle, and she had not once raised hand or voice in anger since that first and only time when she had caught him trying to escape. If he would attempt it again, and fail, she might not be so forgiving. Though it would be courting pain and maybe even death to try, it would be courting more and greater pain meekly to accept captivity among aliens to whom he was nothing more than flesh, an animal to be used as casually as any dumb beast and then perhaps passed on, to serve out his life as a carnal pleasure. Was that really any better than being killed? He needed to regain his freedom, if only to die of it.

Anii, however, had anticipated such a rebellion and had made a point of taking his clothing and every workable piece of cloth with her, leaving him barefoot and naked and with nothing from which to make a rope of any decent length. She had seen the plan behind his previous attempt. Well, he thought, after he had risen from the bed and gingerly washed his bruises in the cold water basin that she kept within the room, if I cannot make a rope, why not a ladder? But another look around the room confirmed that there was no furniture to speak of. Then he would have to use everything that there was. An hour later his carefully piled pyramid of chests and cushions, a few low tables and the raised bed frame, rose nearly half the way to the opening. He thought he could still manage to make a rope that would take him the rest of the way. Using a sharp piece of glass gained by breaking one of her bowls, Padrec sawed and ripped at the thick carpets and cushion covers, savaging what fabric he could, though he cut and tore his own hands in the process. These strips he tied end to end, knot after knot, until his hands were raw and red with blisters. The afternoon light no longer poured into the chamber when the rope was finally done.

But he needed protection from the elements, warmth when night fell—. Rummaging through the things tossed from her chests, he found a garment woven of thick, durable silk, not unlike a pair of trousers, which with a little slitting in strategic places he was able to make fit, thanking his lucky stars that Anii was tall, her figure generous. Two of her tunics were cut to fit, and an embroidered, quilted cloak looked useful enough to take. But there was nothing for his feet, which were bigger than hers, unless ... he ripped out the toes of some slippers and found that they were snug but probably serviceable. Supplies of food and water

found their way into a makeshift pack, enough, he
hoped, to see him to the forest where, he was sure, he
could survive. There was water, and his knowledge of
the plant life there would sustain him, at least for a
while. Long enough to meet the survey team from the
eastern sub-continent if it returned to look for survivors.

*And they will. Rubinsky's wife was assigned to the
main ship . . .*

All that remained was to get away. Anii had not
caught on to his need for a pole, and so he still had the
one he had first selected for the task, a sturdy length
of wood somewhat longer than he estimated the diam-
eter of the opening. After cutting a shallow groove in
the center of the pole, he knotted one end of his rope
to the pole and, clutching his handiwork, he climbed
to the top of the piled furniture. There, he balanced
carefully and took aim.

Padrec knew that his ancestors must have thrown
spears somewhere along the evolutionary scale, but
that skill had not been passed along with the genes
that enabled him to conceive of such a throw. His
hand was willing, his eyes were good, he was strong
enough—but the balance was not there, nor the accu-
racy. Although he had taken care to choose a lightweight pole, and to knot a rope that would not be too
heavy, the thing felt cumbersome and unwieldy. His
first throws did not even come near the opening before
falling back uselessly. He was more in danger of exhaustion from trying than of success. Desperate, fear-
ful of Anii's return, the possible punishment he faced,
imagining shackles the next time, or maiming, remembering the curved blades slicing the fingers from
poor Hayes, Padrec tried not to heed his precarious
balance and put his full shoulder into throwing the
pole through the opening. It went through. He heard
it crash into some growth outside of his sight. Very
carefully, he pulled back on the rope. There was no
resistance, nothing it could grab onto, but he held to
one last hope, the reason for choosing so long a pole.
But it came back to him by its long axis, and fell back

into the hole. Unwilling to be defeated, Padrec tried
until he passed it through the opening again. This
time when he pulled back on the rope, the pole fell
across the opening, securely over it.

Bending down, he retrieved his pack and slung it
across his shoulders, then grabbed for the rope. The
knots held as he swung his weight free from the tower
of clutter and, despite the pain and blood of his torn
hands, pulled himself hand over hand up to the pole.
There, as the dusty hot wind of evening swept at his
face, he swung his feet over the edge of the opening and
onto solid earth. She had built her place underground.

Let her come back now, it doesn't matter—.

Padrec looked around and saw that he had come
onto the plain, although the hilltop he had emerged
onto was covered with stands of shrubby growth, which
kept the opening from being easily discovered. Far
away, beneath clouds turned to flame by the setting
sun, he saw the massive rising towers of the hive. The
nom. It was a word he had heard Anii use, the same
one Toroya had told him. Where was Toroya now?
Sighing, he looked the other way, seeking the best
direction for him to take. It was then that he saw the
dust of a struggle taking place in the bed of one of the
dry gullies not far from him, three creatures, no, four—
one of them golden-haired, golden skinned, being wrestled by the others.

It was Anii.

He recognized the slender bronze Ibisian forms which
had taken her. Neuters, Toroya had called them, bronze-
skinned, smaller, like the Ibisians who had swarmed
the ship, killed Hayes . . . She screamed and tried to
shake herself free but they held her fast. Padrec hesitated. Why should he help her? Like a drug he had
been given but had never wanted to take, she had
taken over his life, at first forbidden and then compulsion, leaving him nothing of his own will or desire. He
did not hate her, but neither did he owe her—or did
he? A voice within reminded him that but for her he
would have been killed, discovered in his weakness

and helplessness at the ship, soon to be dead beside
the others. She had used him—God; yes, she had used
him—but she had saved his life, a human life, and he
could not stand by to watch her killed or captured by
others of her own cruel kind. He would always wonder
. . . and that regret would haunt him, as would her
cries, until his freedom would seem a curse. In the
end, however it came, he would still be dead—until
then he must live according to his own conscience.
And his conscience prodded him with that ancient and
primitive urge to save the woman he had slept with. *I
can still get away after,* he told himself, *if they don't
kill me.*

Arming himself with the pole, Padrec moved down
the low hill, not toward them, but away, circling into
the wind, hoping to take them by surprise. One of
Toroya's admonitions had been that the Ibisian olfactory sense was very keen, that they were more likely
to detect the human presence by smell than any other
means.

As he came upon the scene of the struggle, Padrec
saw something that chilled him to the bone. Lovely
Anii had been stripped, her red garments cut from
her, and while two bronze-skinned Ibisians held her
fast, another older and more female creature was running its hands over her soft thighs, probing her cruelly. *They're animals! They're worse than she is!* He
did not even give the creature a chance to see him as
he swung the pole with all his strength, bringing it
down upon its back. He heard and felt the crunch of
bones breaking as his pole also shattered.

At once the bronze-skinned neuters, alert to him,
released Anii to counter his attack with their spears.
But instead of coming after him, they hesitated as if
confused, holding back their spear thrusts. The bronze
lips parted, human teeth bared in alien grins, arms
jabbing at him to get the broken haft of the pole from
his hands. Instead, he rammed the jagged end of his
weapon hard into the abdomen of the nearest bronze
Ibisian, doubling the creature over, bleeding and

screaming. Out of the coner of his sight, Padrec saw Anii grasp the wounded creature's spear and thrust it through, finishing it. The other one, convinced of danger, swiped at her with its spear butt, knocking her aside, then thrust at Padrec in deadly earnest, its skill abruptly making the difference. A searing pain tore through his side as the spear sliced along his ribs, forcing him to fall back, the neuter jabbing again as he dodged to higher ground, but his feet slipped on the loose stones of a slope and he fell, red hot pain dripping down his leg, stabbing at his brain before a swirling red darkness overtook him and pulled him under to the sound of feet scrabbling on stones.

Anii had left the nom later than planned. Hli and D'nia both had detained her, questioning her condition. She realized too late that she should have mimicked the haggard look of one who had not found a mate. Now D'nia thought her pregnant.

Anii knew otherwise. Had the Stranger impregnated her, her nuptial phase would have ended abruptly after the first few matings. Instead, the phase had lasted its full time. She had not considered what to do if the Stranger had given her a pregnancy, and now she wondered if he even could; the possibility had not occurred to her in the heat of the phase, and for the time being, at least, she did not have to consider it. But in time she would. Of more looming importance was the Queen.

D'nia was jealous of fertile queens in the nom. And although Anii knew she was not pregnant, she had returned wearing the look of one who had mated successfully. Frustration and sleeplessness had not marred her glow; instead the Stranger's ability to mate frequently had heightened the knowing heat in her eyes, added a certain physical awareness to the self-confidence of her walk, the look of one who had taken and enjoyed. She should have known better.

"Where did you find him?" Hli had wanted to know. "Which nom did you raid?" The subservient had been thrilled with her protégée's obvious success.

Anii had merely glared at her. Her success, both real and rumored, suffered from poor timing. D'nia was failing, aging; her last two nuptials had yielded no offspring and the third was late in coming. Soon, very soon, one of the younger queens must move to dethrone her. A young, newly fertilized queen was therefore to be viewed as a rival, a possible successor,

to be relegated to a subordinate position or, if necessary, eliminated before she became a threat. And Anii,
known to be ambitious, would be perceived as a threat.
The rumor merely made her life in the nom more
precarious.

Her audience with D'nia had not gone well. The
Queen had been testy, insecure. Too many warriors
had been lost in fighting the Strangers, all but inviting hostile noms to invade her territory. Twice the
herds had been threatened. And now the young queens
were growing openly restless. From now on, the Queen's
eyes would be on Anii. As her eyes were on every
potential rival. D'nia was failing, yes, but not in
her willingness to preserve her power. But Anii and
other young females knew that D'nia no longer served
to increase the nom. D'nia had long been too interested in D'nia, pursuing her hold on the nom even to
the point of opposing the raising of young queens who
might one day depose her, thereby leaving the nom
ill-prepared to produce future generations. And the
Queen had missed important opportunities to elevate
the nom above its hostile neighbors; including the
mistaken and costly annihilation of the Strangers.

I must find the survivors, she thought. But with
D'nia watching her every move, she would have to
undertake such a thing in secret.

It had been as she was returning to the nuptial
lodge—after telling Hli that she thought it best to be
far from D'nia until the rumor had passed over, though
in truth she had wanted to spend her nights with the
Stranger—that she was waylaid. No doubt the hostiles had been watching her comings and goings, and
although they had not detected her lodge, they knew
her path. And she had been careless, allowing her
mind to wander with plannings and plots that she
would have done better to leave behind. Instead she
had brought them with her, and they had blinded her
to her attackers until it was too late and their hard
arms had grabbed her. Though she fought with her
knife, killing one, the other warriors had caught her

and held her fast, stripping the garments from her body so that she might be viewed. Satisfied that what they had caught was indeed a young queen and not an inferior female, the older female who led the hostiles had then attempted to ascertain if their prize was fertile or already pregnant, the last of great value to a nom in need of a breeder. Shamed, fingers roughly probing at her most secret parts, Anii screamed and struggled, fully knowing what would become of her.

A breeder—a mindless body producing offspring for some small filthy nom with aging drones—.

The female had just finished with her when a blow had felled the hostile from behind, breaking her back. It had stunned Anii more than the two neuters who held her to see that their assailant was a male. Pa-dric! But this was not the Pa-dric of her bed, the light in his eyes was fierce, not submissive. He had attacked with warrior-like strength as they thought to take him as well, a drone to be added to the prize catch of a Queen, but his aggression caught them by surprise, telling them too late that he was not one of the compliant drones of the nomari but of a fiercer race, one in which the males defended. He had felled another, which she had then killed, before the last warrior turned on him, catching him with a spear thrust to the side and again in the leg before Anii could take the fallen one's spear and thrust the warrior through, killing it. She had knelt beside the Stranger, then, amazed, unable to believe what he had done.

He had escaped! Though she had cleared the room of what he might use, he had found a way out of the lodge—but even that accomplishment amazed her less than the aggression he had shown, his ability, his willingness to fight. Though untrained, he had not hesitated to challenge two fully armed Misian warriors! And not on his own behalf, but hers.

He could have left me to my fate, and gained his freedom. And now his blood wets my fingers, red, like the blood of the nomari!

In the amber light before dark, Anii noted that his garments were her own, cut to fit, that he had opted for modesty. He stirred beneath her hand, then fell back with a groan, twisting with pain. The spear wound to his side did not look to be deep, but it bled profusely. The leg wound looked less serious and could be tended. What was she to do with him? She could not leave him here, not even to get a worker from the nom to carry him to safety. There were giant beetles which came out after dark, scavengers which often feasted upon the dead or wounded, and the dead hostiles would be certain meat. She would have to take him back to the lodge.

Bending over him, she touched his face, and his eyes, though deeply laced with pain, met hers. In them, she saw that he realized his failure. He had not escaped her. All his effort had brought him back to her again.

Turning from her, he pushed to his feet and backed away. His injured leg was unsteady, but bore his weight, and she could see that he wanted to run. Anii rose to follow, startled that he could still have such strength despite his injuries, knowing it only meant that he could do himself more harm.

A shrill clicking rose from the blanketing quiet of dusk, a far away reminder that when night fell predators ruled the plain. "Pa-dric, no," Anii spoke to him, tugging at his arms. "There are beetles. Beetles." How could she make him understand? "Bed," she said, using a word he knew, touching her fingers to the blood wetting what once had been her favored garments and holding them up before him, glistening with red in the last light. "Bed."

"Bed, no!" he shouted, tearing away from her. She stared at him in wonder. "No" was not a word she had taught him!

"Pa-dric, wait!" she cried as he ran away into the coming dark. She knew she must go after him, but not unarmed. *My knife,* she thought, running back to her slitted garments and finding it fallen there, forgotten.

She took that and the warrior's spear as well, and set off after him.

Still far away, but from another direction, the clicking renewed its strident summons beneath a purpling orange sunset sky. Padrec stumbled against some rocks and clenched his teeth with pain. It had turned out badly. He should have known that it would ... the damned Ibisians had killed him after all. Only in his case it had taken them a little longer.

He pulled his hand away from his side and looked at the bleeding. Too much. And his leg, the pain was growing worse, severed muscle tissue rubbing nerves raw, screaming at him to stop. He could not run anymore. A loud clicking sounded again, this time from the banks above him. That sound, that sound ... he knew it from the night he had spent gathering his friends' corpses. Beetles had gotten there first, he had found them feasting, first eating out the eyes, the soft tissues ... then they had not bothered him, but now, now that he was weakened, wounded, the blood smell coming from him. ...

Anii had been trying to warn him, suddenly he realized why and of what. He had been too desperate to escape to heed the fear that had stared at him in her eyes. *I'm a dead man,* he thought. *Unless I get out of this gully, onto flat ground ... I can't outrun it, but here I can't fight—there's no room.*

Far to the right he heard stones sliding down the soft desert earth, something heavy scrambling down the sides of the dry river bed. In the rising moonlight, the beetle's shape was massive, a huge, jointed thing, waist high and more than man-long. Its horrible head, long jaws curving at him like scythes, was larger than his own. Unable to tear his eyes from it, Padrec scrambled back along the gully, sometimes falling, searching for a weapon but finding none on the barren dry river bottom. His injured leg buckled and he fell to the sandy floor, groping for a rock to fend off the thing. But as he reared back his arm to hurl it, something grabbed it from behind and sawed into it deeply and

he screamed as the blood poured down and a beetle
clicked over his head. He barely saw Anii as she sliced
at the thing that had seized his arm in its jaws,
killing it by severing the slender juncture that was its
neck. He had a vision of an unclothed, spear-wielding
goddess standing above him as the monster thrashed
in its death throes. Then she stabbed at the eyes of
the other until it retreated, scuttling off, like most
scavengers timid when attacked.

Disturbed stones ground beside his ear as she knelt
beside him, her cool hand on his arm, commanding
him to be still. Bending, she cut off one of the leather
thongs binding her heavy sandals and lashed it around
the arm above the wound, twisting it until it bit deep
into his flesh, cutting off the flow of blood. Looking
up, he saw her working grimly, again, to save him.

"Anii—?"

Her eyes flashed. "Beetles," she said, repeating the
word he had heard her use earlier, pointing to the
hulking carcass still twitching nearby, "Beetles!"

"Beetles," he repeated, nodding that this time he
understood.

She sighed, then got her shoulder under his and
helped him to his feet, bracing his faltering steps on a
halting, slow journey back to the hidden entrance of
her underground chambers. Several times the pain in
his leg became unbearable and he had to rest, and the
jagged gash the beetle had torn in his arm felt as
though acid had been poured in it, eating its way to
the very tips of his fingers, his shoulder. After all his
endeavor, all his pain, he had failed. Ibis had turned
on him, dragged him into its coils from which there
seemed to be no escape. This world was vicious, savage, and he was lost in it as completely as if he had
been swallowed, to be systematically torn apart and
digested. He let Anii take him where she would, the
only safety left to him. She walked holding him with
one arm and her spear in the other, ever wary for
more beetles. But none came. And once he was safe
within her hidden cave, Anii went back to hide the

signs and smell of blood to keep away the scavengers
and other predators as deadly.

Returning, she sat beside his uncomplaining form
upon her bed. In a voice muted by pain, he spoke to
her, the gentle language of his kind that touched her
ears but not her understanding. "I blew it, didn't I?"
And his eyes as he looked away from her were hopeless again and filled with suffering of a kind different
from that of his flesh.

She did not know how to comfort him, though she
wanted to speak to him with words of comfort, reassure him that he was in no danger of dying. Nor could
she. As gently as she could she stripped her garments
from his body, knowing them ruined, begrudging them
not. She regretted only his wounds. When she held a
crock of sweet water for him to drink, knowing that
he must drink to wash the poison from his system, he
did so without protest, and soon after lapsed into a
restless sleep, uncaring, without hope.

She wanted to ask but did not, for he would not
understand, why he had shown her loyalty . . . why he
had taken it upon himself to help one whose kind had
murdered his, she who even now held him captive, her
slave. For was that not what he was? Hers. That
knowledge rubbed at her desire for him, bringing it on
her anew. Her beautiful Pa-dric. Of all her possessions the most desired, the most pleasing to her. A
male with the strength of a warrior and, perhaps, the
intelligence of a female . . . In the morning she would
return to the nom, but that night she tended the hurts
he had taken on her behalf, boiling water with which to
wash his wounds of dirt and poison, bandaging them
with pads of clean cloth, loosening the tourniquet in
an effort to save his life and his arm. Between these
tasks she attempted to restore her chambers to order,
seeking to unravel the disorder of his escape. Her
chests and carriers, her tables and cushions and even
the mattress she had earlier pulled free from him to rest
upon, even her mirror frame, had been piled one atop
the other in the center of the room. Her prized cushion

covers had been slashed to ribbons, the remains litter-
ing the chamber like tufts torn from a scarab's nest, a
rope of knotted fragments lying upon the piled clutter
of her furnishings, discarded. And the pole he had
used against the hostile warriors had prior to that
held her bed curtains! *He is intelligent, intelligent!*
She found herself continually returning to his ingenu-
ity, rejoicing in it. *If one plan does not work, he thinks
of another!* The Stranger was creative. More and more,
Anii knew that he would hold her interest even when
her nuptial phase had passed.

He woke once, when the tallow light had died to
shimmering pools of beeswax in their cups, and when
he saw her, his eyes died again, and he whispered to
her words she could not understand. Her fingers pressed
his lips. "Hush," she said. "It is a dream." And in his
dream he said, "Anii, no—." And so she left him, not
knowing what he had not wanted her to do.

The swell of morning's first light found Anii leaving
Pa-dric in a fevered sleep as she ran across the plain
to the nom. Once there, having brushed past the ever-
present guards who would no doubt report her arrival
to D'nia, she sought out Hli. The aged subservient
knew immediately that all was not as it should be.

"You have bruises!" the older female exclaimed, noting what Anii had hoped her longer than usual garments would conceal.

"I was waylaid last night as I returned to my lodge,"
Anii told her, the memory flushing her face. It had
been her own fault for being so careless! But she did
not tell this to her pale-faced attendant.

"How did you escape?" Hli demanded hoarsely. "Did
you kill them?"

"Yes. Them and one of the beetles." Anii studied the
astonished face of the one who had raised her since
the day she had left the nursery. If she could not trust
Hli, she could trust no one. "You must come with me
to the lodge, Hli," she said. "I can trust no one but you
to help me."

The aged one's shrewd eyes narrowed to orange slits. "What trouble have you got into now?"

"Not I, but one who helped me. I will go ahead. You will come one notch later to the place we have agreed upon. Bring your healing tools and potions and workers who will not be missed and meet me there."

"Perhaps I should bring your warriors as well."

"Perhaps. But I think not yet. The hostiles were a small party, poor and ill-clothed. I do not believe there are others. How many of the warriors are loyal?"

"Enough. But D'nia's phase comes upon her. Surely you saw as much."

Anii had not failed to notice the Queen's heightened color, her increased agitation. The worst time to oppose a queen was during her nuptial phase, for it was then she was at her most aggressive and dangerous, her power over the nom's warriors most compelling. Hli was right; that plan would have to wait. "Can I trust Bekuu?"

Hli twisted her head to one side, marking her young mistress, measuring her intentions. "What are you planning, to call upon the ti-warrior too soon, before you are ready?"

"I need Bekuu's warriors to do something for me. But it must be done in secret. Can they be gotten out of the nom without D'nia becoming suspicious?"

"I think Bekuu can do this. But be careful! What is this thing you wish them to do?"

Anii's delicately colored lips, so fresh from their remembered passion, those of a queen full formed, curved to withhold the answer. "Not yet, Hli. That secret is mine alone. But be patient, my good friend, and you will soon know a greater."

But later, when they met again at the lodge, Hli did not approve of treating the Stranger. She approved even less of Anii's use of him.

"How could you sully yourself with that ugly thing? It is not even nomari!"

"Look at him. Is he not like a nomari drone?"

Hli had pulled back the clean sheeting, scrutinizing

the Stranger. For a male, he was lean and not un-
graceful, and though he was muscled as a warrior, he
was not truly ugly. "He is smaller," she said, referring
to his organ.

"He is durable. There is much to be said for it."

"I still think it obscene."

But the old subservient had tended the Stranger,
marking that his bleeding had been stopped and the
wounds were already scabbing over. "He is of good
stuff, at least," she had muttered, and with the finest
sinews taken from the legs of geduflies, she had painstakingly closed the gaping wound in the Stranger's
arm, slathering it with a salve to keep it from fester-
ing. "Beetle bait!" she snorted derisively. "But I will
grant it is very like a human. The limb is just so. But
his skin—he is as pale as a nebin spider!" All the
while, the workers she had brought with her busied
with setting the chamber in order, polishing its surfaces, freshening soiled hangings and sheeting, making ready the young queen's parcels for her return to
the nom. How lovely she is! Hli thought as she watched
Anii cool the Stranger with cloths sweetened in herb
water. She had the glow that only came from nuptial
nights well spent. He had not harmed her beauty, this
Stranger—Anii knew her power now, the sexual source
of it. D'nia had not given her a mate—and now the
one she had found had shown her too many nights of
passion for her to go without again.

D'nia did well to watch her.

But the Stranger did not look well. Filth from the
beetle's claw had left a fever in his flesh. He had been
bad when first she came to him, and the morning had
still been young. Now the day was growing toward its
end and he was worse.

"You must return to the nom," Hli insisted as the
day gave way, "If you stay away now that your phase
has ended, you will be suspect. And you are already
watched by the Queen."

Anii rose from the bedside, resolved. "Then Pa-dric
must come with us to the nom."

"The Stranger? It will not be allowed!" Reluctantly she said, "Let me stay here with him."

"He will be smuggled into my chambers. There he can be nursed in secret. I would have him with me, Hli."

The subservient glared. "Your phase is past. What good is he to you now?"

"Why, Hli, you would throw him to the beetles, wouldn't you?" Anii watched her companion with her brilliant, narrow eyes, "You would as soon let the spiders feast on his flesh as admit that he might not be as unlike the nomari as you would like to think."

"Make him your pet, what do I care? But you show too much fondness for this creature—"

"It pleases me, Hli, to teach him. Go, and ready my chambers. If you warn others, and they take him from me, you lose your chance to privy chamber a Queen." When Hli had departed, Anii instructed the workers. Under her watchful gaze, one of the largest carriers was opened and most of the things it held removed, replaced by sheeting and the limp, unconscious Stranger and then more sheeting carefully layered in a way that allowed him to breathe. Before the afternoon had grown very much later, the nuptial lodge stood empty, and a train of workers, burdened by long chests and heavy parcels, followed Anii back across the plain to the tall towers of the nom.

For several days Padrec wandered in fever, the alien infection seeping into his brain, trying to kill him in his dreams and out of them. In the end, though much weakened, his body at last fought off the illness to which many an Ibisian would have succumbed. It took days more for him to recover under the stern and cautious eye of Hli, who at first would not let him leave the vast confines of Anii's sumptuous bed. He had awakened to a golden chamber he had recognized at once as being different from the one in which he had first taken ill from his wounds. This chamber was much larger, its walls covered with gold and polished to a gleaming luster, its many appointments much more luxurious. The delicate light reflected from those curved, golden walls played upon a setting too overwhelming to be enjoyed and had a strangeness, an eerie coldness, which he found unpleasant and which kept him to his bed. That bed, with its high, carved posts and rich draperies and sheets that looked as though they had been spun from beaten gold, for a time became his world, the place from which he viewed what was to be his life, learned the language that he must learn to speak. For he belonged to Ibis now.

Anii would come to him those lost nights when one or more of the three moons of Ibis showed through the high round portals, and her beauty would seem like that of the room she had created, untouchable, a goddess beyond reach, too cold and perfect for him to believe that she had ever taken him in lustful abandon. He was aware of her still, but his wounds were healing and she was mindful of them and did not press his response, although sometimes he still thought he detected a certain contained heat in her eyes, the golden gaze which often-times intercepted his across a room. It was not so much as if Anii had lost interest in him as that her interest had shed its overt sensuality, as if she had covered her nakedness with a gown. Instead she would take her place on the bed beside him after long days spent elsewhere, doing, he did not know what, and tutor him in the words she wanted him to know. She demanded his performance in that area no less harshly than she once had in others. And again he lived up to her expectations, learning to speak her language with a speed that surprised him.

Not only that, but Padrec had the satisfaction of knowing that he was able to surprise her. One day Anii brought to him a wooden lattice with many strings of golden beads, twelve to a strand, strung between the slats. He recognized it at once as a primitive calculator and he watched as her six fingers counted out the beads, one at a time, naming the numbers. After repeating them several times, he had mastered the base 12 numerical system and had taken to demonstrating his understanding by employing alternative sets: 2, 4, 6 ... 6, 12, 24 ... 96, 48, 24 ... Her face had glowed while watching his fingers move the beads, creating patterns she recognized as having significance. They had even made a game of it. She would start a set and he would continue it, or vice versa. More and more he saw her reaching out to him, trying to breach the wall of silence that divided his intelligence from hers, and more and more she was succeeding.

The only fly in the ointment was Hli. Padrec mutely accepted the old Ibisian's restrictions, sensing her dislike of him and inclined to return the feeling. Still, her attention was not unkind, only disapproving, and acutely protective, and her potions for all that he did not like to take them did not hinder his healing. Her eyes might glare at him, but Anii commanded her with a fine line, and Anii had made her wishes known. He was the younger female's property of sorts, and the older one had to be content to leave it at that. But that had not stopped her from showing her displeasure. Between Hli and Anii he knew himself guarded, protected, and he could well guess from what. Early in his convalescence he had discovered that Anii had brought him into the nom. One day he had looked out of the portals and found that he stood well above a vast and barren haze of tawny green plain, and far away the purple line of mountains beneath a line of clouds. And below him, the spiraling accesses and honeycombed solar terraces of the nom had spread before his eyes. He was in their hive, a prisoner with no way to escape. Now, in truth, he relied on Anii's protection. That she intended to continue her ownership of him now appeared certain.

One night, when he had recovered, Padrec was roused from his sleep by Hli, roughly bidden to dress in some shapeless brown robes, and placed under the guard of several warriors, who escorted him from Anii's chambers, through passageways strangely empty, patrolled by warriors. At some lower level, he knew not where or for what purpose, a door was opened and he was shoved inside and left there, the door bolts slamming into place behind him, and then again to the outer door beyond. The room was bare, with only a single candle sputtering faint light upon the walls, but there was one other inhabitant, standing alone in a corner.

"Toroya?" Padrec said, unwilling to believe his eyes.

"Morrissey? Is that you?" the xenobiologist came forward into the light. His face was thinner, lined, but he looked little different from the man Padrec had left that day at the ship. When Toroya reached for him, Padrec embraced him with more passion than he had felt for any living thing since his capture.

"Oh, Sam," Padrec whispered, gripping the older man fervently, not holding back the tears that blinded his eyes, "I thought I was the only one. I kept asking for you, but she never told me anything—"

"She?" Toroya asked.

"Anii, the Ibisian who captured me. She used your name once."

"So many of them know my name," said Toroya, "I tell it to any of them who will listen, hoping to get them to communicate. But they always have something else to do."

"What's going on, Sam? It's the middle of the night—"

Still holding him by the shoulders, Toroya pulled away, his dark eyes probing. "I'm not sure. I think we've been put here to keep us safe. Is it true that the ship has been destroyed?" he asked.

"Yes."

"Oh, Padrec, I'm sorry, so sorry. I kept hoping, but I think I knew."

"I saw it, Sam, I buried them. Leveso, Carmeyez—" Shuddering, he closed his eyes, unable to look the other man in the face. "Oh, God, it was awful, so many dead, so many I couldn't bury—the beetles eating out their eyes—"

"Don't, Padrec, don't. It's over. Don't think about it now." Toroya's face had gone pale. "I didn't know. I just didn't know." And he told him how a team had been sent out to attempt a meeting. But the team had been captured, and two members killed trying to escape. Only Toroya had survived, a captive, and brought back to the nom, where for a short time he had served as a curiosity. There, not knowing the fate of the ship or his companions, he had lived on the edge of fascination. The Ibisians were a xenologist's ultimate dream, an intact society, waiting to be catalogued and unraveled. With very little difficulty, Toroya had gradually come to accept his situation, taking extensive notes on Ibisian society, studying them to the extent that they allowed it. Padrec was the first human he had seen since being taken.

"And what about you, Morrissey?" those dark eyes studied him, "What has happened to you?"

"I'm not sure," said Padrec bleakly. Looking back, he could barely remember. His life had been torn from him no less completely than the lives of the dead men he had buried beneath a few inches of Ibisian sod. He often wondered if they would condemn him for the manner of his survival.

"You're barely over it, I can see that," Toroya said gently, guiding him to a bench against the far wall, pulling him down to sit before him. "You told me earlier that *she* had captured you. Do you mean to say that you were captured by one of their females?"

"Yes," Padrec said, because it hardly mattered. "She found me burying the others, and got me out of there before the warriors came back."

"A female? One of their queens?" he demanded excitedly, "Did she keep you? Or did she turn you over to the warriors right away?"

"She kept me." Padrec flushed. He could see that Toroya's interest in him had quickened. "What do you want to know, Sam?" he said quietly. "Didn't you know that the Ibisians keep slaves?"

Toroya shook his head and sighed. "I'm sorry, Padrec. Forgive me. You've been through a lot, haven't you?"

"I guess we all have."

A short time later, to the sounds of the guards being changed in the outer chamber, the older man spoke to him. "The Ibisians have let me study them, so I can tell you what I have found out. They are ruled by females. There is a dominant female and a number of subordinate females. I call them 'queens' because of the similarity of Ibisian social structure to that of the Hymenoptera. Bees, you know, ants and the like—"

"Yes, I know. Pollinators, remember?"

"Of course. In any case, one of the older subservients, a female named Vrisi, who is no longer functional, was given charge of me. She has managed to teach me some of the language, something of the society. I don't understand the biology of it yet, the embryonic differentiation, the genetics of sexual and asexual forms, but socially I've never seen anything like it. They are superbly organized. It's like a hive, exactly like a hive. The caste system is fairly straightforward, but the division of labor is intricate, efficient." Toroya sat before him, trying with his hands to explain what even words could not. His mouth, his usually bland face, were alive with the need to explain his discoveries. "The queens are not the only females capable of reproduction," he told Padrec excitedly, "but, and this is fascinating, the queens are the only truly intelligent caste. The workers, even the breeder-workers, are morons; the warriors have the intelligence of good dogs at best; and the males—well, the males I saw have the mental capacity of a penis."

Again Padrec flushed, violently. Knowing Ibisian females as he did, they required little more. Toroya noted his companion's reaction. He smiled reflectively.

"In this society, the males have been reduced to nothing more than drones. They are necessary only for certain types of reproduction, so very few of them are actually born, and those that are live sheltered lives, pampered and short."

"Short? As in—"

Toroya nodded. "As in they die soon after mating."

Padrec suddenly went ice-cold. "How do they die? Do the females kill them?"

"No, actually—" the look on Toroya's face was almost too scientifically detached, as if he did not consider that he was talking about something that might apply to human beings "—the cause, as near as I can ascertain, is quite natural. Their sexual drive apparently lies dormant until stimulated by the female, at which time they awaken to the sexual urge and successfully mate. Then something, the orgasm, or perhaps ejaculation itself, or maybe even an allergic reaction to the female, subsequently kills them. Or if it does not kill them, it leaves them permanently sterile, and still stupid. In that event, they are killed, since they have ceased to be of use."

"You mean they just mate once?" That would explain Anii's shocked reaction to him just after their brief meeting in the forest. She had not expected him to live—!

"Yes, just once. The big bang, I like to call it."

Is that why you are keeping me, Anii? Because your males die and I don't? Did I pleasure you those nights you would not let me sleep? She remembered. He could see that she remembered. She watched him with a predator's possession. The memory of those nights smoldered at him from behind her icy, stately composure like passion beneath a prostitute's veil. Just wait, it promised, and I will come to you. For all that she had refrained, it would not always be so. *I am hers, and when she is ready. . . .*

The pain of it was like a vise clamping his heart. How could Toroya be so casual? Unless he did not know. . . .

The scientist continued, unwitting. "Very soon after my capture, I was summoned into the presence of one of their young queens. Does the name Hli ring a bell?"

"Yes," Padrec whispered woodenly. "I know her. Anii's subservient." He used the Ibisian word; there was no Terran equivalent. Seeing that his companion had fallen into using the Ibisian language, Toroya smiled.

"It's already happening, isn't it, Morrissey," he observed with horrifying dispassion, "We're being domesticated. We're learning to adapt to them. We have to, if we're to survive. And it might not be so unpleasant. I met your Anii. She was so beautiful she took my breath away. And she is intelligent—"

"Yes," said Padrec, wondering at Toroya's direction, "Anii happens to be very intelligent. That doesn't alter things."

"It could alter things a great deal, if what I think is happening, is happening. The ruling Queen is getting old, my friend, and it may be that her leadership will be challenged. A lot of her warriors must have died taking the ship with its defenses." The look on Padrec's face told him the answer to that. How many thousands had to have died to overload the force shield? Toroya looked triumphant, as at a hypothesis proved correct. "Yes, you see, she lost too many warriors. And the Ibisians follow the dominant Queen. So when the old queen ages, shows signs of weakness, other, younger queens will move to overthrow her, seize the nom. Maybe one already has. I was brought here in the dead of night—and so were you. I think your Anii sent you here to be protected. Both of us. And her warriors stand guard outside. I think a palace coup is in the offing. And your Anii could be the next ruler of this nom."

"You don't seem to understand, Sam." Padrec wanted to wipe the pleased look from Samuro Toroya's face, even though he knew the man couldn't possibly understand his position. "She is not *my* Anii. I'm hers. Her Stranger," again he used the Ibisian word, "that creature *owns* me. And while she might be interested in protecting us, she isn't going to be in any hurry to set us free—"

Noises sounded from the outer chamber, the door being unbolted, swung open. Several warriors dressed

in blood-red silk, their bronze spear points gleaming,
entered the room, followed by Anii. She was in battle
dress, red silk beneath overlying garments of gold-
washed links, elaborately etched insect armor fitted to
her arms and legs, splendidly ridged and barbed as
befitted a young queen of the nomari. A headdress of
polished horns, wickedly curved and darkly gleaming
against the bright gold of her hair, made from the
jaws of some exotic insect, clasped her brow. She looked
barbaric, savage, victorious—and gloriously beautiful.
With her were other young females, equally tall, similarly attired, who kept behind her at a respectful
distance.

Toroya's hand tightened on Padrec's arm. "Bow," he
said under his breath and promptly knelt, putting his
forehead to the ground, before lifting his eyes cau-
tiously and saying with deepest regard in very good
Ibisian, "Royal one, we are honored."

She dismissed him as nothing, turning to Padrec
where he stood, quietly, refusing to bow to her. Her
golden eyes delved into his, asking nothing, claiming
all, and not only the victory.

"Pa-dric," she said coolly, holding out her hand to
him. He came. She could kill him, kill Toroya—to
obey her was his only choice for them both. The warriors parted, their bronze faces impassive, Toroya looking on, acutely observant, as Padrec's fingers touched
her hand and her six closed over his. Then to his
surprise, as the burning eyes of the onlooking females
watched intently, she wrapped her other hand about
his head and pulled his mouth to hers. Deeply humiliated, not daring to refuse her, he allowed her to place
her tongue within his mouth in an overlong, deliberately sexual caress that shamed him to the deepest
core of his being. He was hers, and she was proving it
to them all.

Toroya looked on, aghast with understanding. More
than a slave, he was her human lover! How had that
happened? And what would it mean? Poor Morrissey
. . . no wonder he was so subdued, so beaten . . . cap-

tured by aliens, used in that way . . . the man was
psychologically battered. . . .

At last Anii pulled away, her point proven, the
hard-eyed females openly envious of her possession of
the Stranger. She spoke to him gently. "You are mine,
Pa-dric, and none can take you from me. You are safe
now. Safe. None will kill you, none will take you. For
you are the favored one of the Queen."

"You are the Queen?"

"Yes. D'nia is banished."

He nodded. It was as Toroya had guessed. The old
queen had been overthrown and Anii had taken her
place. He looked across to the scientist and saw that
the compassion in the other man's eyes was only inci-
dental, that he owned a deeper interest he did not
want Padrec to see—consuming curiosity. Well, he
could hardly blame him, but still he felt betrayed, as
women must feel when all people wanted were the
details of a rape, not caring for shattered illusions, the
shame and deep revulsion for that part of oneself that
has been so intimately violated. He closed his eyes,
wanting only to hide from, to deny, the growing realization within him.

"You are weak still, and tired," Anii said, pressing
his arm with gentle fingers, touching the wound she
knew to be hidden beneath the cloth. She ordered two
of the warriors to escort him to her new chambers.
"Rest, pretty one," she said to him before he left,
"Later there will be feasting and celebrations. I would
have you with me."

When he was gone she turned to the guards and
said, "This other one, To-roya, shall go to Vrisi. She
has requested him."

He slept all morning and rose to find that his own
clothing had been laid out for him, cleaned and painstakingly mended. Padrec touched them, disbelieving,
for of late he had worn only shapeless, sashed robes,
the only garments Anii had given him to wear. And

now these. He looked up as the curtain on the far wall was brushed aside and Hli entered.

"Wear them," the subservient ordered sharply, "Now. She waits." Hli had yet to acknowledge that he was capable of understanding anything more complex than simple noun/verb commands.

She thinks of me as some sort of fancy drone, he realized.

Being reminded of the humiliating nature of his captivity hardly gave him any reason to want to please her, but the familiar garments demanded more loudly to be worn than any order to wear them. While Hli looked on, all the while pretending disinterest, Padrec pulled on his silver-gray trousers and regulation tunic, feeling again the familiar touch of fabric against his legs, the welcome snugness of a garment cut to fit, the accustomed pressure in the crotch. He had almost forgotten what it was to wear pants. He had just finished fastening the waist tabs when Anii entered with Toroya, who looked around the room before smiling at him self-consciously, almost in congratulations.

You bastard, Padrec thought suddenly, *you think this is just wonderful!*

"Pa-dric," Anii said, and he turned to her as her eyes scanned him briefly, "You are well? Strong?"

"Yes," he told her. What did she have in mind? Somehow he knew that it did not involve letting them go. Even so, gesturing to the garments he wore, he smiled and said with his small command of the language, "I thank, for this—"

Suddenly she looked acutely interested in him. "Does it mean so much?"

"To me, yes, it means much. I do not like—the others."

"I also like this better," she said, and her lips, too, played at mirth. But he had noticed that Ibisians neither laughed nor smiled, even when, as he had once or twice had occasion to see them, they were genuinely happy or amused. Crossing to him, Anii touched one finger to the fabric of his tunic. The

pressure there was nearly nothing, but it was her, and
he felt it as though upon his bare skin. "There are
others of your kind," she said, "I sent warriors to find
when they came to your nom, and to take them. There
were several—ten—do you understand?"

"Yes."

"That is good. You, and To-roya, must talk with
them, make them understand. There are males, and
females. The males must serve—"

"No!" Hli leaped to strike him for impertinence but
Anii gestured her back. Padrec looked to Toroya, but
the xenobiologist's eyes would not meet his—he already knew. "How can you stand there like that?" he
shouted to Toroya, the words of his own language
sounding discordant in this alien room, "You think
it's fine, don't you? You think this is one of your
xeno-social experiments, damn it—!"

"Morrissey, please listen—"

"Why?"

With a nervous glance at the silent, but intently
watchful Anii, Toroya approached him. "Because our
survival as a race may depend on it. Morrissey, please,
you have to understand—the Ibisians are giving us a
chance at survival. If we make ourselves useful to
them, if they have reasons for wanting to keep us
alive, then we will survive—not just you and me, but
also the other humans who escaped the slaughter.
Yes, yes," he said, as Padrec's eyes sought his with
the question. "Some escaped. I don't know how many,
twenty, thirty, maybe more. I've just found this all out
myself."

"It won't do any good, Toroya. It isn't a large enough
gene pool to do any good."

"Padrec, this group that they captured is from
Rubinsky's shuttles. They must have sent a sled. That
was over a hundred geologists, robotists and technicians. We may have two hundred people to consider.
That's enough. It's all we have left."

"So we prostitute the men, turn our own race over

into alien slavery—and don't tell me that's not what it is—!"

"What makes you think we have any choice? She's not telling us to ask them, Padrec, she's telling us to *tell* them."

"You mean—"

"I hoped my little pep talk would make it easier to swallow. I guess not. Nothing can really make it easier. But it does mean some sort of survival for our race—they want the men for . . . pleasure, and they'll keep the women because they'll need them to make more males."

Padrec looked at Anii. She watched him, her regal beauty hard, unyielding—but not unloving. Yes, he knew that she loved him, but it was not the kind of love that he could invoke against this. Drawing a breath, he shook his head and said to her, "No, no."

"It is good," she said to him, carefully choosing her words. "They will live."

"No. They will die. As will I."

"You do not die—"

"I will."

For once she looked confused. She did not know what he meant. But Toroya did, and his face went pale.

"I have already given them to the others who helped me," Anii went on. "Tonight they will be chosen. This, you will explain to them."

"I will not."

"If you will not, then who will?"

Padrec saw then the terrible choice. What would these men think, what would they do, if, knowing nothing, they found themselves being examined, chosen, dragged off to some alien lair without explanation, not knowing what would happen to them? Could he put any of his fellow men through even half of what he had gone through, because he did not want to have to face them with the truth?

It's my fault. If I had died with the others, if Anii had never found me, if I had not rescued her from

*those neuters ... I have brought this upon not only
myself, but others, now, as well—.*

And now they wanted him to make it easier for
them.

He looked away and said nothing, his throat worked
but he couldn't speak, his voice had left him. Vaguely,
he was aware of a concerned-looking Toroya indicating to Anii that the behavior was submissive, that
Padrec would do whatever was needed. But it didn't
make it any easier on him when, a short while later,
he followed Toroya into a large circular holding room
in one of the lower levels, and found himself face to
face with a handful of bewildered, frightened men.
The sight of the two former crewmates, in uniform,
was greeted first with astonishment, then confusion.

"What the hell is going on here?" the red-haired
leader Rubinsky demanded of Toroya, whom he remembered and knew. "What happened? The ship has
been gutted—!" The man looked haunted and Padrec
remembered that his wife had been among the crew.

"Yes we know."

"Those savages took the women—" another man
interposed, referring to the female members of the
scouting party. But Toroya only nodded, made a sooth-
ing gesture. "The women are fine, Lars. We've seen
them. They're housed in an area not far from here,
and being treated very well."

"Can you promise that?" Rubinsky said darkly.

"I can," said Padrec, defending what he knew of the
Ibisians. The women were completely safe—so long as
Anii wanted them to be.

"Who's this?"

"Senior Biologist Morrissey," Padrec answered dully.
"Planetary Phytology, PES Secondary."

"Oh, right," Rubinsky said, "I remember. Vladov's
young protégé. So they got you, too." His mouth twisted
into a wry grimace. "Not much to smile about anymore, is there, young fellow? By God, Sam, tell us
what happened—we got transmissions for weeks, then
suddenly, one day, nothing—."

"It happened very suddenly. Martin, please, you have to tell us first—your people, what happened with you. How many of you are there?"

Martin Rubinsky frowned. He was a big man, and bearded, unlike most PES personnel, who preferred facial electrolysis for the sake of convenience. Padrec himself had never worn a beard and even the thought of doing so was alien, and now impossible. But the reddish stubble on the research captain's cheeks gave his masculine authority that much more impact, something he counted on in his position. "One hundred and forty-three men and women," Rubinsky told Toroya, reaffirming what Toroya had said about the number of survivors on the eastern sub-continent. "We lost two surveyors to a geo-accident, but none landing. But you know that. We kept contact with the ship. When we didn't hear anything—we had to come, even if it meant tearing down one of the shuttles." His face showed what it had cost him to do that. "We found the ship—" he choked, unable to hold back on the throb in his voice, "You know what we found. We thought that maybe there were survivors—that if there were any maybe we could find them—" He looked up, desperately hopeful. "Helen—" he gave them his wife's name. "Do you know—?"

"I'm sorry, Martin, really, but I don't know—" Toroya was vaguely sympathetic.

Touched by the man's pain, his unwillingness to relinquish hope, Padrec added, "I—I found the dead, Captain Rubinsky, and I did manage to bury a few. She wasn't one of them."

"You mean she might still be alive?"

"There were a lot of bodies I never found—" Padrec began, not wanting to be too hopeful, but another of the men said softly, forestalling him, "Let him hope, will you? It's all he's got left."

It was painful to hear Toroya tell them what had happened. Painful to relive it, if only in his own mind, the smoke, the screams. Leveso dead. The ship overrun, plundered, burned—Hayes dismembered before his eyes—attacked by aliens who did not even know what it was they were destroying, Ignorance, paranoia, fear—that was what had moved the Ibisians to eliminate them. Padrec knew that now, knew it as a hard knot of reason that had no power to dissipate his pain, only to contain it, to keep it from spilling over and causing him to hate those who had brought it to him. He did not hate the Ibisians for protecting their world, though he disagreed with and hated the way they had done it. And it terrified him that Toroya's explanations, rationalizations, made an obscene sort of sense, as if in some way they deserved this for having fallen into something in which they had no place, no right to be. It was also painful to explain why these same Ibisians were now content to let them live.

For the same reason our savage Terran ancestors let captive women live—.

But Padrec did not say this. He said nothing. He just stood there, silently containing his pain as Toroya laid down the terms of Ibisian capture to seven stunned and angry men. He only knew that he did not want to be there as a strangely dispassionate scientist told this handful of proud, intelligent and independent human beings that they were now possessions, their sexuality little more than prime barter. He was hardly surprised when the men turned on them, enraged, striking out at them as traitors, a hard fist from one man knocking Toroya to the floor without warning.

"Don't!" Toroya shouted as Rubinsky, with a threatening snarl on his face, pushed Padrec to the wall, taking his silence as being in support of Toroya's proclamation. At once several spear-bearing warriors appeared to force him away. "Threaten him, and it could well be the end of us all!"

"What?" the big science officer demanded. But he stared respectfully at the spears and the pale-haired, bronze-skinned warriors still carefully attending his every move with spear tips ready.

"This nom's Queen, Anii—" the scientist explained, "He belongs to her."

"Good God!" Rubinsky stared at Padrec, his face flushing with anger. "You mean—him? He's actually slept with one of those things?"

"The queens—the females—are very human," Toroya hastened to explain, as the revulsion of his fellow humans brought Padrec very close to breaking down completely. "They are also very beautiful. At first glance, any man in the universe would think them Terran women. Morrissey hasn't done anything we won't be doing ourselves in a few hours—whether we want to or not. He had no choice. And neither will we. It was explained to me. Ibisian females have evolved pheromones so powerfully enticing that no human male can refuse to mate once he is under the influence of them. These pheromones are necessary in their own species to stimulate the dormant testes of the Ibisian male and ready him for mating. To our species, they are the ultimate aphrodisiac."

"But if they have males of their own," Lars Hanson protested, "why don't they use them?"

Toroya answered simply. "Their own males die once they have mated. And they don't have very many."

"So—"

"Morrissey didn't. We won't. We're reusable."

The silence that followed was awesome. Rubinsky turned to Padrec again, and the look on his face was thick with loathing. "You godless bastard—I'd kill myself before I would crawl into some alien female's bed!"

"You would do well not to talk to him like that," Toroya said. "You'll be doing the same thing very soon. And if he hadn't fallen into her bed, you wouldn't be alive to rant about it! You'd have been killed outright, the moment the Ibisians caught wind of you!"

"And better that way!" Rubinsky hissed. He glared at Padrec so fiercely that the Ibisian guards readied their spears in warning. "God!" he swore, disbelieving, "They're guarding him, not us!"

Though Padrec wanted to agree with him that it would be better to prefer death to slavery, he knew that saying it wouldn't help. Nothing he could say at this moment would help, nor did he think they would believe him. He merely stood before them, mute evidence that such a life was livable, if not the optimum of human conditions. And that was as much as he would do to ease the horror and dark desperation of what these men were feeling. He couldn't tell them to be happy with their lots when he knew that they would not be, could not be. The other queens would not be as kind to them as Anii was to him. He couldn't tell them lies, and they did not want to believe the truth, and would not believe the truth until this evening when it confronted them.

Just before the warriors led him away Rubinsky shouted at them in parting, "You sold out! For your own crummy lives, you sold out! And now you're selling out the rest of us—!"

Those words rang in his ears, damning him, even when the other men were gone.

Anii paced the vast confines of the royal chambers and worried. Something was wrong with Pa-dric. During his recovery, he had come to accept his captivity, his place with her. Her company had pleased him, she knew this, and he had made no further trouble, no other attempts at escape, and had passively submitted to lessons aimed at teaching him the ways of the nomari. Her touch no longer horrified him. He did not shrink from her fingers now when they touched his and more often of late he would let her stroke his hair, his limbs, with gentle wonder and appreciation of his alien beauty. Even last night, when she had come to him in victory, and had forced him to perform the gesture of submission in the presence of others, even one of his own kind, he had allowed this. And then this morning, following his sleep and dressed in the garments of his captured kind, he had looked at her and she had detected *something*. Pleasure and perhaps warmth, maybe pride. Something, she sensed, of what he had been. Her heart had soared at seeing his sadness lifted, and in knowing that she had, even in so small a thing, pleased him. She had forgotten how appealing he could be in those garments that showed the shape of him, the easy grace of his movements. Yes, she did prefer those garments to the others—perhaps, for her pleasure alone, she would allow him to wear them.

But when she had told him that he must talk with the other males of his nom who had been captured, to explain to them that they must do as he did and live as the personal captives of nomari queens and not the slaves of warriors or drudges in the pits, he had not accepted it. Like a knife to her heart, the earlier sadness had returned and, if anything, deepened. And to To-roya, with whose presence she had thought to please him, he had shown only anger.

To-roya had told her that Pa-dric would not like it.

"For our race it is—unacceptable—to mate outside our own kind."

"But you say that we are of the same kind," she had pointed out. "You say that we, and you, are Hu-man."

"Human, yes. But not the same."

She had pondered this and known it true. The nomari and the Strangers had many differences no amount of similarity could overlook. Had she not wondered herself, at first, as to the naturalness of taking Pa-dric as a mate? Perhaps it was not, quite, natural. Perhaps it was not natural for two queens to pleasure each other in the absence of a male, for certainly such things happened, or for a queen in desperation to entertain a warrior's services, for that too was known to occur. Of the three, taking pleasure of a Stranger more approached the sexual norm.

"Pa-dric delights me," she had told To-roya then, "You and your captured companions shall delight others. It will not be unpleasant. Pa-dric, as you see, is cherished and well-treated. I have allowed no harm to come to him."

"Yes, Most Royal Queen," To-roya had responded,

bowing low. His manners pleased her. "I̶
harmed. It harms him to be without ch̶
freedom. Our race does not take or keep
forbidden."

"Why?"

"We think it wrong to—take away, an intelligent creature's freedom of action or will."

She had not liked pondering that key concept. On Mi it was universally held that for queens slavery was the most odious of captivities, the bondage of one who gives life, the shame of being made to bear for others and not one's own. That the Strangers, too, might suffer similarly had occurred to her, but she knew that she must not allow such considerations to stand in the way of the nom's greater good. To accept its tenets would mean giving up not only her path to power but also the Stranger she had come to treasure fondly.

"All captives are slaves," she had explained to Toroya. "All who are not of this nom must be slaves of the nom or die. You surrendered yourself to the warriors and lived; your companions who did not, died. I found Pa-dric in his weakness, and took him, and he knows himself my slave now because he wishes to live. Your males who wish to live will do the same, for there are other types of slavery, none of which they would survive."

"But must we be—enslaved?"

"You must. That which is not nomari on Mi is either food or sport. Your kind would do well for either. Already other noms have hunted your survivors. My warriors saved these, because I ordered it. I wanted more of your males for my nom. You see, I would keep the one I have. A male who can mate many times would be the treasure of any who owned him. Young queens without access to drones, and no way to mate, would kill for such a prize. Well do I know it! I have therefore decided to give them Strangers of their own, and in that way satisfy their urgings che nuptial chamber, not in the heat of a royal coup."

"You are wise."

"I think so. I owe my throne to the promise of these males to those who supported my overthrow of D'nia. You understand my plan for your kind?"

"Yes. I am an old man, and a practical one. I can accept enslavement to save the race. But Padrec is an idealist—he never will."

"He is less intelligent than you?"

"Oh, no. He is very intelligent. But he is an ethical man, one who will abide by his beliefs. He will not easily accept slavery, not his own and not that of his fellow humans. I can admire that in him."

"What is this ... ethical?" she had asked, for To-roya had used a word of his own language. If it was something his own kind admired, she wanted to know of it.

"He believes in a set of values whereby certain things are good or bad, right or wrong—acceptable and unacceptable. Human slavery is bad, wrong, and unacceptable."

She had leaned back then, amused by this man of contradictions. "But you do not think that it is wrong to make slaves of your kind?"

"If it serves to save the race, I can accept it."

"You are to be included."

Again he had bowed, showing acceptance, but she had seen the uncertainty that had dropped his eyes too suddenly from hers.

"Do not worry, To-roya, you will not die. I used Pa-dric many times and he suffered little."

"Alas," To-roya had said, "Padrec is a young man still. I am much older. How many times in a day did you mate him?"

When she had told him, he had stood silent, then he had swallowed and said, "Older males are not capable of such frequent matings. I am not even sure he is."

"Perhaps not. After the first several times his performance declined. Is this to be expected in your race?"

"Your males die with but one mating," To-roya had pointed out. "We Strangers can mate more often, but not without limit. I find Padrec's performance extraordinary."

So it was true, she had used her pheromone-enslaved captive to excess. Anii had explained this to To-roya, emphasizing the effects of the royal pheromones in the mating ritual. His dark, alien eyes had widened with the significance of that discovery.

"Pheromones! He was compelled, then—"

"Yes. All are compelled by the nuptial need. If at that time a male and a female are together, the female must mate the male and the male must mate her."

"Even if he does not want to?"

"Ah, but he has no choice, To-roya, because by then he does want to."

As she had wanted to pull Pa-dric down to her upon the moss, an alien, a Stranger, and so very much a male as he too had answered to that primal call to mate. And in the nuptial lodge, for three days and nights, he had been her willing slave, her every desire fulfilled. Remembering, she had felt again the stir of those many hours, and she had grown impatient with counting the moons until her nuptial phase would return.

And To-roya, unable to look upon her desire, had bowed deeply and backed away. Later, together, they had approached Pa-dric on the matter of convincing his fellow captives to give themselves passively, without the need to dominate them as she had had to do with him. He had refused, and in that strange tongue of his had argued with To-roya, to what end she was not certain, only that To-roya had pleaded with her after not to press him. And such was his agitation that she could see for herself that it would be a mistake. Pa-dric, his eyes dull with pain, had somehow taken the notion that he would die. She had thought that maybe he had heard some rumor of how drones died in the mating heat, but To-roya had said no, that

Pa-dric's state was one of mourning for the slavery to which his fellow creatures were being put. Only then had she understood what To-roya had tried to tell her.

He has the pride of a queen, and the intelligence to suffer for it, and I have made of him a slave. And now I would use him to enslave others of his kind. That he could feel such empathy for his fellow beings both dismayed and moved her, for she was set upon this course. *Tonight my nomari sisters will anoint their skins with the sweet oils and scents of the nuptial female, and they will draw his companions down upon their couches, and they will press on them the gesture of submission that I show to them, and tonight we will celebrate this discovery. Never again will it be necessary for a female to revolt simply to satisfy her need to have a male in her arms, nor to die in raiding a hostile nom—I will see to it that all have Strangers to pleasure them.*

And Pa-dric knows this, he reads my full intention.

She was adjusting the filigree clasp on her girdle of irisfly wings when the curtain to her bathing chambers parted and Hli entered. Behind her, Pa-dric looked as exhausted as he had on that first morning when she had found him, again the tears on his face, that haunting sense of pain. *Is it really so terrible for him?*

Hli's coppery eyes flashed. "It was nearly a disturbance! The guards had to step in to keep them from killing him!"

Angered that To-roya should not have warned her of this danger, Anii looked to Pa-dric. But he only shook his head, and said, subdued, "Not me. What you wish. They are humans, not animals. They cannot accept what you wish them to do."

"Neither do you accept it, I see." With a motion of her hand, she directed Hli to bring some garments from a nearby holder. "These are for you," she said.

The frowning subservient placed them in Pa-dric's arms and he looked at them, fully knowing what they were. What he held was yet another loose gown of the type she had lately seen him wear, but woven of the heaviest, richest of red silks, thickly luxurious, lanced with costly barbings and embroidery—garments fit for a queen's new favorite.

Anii watched to see his reaction. Why did he hesitate? Did he think the garments ugly, too fine, too garish? Perhaps he did not like the color red ... or maybe he was thinking to rebel again, by refusing to wear her gift. When that dark head lifted, and those tortured blue eyes met hers with reflections of shame and thwarted defiance, she knew the answer, and anger suffused her cheeks with deep bronze beneath the gold. She suppressed the urge to strike him. "Why must you act as though you are ashamed to be mine?" she snapped at him, "Is it not some justification of your worth to me that I want you, and not one of those others? I could give you to another less patient with your ways!" Abruptly she regretted having said this, for his eyes flashed back at her defiantly.

"Why don't you?"

She set down her brush as Hli looked on in amazed silence. It was unheard of for a subordinate, a mere male, to so defy the orders of his queen! The long girdle of a thousand dancing irisfly wings rustled lightly as she crossed the room to stand before him, and with fingers sure with prior experience began to undo his alien garments. "Because," she said, ripping free the neck tabs and front binding, "it is you I wanted to speak so that I might know you; and you who first taught me the lessons of Strangers. You it was who saved me from the hostiles and you I saved from the beetles; you I play numbers with late at night; and you I claim. Leave them the others—I will have you with me tonight, my dark-haired beauty, your eyes the jewels of my treasury, the envy of them all. Because you, beloved Pa-dric, are you, and when you are all sweetness in my arms I will want nothing more in this world or any other."

Why did he tremble beneath her hands? "Anii," he whispered, and her hands stopped upon his waist, "take me, if you want me—I will be yours. I—am yours for many passages now. I, too, know you, and for me it is—I can accept this. But, my people, the others, let them free, let them go."

He was begging her, something he had never done for himself, pleading with imperfect words, but in his intelligent eyes that plea was repeated a thousand times more passionately, his pride dying with every moment that she looked into his reasons for asking her to give him this one gift, this one proof of her affection for him. She put her fingers to his face, touched his tears. "Beautiful, beautiful one," she said, "I cannot. You must learn that your place gives you no privilege to decide my policy. Hli knows this lesson. You must learn it. You cannot barter yourself. That, too, is already decided."

And gently, taking her privilege, she touched her mouth to his and tasted the tender victory of his hopeless submission. And yet it was not victory. She could feel him running from her, the horror with which he pulled away, the hopelessness which held him captive. His mortal despair struck at her with lightnings, as if the entire nation of his people stood between them.

I must find some way to heal him. To make him mine freely. Then he would not be a slave, and he would not suffer so. He would know I am not using him, that I have come to cherish him above all other creatures.

When she pulled away, satisfied with his passivity, Anii ordered Hli to proceed with the preparations, to attire him as Anii wished him to be attired. He dully submitted, but his eyes would not meet hers, nor did the expression on his face change, but remained blank with pain. Even Hli ordered him with gentleness, attending both her Queen's desire and the Stranger's odd listlessness with care. When all was done, the subservient bowed and left them. Though Pa-dric's silent companionship gave her no joy, Anii found that she could take pleasure in the sight of him. The garments the silk-workers had made for him played to his strange alien beauty as she had planned that they should: a color to give fire to his paleness; dyed barbs to bring out the color of his eyes, the darkness of his hair; a wide corded sash at his waist to accentuate the body beneath the cloth. Her purpose in displaying him to such advantage was two-fold: to present a tempting picture to her subordinates, and to show that she, Anii, their new Queen, owned the most desirable Stranger of all.

Pa-dric was her slave, yes, but he was also her beloved—the paradox was not lost on her, for all that its discovery was unexpected. Queens occasionally become attached to a particular male, but such liaisons usually terminated abruptly, when the male died at the inevitable mating. No provisions, social or emotional, had been made for longer relationships, leaving her confused as to how to proceed. Clearly it demeaned him to be treated as a slave, for his intelligence and pride could not accept such treatment. But neither could she treat him with the usual solicitous reverence reserved for the beautiful, doomed creatures favored by great fortune to live a few short moons as the chosen mates of a nomari Queen. And for tonight, at least, he must remain the slave.

Beneath the high, golden ceiling of the Hall of Eshunn, Anii held court that night. Enthroned on a raised dais of onyx and ebony, lying on her shimmering cushions of spun gold and sapphire and queenly scarlet alongside a low table laden with delicacies for every sense, she who but the night before had wrested power now received the fruits of victory. At her feet, in a place of intimacy without honor, Padrec sat unmoving, unable to look away from the unfolding spectacle on the floor just a few steps below, where seven human males, apprehensive and dressed even as he was in garments alien to them, had assembled in a tight knot. His friends! He barely knew them. The geo-survey unit had never had much contact with him, had kept to themselves—but they were his people, men like himself, and he felt their confusion and pain as if it was his own. *And I cannot help them. We've been plunged into a nightmare where our own society no longer exists—*.

Anii touched him, and he glanced into her goldening eyes. "You shall learn the ways of the nomari," her rich voice reminded him. "We are your people now."

He shook his head, and looked elsewhere. "Those are my people. My *nomari*."

Unexpectedly, she made no move to challenge him. Instead she quietly poured a draught of strange dark nectar into his cup and this she handed him with solemn, almost ritualistic, attention to his taking of it. Though he lifted it to his lips, enough to know that the drink was sweet to the taste and heavy, he did not swallow, wary of her intensity. He had noted it first early in the evening, before coming down to the Hall, as she had wandered in her chambers, ever watchful of him, dabbing at her skin with a tiny vial of sweetly scented oils. Now when she leaned near to him, he felt the beginning stirrings of what once had claimed him completely. Ibisian pheromones, that provocative summons no man could refuse—and she would be wearing them tonight. One touch of those oils upon his skin, and his blood would answer. Already she had it in hers. And all evening he had been aware of her, beneath the skin, the surface awareness of his mind. Before, when she had been in her mating heat, her body casting off pheromones as swiftly as she had produced them, the effect had been devastating, immediate, compelling. Now it was muted, the preserved pheromones more subtle, less potent. Seduction, too, would be needed tonight. But he did not doubt that, in the end, she would seduce him, nor was he sure he did not want her to.

To feel her again—. Raggedly, he looked away and tried not to be aware of her, her breasts moving softly, unrestrained beneath her gown, her lovely arms, the ways her lips curved with remembered passions whenever her shining eyes caught his. Every time she looked at him he felt like a virgin before his first woman. . . .

It had been worse to endure the sight of his fellow scientists being led to their new masters, who had chosen them ahead of time, out of his sight, in what manner he did not know. But he was sure Toroya knew. He could see the stooping scientist serving as translator between the men and the queens who owned them, doing his best to ease the transition amid bowls of nectar and platters of sweet grubs used to tempt the captives. *Why do you try to make it easier for them? You can't. You can't make men accept this state, just because you are able. Toroya, you are wrong.*

Only Rubinsky showed signs of being a difficult captive, with his hands bound before him with golden cords. Once Padrec met his eyes across the room, and the hatred there had burned at him, damning him, and he had not dared to look that way again. *Can't they see, even now, that I am in the same straits they are in? That I am not here by choice?*

Food and drink gave way to music, and then the dancers came, Ibisian warriors of a specialized caste, as elegant and supple as reeds in wind or vapor swirling at first dawn, at first haunting, then vigorously savage in their leaping, spinning dance. Streamers trailed from their shoulders like wings, from their hands like flame. Slowly, the music died down to flickering embers—but not the heat in Anii's eyes, nor in those of the other gleaming, golden-skinned females who watched with understanding the unfolding petals of this evening, seeking the nectar to be found at its center. All else—food, drink, dance, talk—was but the prelude to their celebration of victory, the doorstep of a discovery all queens hoped would free them at last from cruel constraints.

He could not bear their eyes. He felt like an animal, or worse, an inanimate thing, and it was all he could do to keep from cringing whenever Anii touched him, her fingertips reaching to stroke, carelessly, without meaning or malice, whatever part of him was nearest

her, his arm, his cheek, his hair, reminding them—
and him—of her physical possession. He had not seen
Anii so much as touch the vial of pheromones that
hung about her neck, dipping between her breasts
like a dangling threat and promise, but somehow the
scent of it lingered in the air, warmed by the rising
temperature of a room heated by dancing fires and
pressing bodies. Drawn from some golden dream, Anii
leaned to him and placed the drink he had earlier
rejected again to his lips, and this time he could not
pretend. The honeyed drink, thick and sweet, flowed
down his throat to line his stomach, leaving a residue
in his mouth, the last traces glistening on his lips. He
felt sick, knowing it red, like blood, the nuptial color
Ibisians loved, and he moved to wipe it from his mouth,
but Anii stopped his hand and, placing her mouth to
his, licked the honey sweet taste from his lips as the
heady scent of her surrounded him, no doubt as she
intended.

"Pa-dric," she said, her lips still touching his, "burn
for me, beloved—"

"Anii, please—," he answered huskily, because it
was true. He did want her. Especially now, her golden
skin inviting touch, her golden eyes his surrender.
"Please don't make me—" How could he tell her he
could not respond to her in front of others? If she
asked that of him, or demanded it—.

"Is it too soon?"

"I cannot, before these others."

Her eyes glowed, laughing at him. "Is that what
you fear? No, pretty one, I will not take you for all to
see. None but I may know what it is like to be with
you."

Could she possibly understand what it would mean
to him? Anii would not intentionally shame or humili-
ate him, time and again she had proven that she could
be sensitive to his needs. Her use of him was never
deliberately cruel. But his eyes strayed to the other
men, some of them already pheromone-affected, their
eyes glazed and stupefied as their robes were loosened

and drawn from their shoulders, their bodies, alien hands taking possession . . . even Rubinsky, his hands still chained, his red head bent as a long limbed Ibisian queen ran her hands through his hair, pulled at his beard . . . He shuddered, and Anii, to take his eyes from them, drew him to her in a movement that caused him to bump the low table, knocking from it a bowl which clattered dully down the broad steps to ring upon the floor below. No more the delicate kiss. Her fingers, moistened in the secret oils of the tiny vial between her breasts, traced a burning path down his throat, across his shoulder, anointing him with phero- mones as deadly to his will as cobra venom to his blood, and he yielded as with her other hand she angled his mouth to hers, performing again that deeply probing kiss which for some strange reason symbol- ized her possession of him. Her deliberate seduction, his obvious acceptance, drew murmurs of approval from around the chamber. "Oh, God—" someone moaned, and Padrec, ashamed that the others should see him so easily used, tried to pull away, but Anii sensed that attempt at escape. "No," her lips moved upon his mouth, "This alone I will ask of you before them," and so he remained, frozen beneath her touch, submitting to her hands, her mouth, her probing tongue, as she bent over him and demonstrated her possession. Mortified, he allowed it. Only then did she release him, reluctantly, her purpose attained, if not her desire.

Padrec sank back, shaken, humiliated, angry—and throbbing with sensations that had nothing to do with any of these vastly conflicting emotions. She had just assured him of her care, and now this—public embar- rassment! *Did she mean it that way, or was it neces- sary, some sort of expected behavior? It was only a kiss, after all—.* But he blushed furiously, knowing that every pair of eyes in the Hall had watched that kiss, fully knowing the final act that, ultimately, must follow. Looking up, across the room, he saw the faint smile on Samuro Toroya's face, as though he had seen something that had made the evening shine more brightly.

But that night at least the Queen held him chaste, her own, the vestal virgin of her own very brightly burning sexuality by which the nom now was to be ruled. He was hers and no other's ... Not for thine eyes, she as much as said, but for mine alone. But he had seen the other men used with less care. Rubinsky, especially, that proud hard man, crudely enslaved by alien biology, mindlessly coupling beneath the glow of the midnight fires, the heat of sweat on his gleaming body, in full display of all. No such gentleness was shown them as was shown him, and Anii in no way tried to keep him from seeing the manner of slavery into which he had unknowingly led them. But as the night fires burned low, and the dancers one by one dropped to the floors with exhaustion, and the Hall fell into a languor of food and drink and spent desires, Anii's fingers became bold, touching him in ways she had not pursued when the night was young and other eyes upon them, awakening in him the slow burn that had long ago consumed the others. In the end it was he who pulled her to him, desiring the embrace.

"Take me now—" he had whispered.

"So sweet," her low voice caressed him, and her kiss had stolen his very breath away. "Now you know what I intend for you—"

She was in his blood, and he was no better than the others for wanting her. But she had waited, and later, in the vast confines of her queenly bed, beneath a conical ceiling softly afire with tallow lights, he had appeased the shameful hunger of his body, now recovered and intent on its own release. Smoothly, as though entering silk, he had felt golden Anii welcome him, her arms enfolding him, her thighs clasping his, exercising her ownership of him by allowing this gentle possession by the object of her desire. In the aftermath he could not even feel used, such had been his active participation.

"You are not ashamed to be mine?" she had asked

softly later, much later, when all lovemaking was done.

"No," he had answered, truthfully, "It does not shame me to be yours. I would be yours—before anyone's."

He wondered if she knew what that admission meant.

He did not know how well she knew what the release had meant for him. Toroya had told her about Stranger males, the strange and wonderful hungers of their bodies, with mating needs of their own apart from those of the female. A male Stranger, he had told her, seldom went many passages without mating, though the matings that resulted were less intense, less sure to produce, than those of the nomari. A male, constantly aware of a female, he had said, would soon desire to relieve his sexual tension. As Pa-dric had done with her.

But that knowledge had given rise to a problem. A Stranger was not like a nomari male, ready only when the female required him. And tonight she had tasted the heated urgency of her beloved's need, his readiness that went far deeper than the pull of the drug upon him. She had not taken him so much as he had taken her. The feel of his trembling body, so strong, so powerfully driven, so giving, had been the reward of all her patient waiting. But it had been easy for her to wait. When not in the nuptial phase, a queen's sexual urges were quiescent, submerged, unless aroused by *muhra,* as she had done this night, or the pervading sexuality of the ruling Queen's nuptial phase upon her followers. She would take him, she knew, for the pleasure of it, for sensuality, for love of the way he wanted her. But soon she would enter her nuptial phase again, and then she must take a mate of her own kind to provide for the nom.

That alone did not worry her. The one desire did not threaten the other. But afterward she would not wish to mate, not for many passings of moons, not while her pregnancy lasted. It was Pa-dric's welfare that concerned her. His needs that Toroya had described to her must be seen to, but how? To give him to another queen, even temporarily, was out of the question. Even if her jealousy could allow it, the other queen would, by using her male, threaten her dominance, and that could not be allowed. Nor did she think Pa-dric would consent to ownership by another; the bonds they had built between them allowed him to consent to her ownership, but he would not consent to belong to another. He had only now said as much. She reached out her hand and lovingly stroked the long, hard muscles of his thigh. He was younger and more beautiful than the others. Perhaps one of the female Strangers could be found for him—. Yes, the idea appealed to her. Perhaps Pa-dric, too, had need to mate with his own kind. . . .

"She loves you! Don't you realize that, you proud, stubborn fool?"

Toroya studied Padrec Morrissey across the light-filled confines of this garden room attached to the Queen's private chambers. It was an extravagance, and it dripped, but it had the smell of soil and greenery and at least an approximation of the world outside. There were times when even the harsh desert plain would have been a welcome change from the unending corridors and high conical ceilings of the vast, self-contained nom.

"Do you know what you're saying?" Padrec replied, though his question was strangely restrained, as if the answer were known.

The older man sighed. "Yes, I know what I'm saying. Is it so impossible? That lovely creature is obsessed with you, she wants to know what's going on inside your head. She keeps fishing for ways to understand and please you. Our talks inevitably revert to *Padric*." Somehow his tongue was able to reproduce exactly the peculiar lilting twist that Anii used. "If I were your father, Morrissey, maybe I could help her, but I'm not."

"Hell, Toroya, you're not even my friend—"

Toroya's face went slack and hurt, and his eyes died just a little. "Look, Padrec," he said quietly. "I know you don't approve of me, of some of the positions I have taken. It hasn't been easy for you to accept—I can understand why. I want your approval and I know I shall never have it—and you don't want mine, though I will tell you now that it is not for me to approve or disapprove of anything you do. What happened between you and Anii is quite separate from my judg-

103

ment, but it may well have saved the future of the human race on this planet."

"Saved? Is that what you call it?" Padrec barely controlled his anger, not even trying to hide his contempt for the older man he had once admired so greatly. "Tell me who was saved when you set the Ibisians on the trail of Rubinsky's secondary rescue team? Or when you told the warriors how to round up survivors like so many cattle?"

"It's necessary. I want to save them."

"And so do I. But not as Ibisian herd animals, fodder for their damned queens. And who are you to declare that the Ibisians must decide the shape of human society? There aren't any Ibisians where Rubinsky landed on the eastern sub-continent—and why not gather what is left of our people there? We could live our own lives, wait for rescue—"

"There won't be any rescue. That space fold plucked us out of reach, maybe out of time itself. We just don't know. But don't you think the PES would have come by now if they were going to? They aren't coming, or maybe they did—and we weren't there." His manner seemed to appeal fervently for understanding. "We are going to stay here, Padrec, and we are going to die here, and our children if we have any, and our children's children for as far into the future as you care to imagine them. And we are so few, so poorly equipped to survive—"

Impatiently, Padrec refused to listen. "For crying out loud, Sam, humans once survived an Ice Age with stone knives and bear skins!"

"Hundreds of thousands did—other hundreds of thousands did not. And we are only, at best, two hundred. Including those still on the eastern sub-continent, there are maybe one hundred and sixty men and only forty women—"

It was an argument he had heard before. He had not swallowed it then and he could not swallow it now. "We don't need the Ibisians to help us with *that* problem!"

"They can insure our survival."

"They would make us a sub-class of craftsmen and pleasure slaves!" He caught the glimpse of renewed startlement in Toroya's eyes and laughed shortly, with a burst of bitter amusement. "Yes, I've thought of what would come of it. For God's sake, Sam, do you think I spend my time polishing my nails and worrying about my looks?"

"I never thought you needed to. Frankly, I can understand what she sees in you."

Padrec turned away. He knew what Anii saw in him. Her touches betrayed her and, now that he understood her language, so did her words. Pretty one. And for all of that he had never considered himself especially good-looking. He had always been ordinary, though young and healthy and maybe even handsome in that vital way most young men tend to be. But women had never swooned over his looks; his few relationships with them had been based more on friendship than lust, the occasional sex casual and pleasant. Typical Terran couplings, two lives briefly touching, then going on in the morning as if nothing had changed—because nothing had. Until Anii had taken him in an act that had bordered on rape—what the hell, it *had* been rape—tearing him out of his sterile, becalmed existence and pulling him into her violently sexual world where mating was akin to life and death itself. She loved him with a passion found in the pleasure of their two bodies meeting in a pheromone-induced heat, her hormones leading his in a biological dance of death which he survived. But, more, she loved him apart from her physical use of him. He sensed this and was confused by his own responses. He was not just an animal to her, but someone she protected and cherished with careful attention to emotions and attitudes she could have as easily dismissed as unimportant—and for his own part he was not sure he did not love her in return, or if it was just gratitude on his part that she did not treat him as he knew other queens treated their human bed-partners, as dumb animals to be used solely, and often abusively, for pleasure.

He looked again at Toroya, wondering what the man was trying to accomplish. Since the coming of the humans to the nom three standard months ago—men and women, not all destined for the beds of queens—Toroya had assumed the task of overseeing the small community, helping it adjust to life alongside an alien society which kept many of its members in close-held slavery. Padrec rarely went to the human quarters, a cramped compound on the lowermost and outermost levels of the nom. Anii frowned on such visits, for they took him from the security of her own vast quarters, where the disapproval of his fellow humans could not reach him. Twice he had returned, deeply shaken by the conditions in which he found his former crewmates, abject, despondent, men and women who had been trained for scientific work reduced to glazing pottery. They had stared at him at first, before realizing who he was, for Anii no longer let him wear his service uniform outside of her quarters and he had appeared in one of the knee-length, sashed gowns he had taken to wearing in its stead. It had not taken any special genius to read what they were thinking, it stared at him from their eyes and whispered from their lips behind his back.

Morrissey. The Ibisian mare's prize stallion . . .

He could only imagine what Toroya had said to them, trying to persuade them that it was somehow acceptable for their males to serve the Ibisians as human mates. A few had been cordial, those who had known him before and were glad to see him among the living, but most had merely stared and the overall welcome had been restrained, unfriendly. It had hurt more deeply than he had ever admitted, but he had gone back. And each time Anii had noticed that he returned to her subdued, driven by feelings he could not explain to her. How could he tell her that he felt as though he were betraying them, had betrayed them from the beginning—that he should be there with them, not warm in her bed, safe, secure, her hands hardening his ardor in the fire of an alien lust.

I am human. I belong with them, not you.

But the choice was not his. Had never been his. Even being human had not been a matter of choice, but of birth, a biological quirk.

He saw Toroya drop wearily onto the low ledge of the condensation catch which ringed the outer walls of the garden room and alongside which they had been speaking. The scientist looked old and faded, not only from lack of sun and fresh air. He, too, suffered the disapprobation of his fellows, and he was forced to suffer it daily, unlike Padrec, who need not face them unless he wished it.

Pedrec went and sat there beside him, Toroya looked up, surprised, pathetically hopeful.

"I always liked you, Padrec. Honestly. I always did, I still do. You're a decent human being—don't turn away, humans rarely aspire to decency. But you—" he smiled faintly, remembering—"you were a quiet one, like your plants, always looking on, trying very hard not to be judgmental. That was refreshing, to an old cynic like me."

"Look, Sam—"

"No, Padrec, please, let me finish. You have earned the right to hear this, and I think—I hope—maybe you can understand. Ibis is my lifework. When the ships were forced to make landfall, I wanted to get off no less than any of us—and if it could still be done, Lord knows I still would want to—but I knew I would come back. And funny thing is, I think maybe you felt the same way."

He nodded briefly. "We talked about it, once."

"I am a Xenologist, a xeno-biologist with xeno-sociology secondaries—and if I'm lucky, I might come across a semi-intelligent species once in my lifetime, they are that rare. The Ibisians are all I ever wanted to come my way: they are sapient, social beings with a fully developed society and culture. I can spend the remainder of my life studying them, learning to understand them, to see first-hand the impact of humans on their system—"

Padrec stared at him, repulsed and yet fascinated. "Sam, don't you see what you are doing? You're making a scientific killing at the expense of your own people!"

"No, Padrec, no, that's where you're wrong. Not at their expense. I am trying to make it as painless as possible—"

"You approve of their slavery!"

"It allows them to live. We can become a sub-society, living alongside this one. And if the men must sometimes be taken as mates by the queens, well, you know that it is not necessarily hell on earth—or Ibis—to be one."

"Tell that to Rubinsky. Or Ebert. I saw them the other day, on *leashes*, sitting at the feet of their *loving* mistresses—" With difficulty he controlled the swelling knots that rose in his throat. Tears nearly rose to his eyes. "They looked sick, Toroya, haggard. Their eyes—Ebert didn't have any hope left. And Rubinsky was damning me, just damning me, because he *knows* that he's found hell on earth."

"It takes time to adjust. You didn't look so well the first day I saw you again—"

"I really had been sick, Toroya. And I am sure Anii told you why." Toroya had seen the scar on his forearm, well-healed now but not then, where the beetle had sliced nearly to the bone. How these primitives had managed to mend such a wound, so well that it now gave him no trouble, Padrec dared not even guess.

"Yes, yes, you're right," the other man said, to placate him. "But don't you see that her devotion to you is an asset we can ill afford to ignore? Our species has a better chance at establishing itself alongside the Ibisians here and now, at the start, than if we made a stab at surviving on our own, in the wild, hunted, victims of accident or even another vicious attack by some other nom which feels itself threatened. I've spoken with Anii—she wants to see us assimilated, content, properly employed. We can be craftsmen—why not?—we have the intelligence, the creativity as a race, to manufacture objects of beauty, things for which their own workers and warriors are not so well suited. We can make ourselves not only useful but indispensable, in time."

The poor man was mad, Padrec saw. He barely knew truth from fantasy. Toroya had vanished into his own warped realm of xeno-sociological experimentation and theory. He didn't even realize what he was doing wrong, or even that it wrong. Or was it? Padrec no longer knew if he had the objectivity to make such a judgment. For all he knew, Toroya was right, humans could not survive on their own. Life outside the nom could be harsh, even cruel; certainly it would not be easy. *But wouldn't it at least be ours?*

He became aware that Toroya was shifting beside him, looking uncomfortable. The xeno-biologist's dark eyes avoided his. "I—I've started fostering genetic spread in the community, I suppose you know that."

Padrec's mouth firmed. "If you are saying that you have started a human breeding program, then yes, I have heard that."

"It's needed, you know.We have to expand the gene pool if we're to survive as a viable species. We aren't interfertile with the Ibisians; we must breed among ourselves in as many combinations as possible to fend off the consequences of inevitable inbreeding in the population. It's, ah, cold-blooded, but—"

"I know, I know," Padrec sighed, "It's necessary."

"Please, this isn't easy for me. It's even harder now that I have to do it. Anii thought it would be better, coming from me. Now I'm not so sure."

Something cold touched Padrec at the back of his neck and crawled along his nerves. "Thought *what* would be better?"

Toroya looked him coldly in the eye. "She's going into her nuptial phase in a few weeks. She'll want you for a few nights, of course, but then she's planning to take one of the drones in a mating that should leave her pregnant."

Anii, pregnant, swollen with more of her own kind. A hardness settled in him, closing about his most cherished illusions, squeezing them dry. In a way, he knew, he had been pretending she was human, that she wasn't really one of *them*. Now that defense, too, was being taken from him.

"What is she going to do about me?" he asked stiffly, knowing that Toroya would not be addressing him now unless he knew that she did have plans for him. Plans she did not want to present to him herself. Or perhaps, and more likely, she had wanted someone to explain it to him in his own language, to be sure he understood.

"She's not getting rid of you, if that's what you're thinking," Toroya assured him quietly with that faintly envious smile he had often taken to wearing in Padrec's presence. "Though no doubt some of the other queens will want her to. No. But she will lose sexual interest during her pregnancy and she is concerned that you will require a mate during this time. She wants you to take one of the girls from the compound—"

A claxon of warning went off in his head.

"Whose idea is this, Sam?" he asked coldly. "Anii's? Or yours?"

"Hers, to start," the xenologist admitted bluntly, and for once Padrec could sense he was being totally honest. "She wants to provide for you."

"Neither you nor she has any right to do that!"

"I can see this was a mistake. There was really no tactful way—"

"Rubinsky was right. You're no better than a procurer—!"

"This is important. This is the survival of the race we are talking about."

"Count me out, Toroya, I'm not contributing." Rising, he left the man and walked to stand in front of the louvered windows which provided this place with light and ventilation. As the air from outside the nom

filtered past him, Padrec caught himself remembering
the dry essence of the plain, the dusty winds heated
by that amber sun. Rainshowers from the day before
had brought forth the hidden flowers and even from
here he could see those jewel-like patches beckoning.
Beckoning, and he was not able to answer their call.

"If you won't, if you don't want to, I can't make
you," said Toroya, coming to stand beside him. "And,
after all, it isn't men we're lacking. Believe me, I
didn't mean it to sound like you were being put to
stud. I wouldn't do that to you. But I wouldn't turn
down the opportunity. Your genes are as valuable to
me as anyone else's."

"I'd like to tell you what to do with your damned
genetics—"

A badly concealed smile twitched at the corners of
the xenologist's mouth, surprisingly bitter. "An al-
together normal reaction, I suppose, and you are hardly
the first to refuse me. But we are going to be here, on
this planet, for a very long time. I hate to think of
how our human descendants will degenerate if in these
first few generations no effort is made to bring every
possible individual into the gene pool, to see that each
woman has offspring by a variety—and not just one—
male. Inbreeding has been known to turn up some
very nasty surprises."

Despite himself, Padrec nodded. In a world without
the corrective measures of advanced technology simple, easily correctable recessives could become the norm
in a small, inbred population. with the ship records
destroyed—or at the very least unavailable—there was
no way of knowing which crew members harbored
undesirable genes, and no way to avoid them. But
why have offspring at all? Shipboard personnel, to
prevent inconvenient and medically inadvisable conceptions and pregnancies on long space voyages, undertook temporary sterilization . . . but Toroya was
right again: the drugs wore off; there would, eventually, be conceptions. And with fewer conceptions, fewer
births, fewer individuals—and the smaller the result-

ing gene pool for each surviving generation. In time recessives could take over and weaken the race, leave it blinded, deformed, infirm. There would be humans on Ibis—yes, that was probably inevitable, now—but would they be a strong, vital people, or a pathetic, degenerate race?

"I suppose it's necessary," he finally admitted.

"Yes, it is."

"But you don't want mine." He was moved to grant the other man a slightly embarrassed frown. "Near-sightedness. I've been fitted with corrective cellular lenses, as good as the real thing for me—but any children will run the risk of turning up with it."

"Hardly a major defect, even in a backward society. Lens grinding is not a lost art, you know. Any diabetes? Heart defects?" Although angered and humiliated by such questioning, Padrec merely shook his head. Toroya's grin was stillborn, the attempt at levity forced. "If you ever feel the urge—"

"Forget it."

"I might be willing to do that—but Anii won't, and don't look to me to talk her out of it." He shrugged, spreading his hands a little at the betrayal he had just voiced. "I'm sorry, Padrec; I know I'm not popular this year. But in the end, you'll see. It will turn out for the best."

"Not the way you're going about it. You're killing them to save them. It won't work. What kind of salvation is that?"

"Don't you understand? I am trying to give them a race worth saving."

"Them, Sam?" Padrec said quietly. "Or Ibis? Who is it you are saving them for?"

"**I** want to go outside the nom."

Though he presented the request quietly, Anii could detect Padrec's resolve; she had learned to recognize the unspoken language behind his words, the subtlety of translation which granted her a better understanding of him. "What for?" she asked. He stood opposite her, stiff and wary, sensing her refusal even before it came. "Do you lack for anything, that you must seek it elsewhere?"

"I wish to look for objects from the ship—the place I came from." He corrected for the Terran word.

"The nom that flew?"

"Yes. I—had possessions there that I would recover."

"Possessions?"

He paused, uncertain of his ability to explain. He felt that once she understood, she would allow him to go. Recently she had shown herself unusually willing to please him, perhaps because he had asked nothing of her since she had refused his request to free the captive Terrans. As she looked at him now, he saw in her eyes that she was willing, if not wholly inclined, to consider his arguments.

"I came to Ibis—" again he corrected himself, this time using the native word—"to Mi—to study the plant life. That was my function, to study the plants, and I would like to continue that work. But I need to go outside the nom—and I need my instruments."

Anii pondered him, curiosity touching her perturbed frown. "But were not such things destroyed when the nom that flew was burned and plundered?"

"Perhaps, perhaps not," Padrec said, "I will not know until I have looked for them."

"And if you do not find them?"

"Then I will make others, where I can. But I do not

have the skills to recreate the instruments that I had before. If I could find even a few of them—"

Anii smiled that loving smile of hers, that warmed her eyes but not her lips, which insisted still on frowning at him. "I have noticed your restless mood of late. Does it truly give you pleasure to pursue your function? You tend the greenhouse well. It thrives under your care."

Conscious of the praise, Padrec lowered his gaze, realizing that he was getting nowhere. Anii had difficulty comprehending that he was a scientist. His interest in plants she considered to be but a chosen pastime and he doubted she would ever understand how important his work had been, how advanced his training. As a male in an Ibisian society, his functions were assigned by sex, his abilities narrowly defined within that context. He was ready to do anything, anything at all, to get out of the nom even for a few minutes, just to get away from it, to feel the hot wind on his face, to smell the dusty sweet scent of earth and not the noticeably nonhuman odors of the nom. That, and his need to remember that he was educated, and highly skilled, more than his desire to track down irreplaceable scientific instruments, had prompted him to confront Anii with his request.

"I must—have a function, apart from you," he told her, daring to be blunt, wondering what her response would be. As Queen, even the nom revolved around her, and he had been made part of that vast order, singularly focused and obedient.

He was not surprised to see Anii's golden eyes darken with displeasure that was stern, though it did nothing to deny her pleasure in his presence. "You have no function apart from me," she reminded him. "Whatever functions you may learn to serve within this nom, they shall be because the performance of them pleases me."

Daring again to look her in the eyes, Padrec said, "Does it please you that I should be inactive and bored—and unhappy?"

Anii looked at him sharply, then waved off the hovering subservients who attended her. She rose, a vision in jewel-webbed gossamer, and slowly descended the padded steps from her dressing table, walking toward him. "Are you unhappy?"

He wanted to say that yes, he was unhappy—but that he was not unhappy to be with her, only with his circumstances. But he did not need to say it, Anii saw in his face, his eyes, the truth of what he had said.

Padrec tried to explain. "You see that I am restless, but can you not see why? I need something to do, to occupy my time, my body. I am healthy now—I need something to do."

"You have something to do—."

He flushed with embarrassment, and a frustration rapdily reaching the point where it would become anger. "Not that. I need something more. I am not a drone, Anii, I am a *man*," he used the Terran word because the Ibisians had none that suited. "Can't you allow me to be one?"

At last taking him seriously, Anii asked, "What would that entail?"

"My studies—and activity, exercise. When I wish to be active, my attendants refuse to let me exercise. Look at me—I am getting soft, flabby—."

Anii looked at him, but saw no reason to complain. True, he had lost some of his muscular hardness between his illness and his present inactivity, but she secretly found his new softness pleasing and did not compliment him on it only because she knew he did not feel as she did, that a male should be hard only in the right places.

But Pa-dric was right to remind her that he was not a drone, stupid and indolent, living for one purpose only. He had served his own kind in other capacities, and his physical conditioning had once saved her life, and his. Perhaps for health he must be exercised. And certainly his intelligence required stimulation. How frustrated might she become if captured by hostiles and held inactive, totally confined, with only occasional matings for release from boredom? If given no other outlet, was it not possible Pa-dric might take the course of rebellion, if only for the stimulation of conflict? Yes, she must remember to treat him not as a drone but as a captive queen, for that had by far proven the best means of handling him. What harm was there, after all, in letting him seek his simple pleasures?

She touched his face, glad that he allowed it. "Above all things, it pleases me for you to be content. You may go to your place that was destroyed. Hli will go with you, and a party of warriors, and workers should you need them. But Pa-dric, do not run from me." In his eyes she saw his compliance, and knew that he would return, willingly, to her. But his unbidden joy was for his freedom. *Oh, beloved,* she thought, *I treat you too leniently, just for that look in your eyes!*

That day was filled with plannings. During an audience with To-roya, she forced herself, through a veil of jealousy, to examine the female Stranger he had selected to relieve Pa-dric's mating needs during her nuptials. The one chosen was a pale-haired, colorless creature with spirited eyes who possibly might interest him. Whether she did or not was not really important, so long as she did not wish to pursue the mating after it occurred. Only when To-roya had assured her of this, did Anii, flashing a narrow, golden-eyed warning at the Stranger, give her approval.

But later, when Hli arrived to report on the progress of the nom, she marked the queen's preoccupation. And, more importantly, the coming nuptial phase already written in the queenly complexion.

"Do not waste this phase on the Stranger," the loyal subservient said at once. "Get rid of him."

"No." Anii turned away from her old friend, moved across the room, shaking her hair in defiance. "I must keep him."

"Why?"

Anii glared at her subservient sharply, the morning having done little to improve her temper. "It pleases me to keep him. I do not need to explain to you why. There is more to Pa-dric than you are seeing, Hli."

"I doubt it."

"What of the other Strangers?" she asked, going on to matters more important. "Are they adapting?"

"Poorly. They are a difficult race, more trouble than they are worth—you are singularly fortunate to have found one with good temperament."

Anii knew this was true. Her conversations with Toy-roya had confirmed that the Strangers were prone to discord, and that Pa-dric's gentle ways were his alone. The Strangers, unlike the nomari, were a society of individuals, and thus highly unpredictable. It was like dealing with a whole nest of queens.

"Have you discerned the leaders among them?"

Hli made a noise of disgust between her teeth. "We knew before we undertook to destroy them that they were ruled by dominant males. That has not changed. A few of the females display dominant behavior, but they too defer to the males. Do not ask me why, but it may have something to do with the males being aggressive and unruly. If they do not die with the mating, their hormones poison their systems and they become this way."

"The Goddess was wise." Anii murmured.

The subservient muttered the response, though her agreement was complete.

"And what of To-roya?" Anii directed, "He is in charge of the Strangers. Has he had any success at organizing them?"

"They obey him reluctantly. They fear our warriors and work only to escape punishment."

"So long as they work. They are intelligent, and have the ability to create useful objects. The crafts they produce will soon rival our own in beauty." Anii gestured to a set of porcelain cups on a tray of lacquered wood. Though the making was still crude, the tracery and glaze showed a promising delicacy of design and color.

"Yes," even Hli was forced to recognize the Strangers' superior workmanship. "Our workers do not have such eye for color. If ever they attain excellence, they will increase the wealth of the nom through the trading of their goods."

"That is my hope. The Strangers will serve us in many ways, Hli."

"There are many who think them best suited to the nuptial couch."

Feeling her own phase so near, already stirring in her brain, Anii allowed a smile to come to her eyes. The pleasures of the nuptials were deservedly famous. "That, too," she admitted. "But that is not always. The newness will become common, and the Strangers must have other uses. To-roya insists on this, and Pa-dric just now told me of his need for other outlets."

"He has the greenhouse—"

Anii nodded, lost in thought. "It seems his interest in plants goes deeper than the enjoyment of them."

"He identifies them well and accurately," Hli judged.

"He says that he came to Mi to study the plants."

Hli's brows crowded to the bridge of her nose. "He speaks like To-roya. To-roya says the Strangers came to Mi to study *us*."

"To study Mi," Anii corrected. She had discussed this with To-roya at some length before understanding it.

"What for?"

Anii could not answer, because she was not sure. Other stars, other planets—it sounded too familiarly like the tales of the High Ones. Only the Strangers were not the High Ones, and knew of them only vaguely, through tales not unlike those known to the nomari.

"They are not natural," said Hli again. "This will not work."

"It will work." Anii voiced that opinion without hesitation, certain of it. "They will contribute toward our stability, our prosperity. I will see that no other nom has the Strangers. I have sent envoys to the other noms, with orders that they find and bring to me any Strangers they find captive. Thus we will have them all. In this way we will have a lock on them, on the most valuable commodity of all. Our young queens will not be forced to risk instability in the nom to satisfy their nuptial needs, and the Strangers who are not needed by the queens will be productive in other, no less valuable ways. Tell me I have not implemented a satisfactory solution."

Grudgingly, Hli decided not to argue the policy. There was no questioning the role of the Strangers had played in establishing Anii's dominance. "D'nia might have done you better to attempt it," she conceded.

Anii detected the stressed irony in the old female's remark and found herself amused. Hli would always point out the subtleties. "You see, Hli, how much we need them. Now that my queens have tasted freedom, how shall I take it from them?"

"But will our reproduction suffer, now that drones are not needed to satisfy the nuptials?"

"I will still foster breeding among loyal subordinates. And promote emigration when needed. You know as well as I do, Hli, that nuptial madness in young queens is more likely to result in deaths by raids that do not succeed, or revolts that fail, than in successful breeding."

Hli nodded slowly, gauging her young Queen with growing approval. "You show much thought to this."

"I have thought it out thoroughly," Anii assured her. "The Strangers will serve us very well indeed. Pa-dric shows me the way."

"I would question that. The other Strangers do not follow his example. They are contentious and difficult. Many have had to be chained, others beaten. They will not mate when it is required of them, or they seek to escape."

"Pa-dric tried to escape when first I took him. I think it is expected behavior for them. Mating for them may be a choice they agree to. As with a nomari queen. If captured by a hostile nom and forced to bear,

she will seek to escape. Since Pa-dric has agreed to b
my mate, he has given me no trouble about it."

But other queens had encountered more problems
Most of the other Strangers had proven less tractable
given to angers and physical aggression, and had re
quired harsh measures before they could be managed
Knowing how such things affected him, Anii kep
Pa-dric from this unpleasantness and did not speak to
him of the treatment of his fellow creatures. But hi
visits to the lower levels had taught him that all were
not as well-treated as he. For a time she had consid
ered restricting him, forbidding him to see his kind
But To-roya had told her this would be unwise. "He
would resent you for it, and imagine worse things
And it is good that the others see him treated well.
Because she had not wished Pa-dric's resentment, and
because she had assigned matters pertaining to the
Strangers to To-roya, she had followed that advice.

"Other queens have had trouble," Hli reported, "The
red-haired one given to Bhi'hia nearly strangled her
and she had to beat him severely. The next day he
tried it again."

"She has given him up, and taken another," Ani
said, "I gave her first choice of the new ones."

"Yes. She is consoled. But only because he is more
beautiful—I have heard her say that he, too, must be
beaten."

It was also true, Anii reflected, with a sigh, that
other queens did not seem to appreciate the sensitivity and intelligence of the Strangers; too often they
treated their exotic slaves more as useful beasts to be
ridden than as thinking creatures to be fostered for
other riches. She, too, had struck her captive—and for
weeks he had flinched from her touch, even in his
dreams. Had she treated him more cruelly, how then
would he have treated her?

But could she tell the queens whose support and
obedience she had gained by promising them sexual
freedom with the Strangers, how to treat the partners
she had given them? No. No queen ever provoked

another over a male, except to take him from her. And her dominance was still tenuous, untried, too uncertain to attempt to interfere in matters so delicate, so near to the heart of rebellion.

Only by example could she determine the way she wished them to go.

I will make the Strangers part of the nomari; as warriors fight that the nom be secure, and workers toil that the nom should prosper, the Strangers, too, will have their place.

Part of that day was to be spent seeing to the functioning of the incubator-comb, that vital chamber where her partially developed young, once born, would be nurtured until mature enough for the nursery. With Hli and a party of warriors to guard against the possibility of a rival challenging her yet unsecure position, Anii descended the nom along the royal passages, the spiraling ramps that gave access to the nom's innermost and most secret chambers. In the spacious honeycombed chambers below her own were the luxurious confines of the drone sanctum. And below these, the storehouses. But most precious of all, buried deep in the fastness of the nom, the last place an enemy could reach, were the combs where the next generation slept until the second birth.

The light was that of the central core, the amber glow of which reflected throughout the nom's inner heart, directed by mirrors downward and throughout its myriad chambers. The worker-breeders, swollen with the multiple young that were their sole function, hurried about the chambers, grooming and providing, feeding the warrior-overseers. The comb-watchers turned their eyes on her, marking the new Queen, the one whose scent even now ruled them as it did all others in the nom.

Anii walked to the first nutrient chamber, peered within. No young resided there; she was relieved, for had there been any, she would have had to order them destroyed. Her own young must supplant all others. But D'nia had not produced in three nuptials, nor had she allowed any of her subordinate queens to mate.

"Are the chambers functional?"

"Yes, Great Queen," the *ti* warrior who was prime overseer assured her, "The nutrients have been injected."

"How many were needed?"

"Two. And a queen-chamber, of course, was prepared from the jelly of the deposed one. Unless, of course, you will be allowing others—" But the speaker stopped abruptly. It had been a stupid question, spoken out of habit only.

"No."

Hli glanced into another of the chambers. "This jelly looks depleted—.

The overseer paled at the implied neglect. If a batch of young was lost, the chambers would be purged of those responsible. "It is the right color."

"Be sure of it."

Anii allowed Hli to check the specifications, trusting to the subservient's greater experience. Her own was very little, for D'nia had never allowed her, or any other queen she had not allowed to breed, to visit the incubation combs. Hli, as an areproductive female, a queen who had not been allowed to fully form, had once overseen D'nia's predecessor's offspring. Her intelligence had prompted D'nia to spare her as a nurse after the purge.

Using a sampling tube, Anii sipped a portion of the jelly from the queen chamber, tasting it, even as Hli did the others, for imperfections. The tiny sample slipped into her mouth, a thick and unpleasant clot of a substance that tasted of the liquefied flesh from which it had been formed, a sort of gelatinous broth.

So this is what was once D'nia. . . .

In the jelly of the queen she discerned its complex essence, the single notes within the hormonal tune that would dictate to the embryos within the specialized characteristics that would make them female rather than warrior. Of the female young, only a few, to be nourished at their mother's breast, would ever become queens.

"It is well," was Hli's verdict several minutes later. She returned, completely satisfied, the overseer shuffling behind, its work having been approved.

"The neuters will all be warriors to start—?"

"All but a few. You will need *ti'* warriors of various castes—if only to oversee the incubation should this dung worker of a *ti'* ever fail in its function."

"I wonder how many females there will be, how many drones?"

"One never knows," Hli informed her, "Sometimes there are none, if they are reabsorbed. The sexed embryos often fail."

"Why?"

"We don't know that. Maybe your Strangers can tell you. To-roya has an interest in such things."

Leaving the incubator chambers to the comb-watchers, Anii and Hli returned to the high royal chamber, walking the winding path that for centuries had served as the passageway of queens, the road to power. Halfway, beneath the lofty arches which decided the spiral of the walls, Anii told Hli of her decision to allow Padrec outside the nom.

"Is that wise?" the old subservient asked. "Unless this is your plan to be rid of him—"

"You would like that too well, but no—he wants the tools with which he studies plants, and I have told him that he may go to find them."

"Why do you encourage this?" Hli thought little of Padrec's occupation, equating it with sniffing flowers from the fields. "What do you hope to gain by it?"

"Maybe little, maybe much. If nothing else, Pa-dric will be content—and that means much to me. And I have been thinking: the nom depends greatly on grains for food and trade. It may benefit the nom if Pa-dric, in using the Strangers' methods, is able to improve our knowledge." She shrugged, the new thoughts too untried to carry much conviction. "You are to go with him, to see that he does not escape, or come to harm. But it is important to him, to visit this place and seek to continue the function he had as a Stranger."

"This does not make sense, that a male should have any function at all—other than that the Goddess gave him."

"The Goddess did not make the Strangers, I think."

"Then are they, like the Goddess, Children of the High Ones? I think not. If so, they would be gods themselves—"

"No, not that. I do not know what they are." Pa-dric and To-roya both had attempted to explain this to her, but she had yet to understand it. She preferred to think that they had been sent by the Goddess, to serve Her nomari daughters. And that was the myth she allowed to spread among the others.

"But Pa-dric requires activity; this I know to be true. I do not think I want him to become sloth—I like him too well as he is, with his unpredictabilities."

"Beware, then, if one day you do not like the surprise."

"Do you really think him dangerous?" Anii tried not to remember how he had attacked the hostiles, breaking one's back, spearing another—.

Hli's eyes glowed lambent orange in the low light filtering from the core. "All creatures are dangerous until they are properly controlled."

"Pa-dric is controlled, Hli. The pheromones rule him, even as they rule the nomari."

But even as she said it, bravely, Anii knew she claimed a mastery that was far from certain.

The next morning Anii watched from the high terrace of her royal tower as the line of the expedition wound away from the nom, cutting across the tawny plain toward the distant hills. All morning she had regretted her decision of the day before, and would have withdrawn her approval but for a haunting sense of Pa-dric's need. Always, since seizing the nom, she had kept him near at hand, allowing only short visits, always under guard, to his own kind. She used no chains on him, neither did she need to threaten him—it pleased her to possess him freely. Jealousy, in the deepest secrecy of her heart, she resented his restless need to escape her, in spirit if not in fact; for she, too, longed for the dusty expanses of the plain, the tall sky and vast spaces. To deny him this, after having promised it, would be to deny the love with which that promise had been given. But the Queen did not leave the nom, except in catastrophe or upon provocation. And so she could not go with him, or show him the Valley of Forest and the place of the tall trees where first she had seen him, that secluded clearing where the purple rza'li draped the high branches with veils of purple blossoms. He had climbed those towering trees for the sake of those exquisite flowers. Her heart beat with a sudden desire to have taken him there. *Pretty one, you shall have your flowers, and your growing things, if that is what you must have to make you content to be with me.* She smiled and turned away.

Her nuptials were near again, a certain heat and renewed interest. Pa-dric had not ceased to attract her; indeed, she cherished him more for being willing, for sharing with her an alien yet provocative sexuality. His passion at times alternated between exquisite tenderness and a sort of restrained violence, consuming and then consumed. Would a drone of her own kind please her so well? Days ago she had known that the time had come to choose a mate of her own kind. Respectful of the importance of the ritual for which she prepared, Anii donned garments of a restful color, with veils that reached to her ankles and long sleeves that floated above the bracelets that locked the fabric at her wrists. No queen enticed her drones without cause. Taking with her a tray of sweets and simple presents to delight them, she proceeded to the inner chamber the queen alone was allowed to approach and enter. This place, so well guarded, was the treasury of the nom's well-being, where the drones were kept and tended. Once she had shown Pa-dric this place and even, briefly, had considered keeping him there—but he had been horrified by the stupidity of the drones, their beautiful idleness, and she had seen at once that it would be a mistake to put him with them. The doorway to the sanctum opened inward as the guards, the fiercest and most trusted of her warriors, bowed low to acknowledge her presence and her mission.

How small they are, she considered when she saw them again, the drones whose pale, golden eyes watched her from across the sumptuous chamber. The specially trained neuters who groomed the drones and attended to their needs made their obeisances, but the drones themselves either stood in confusion or cowered back upon the cushions. They were not as small as at first they seemed, though the head of the tallest one would not have reached Pa-dric's shoulders. But their race was nomari, and they had hair of golden light and eyes cut from the finest topaz; their delicate skins, unblemished by sun or the harshness of the elements, were like flawless garments upon the loveliest of limbs. Beautiful, beautiful creatures, beside which Pa-dric for all her love of him had looked coarse, unfinished, an imperfect suggestion of malehood. But there was no light of knowledge in these innocents' eyes, no understanding in their minds or speech upon their tongues—the lovely creatures regarded her mutely, some wimpering already for their nurses, who hurried to quiet them and tidy their appearances. The oldest ones were quietest; the youngest drones, those who had just entered their adulthood, had not yet grown accustomed to intrusions. All at once Anii felt a rush of tenderness. "My beautiful ones," she said softly, proffering sweets to draw them to her, granting loving touches to those she favored. For some were lovelier than others, or had other qualities which endeared them. Her fingers trailed through heads of hair as fine as silk, and her lips brushed the foreheads of uncaring faces which smiled up at her blandly, as trusting as children, wondering at this marvelous, goddess-like creature who had come among them, bringing to life the long buried meaning of their lives. They were all so beautiful. So innocent, their maleness awaiting only her awakening. How could she choose just one?

One young drone who had stood when she entered, and who looked at her with some understanding, if only that of a child, drew her. In a sort of loving dance, the servants folded back his garments so that she might look at him. He was perfect; a well-formed, well-developed male, suitable to her needs. Gently, she bent and touched her lips to his, the gesture of submission she now preferred above all others. He stood unmoving, confused by her attention, but his eyes closed and he was compliant, though his heart and breathing quickened beneath her caress. Ah, beautiful . . . and there was the light of some small intelligence in his eyes. A good choice to make her daughters.

She turned to the richly gowned subservient who headed the sanctum's attendants. "Each day you will bring him to me, that he may come to know me."

"Beloved Queen." The subservient bowed deeply to soften the impertinence of the remark she was about to make. But the Queen was new and young and perhaps did not know. "Do you not wish him to be with you?"

Anii was tempted. The young drone was indeed beautiful, a golden blaze of adoring innocence, a worshipful slave to her wishes, wanting only her glance, her touch, her presence to bring him happiness. If Pa-dric was so unhappy, why should she not turn, for a time, to another? *Because I want them both, and this one will not know the difference.*

This one I will not keep; he is but a lovely creature I will treasure all too briefly before he dies in my embrace, my use for him done, his purpose on this earth fulfilled. My pleasure in him will be as short as his life.

Again she kissed the adoring male, who this time parted his lips beneath hers, giving her a taste of a sweet, childlike sensuality, unknowing of its own promises. "You must wait my beautiful, chosen one," she told him softly, lingering, savoring the virgin beauty she would soon see extinguished, that it might be reborn in the young he seeded, "There will be time for you."

Having chosen her mate, Anii left the chambers of the drones for her own bright rooms that now seemed vast and empty. And there she remained until evening, awaiting the return of one who would satisfy her restlessness, now that he would have satisfied his own.

When Padrec first saw the ship again, he was reminded of an ancient place he had once walked upon a planet whose name he had forgotten. Time had started its inexorable work upon them both. Gaping and blackened, the vessel still looked out of place, but less jarringly so than it had while intact, its struts once etched upon an amber sky above the creeping edges of the wooded grasslands cleared from its perimeter. That grassland now reclaimed its own, and years from now the taller growth would follow. And the metallic shell of what had been a starship would gradually be covered over and forgotten. The corpses were gone and had been for many months, Ibisians or insect scavengers having seen to that task, and he approached the vessel where he had once worked and lived across a land eerily cleansed of the scattered remains of its passing. With Hli following his every step, Padrec combed the wreckage of the ship, trying to uncover anything of value overlooked in the destruction and subsequent plundering.

The ship had been breached, not by internal explosions, but by a massive boulder barrage. How many Ibisian workers, their incredibly tough bodies strained past endurance, had it taken to lug so many huge boulders from the quarries to this place? So much effort, to destroy a people who had meant them no harm, who would have gladly left this planet if only they had been able. *You may never know how well you have destroyed us. Our ship and now our lives. . . .*

Followed by Hli, he entered gutted chambers he barely recognized—the hospital, the labs, what was left of the personnel quarters—sifting through the charred debris. Precious few instruments had been spared by the fire. The Ibisians must have hauled off anything that remained intact. If it was still stored at the nom, perhaps Anii would let him look at it. But what he sought now the Ibisians would not have known to look for. Simply because he knew where they had been stored, he found the data files. One by one, he pulled banks of data chips from behind blackened panels, the painstakingly gathered knowledge of the Terrans embedded in rods of resonant crystal. He gathered as many of the rods as he could find, placing them carefully within one of the storage cylinders the Ibisians had overlooked. There was no way to know what the data rods contained—he might have recovered personnel files or engineering graphs, Toroya's studies of the Ibisians or weather maps or even his own compilations of the planet's plant forms—nor was there any way to retrieve the information stored there. All data retrieval systems had been destroyed. *But maybe, someday. . . .*

Hli, however, was excited by his discovery. "Are these the jewels of your kind?" she asked, carrying one of the rods to the nearest portal and holding it to the sun. "Ah, yes! Look how the sun shines through them!"

"Don't do that—" he stopped short, realizing that his abruptness smacked of impertinence, something for which Hli had little patience. But he had to stop her from damaging whatever data remained. "The sunlight is not good for the crystal," he explained.

Obligingly, Hli lowered the rod, returned it to the storage cylinder, but she insisted on retrieving all the banks and assigned workers to the task now that he had shown her the way of doing it. Only later, in the ruined husk of what had been his laboratory, searching compartments the Ibisians had not known to open and which had survived the fire, did Padrec find anything he could actually use: a microsynthesizer that seemed to be undamaged, several miniature power cells, a microscanner and even a spectrometer that could be repaired. But all else was blackened, overturned, his charts curling from the walls, racks of specimen plates and reagents spilled from their bases. Beneath a late afternoon sun, Hli's shadow looming impatiently over him as he got down on hands and knees, Padrec sifted through the desolation for any plates not scorched or trampled and vials of research chemicals that might have escaped breakage. Most of the plates were blackened beyond use; but the chemicals, the preservatives and stains . . . with those he could still continue his studies. Though he discarded each jar that had cracked or showed changes from the heat, he found several which were intact, usable, but Hli, seeing the vials in his hands, knocked them from him.

"No," she ordered, "You have enough."

Tautly controlling his first response, which had been to grab the vials back from her, Padrec answered simply. "Anii said I am to be allowed to take whatever I need."

"You take much for one male."

"These things are important to my work."

"Your work does not exist. She allows you your diversion, but no work. Your function is to pleasure her. Do that, and forget this madness." The subservient tossed the vials aside and, grasping him roughly by the arm, hauled him to his feet. "It is time to go now."

But Padrec was not prepared to leave without the vital chemicals that had until moments before been within his grasp. The bottles glinted in bright spots of color on the floor close to where he stood. Tearing free from Hli's hold on him, he moved toward them. The subservient, however, had anticipated rebellion.

"No!" she said, and drove the butt of her spear into the cinders where a moment later his hand would have been. A spray of tiny fragments tossed up by the impact rattled loudly as they spattered against the walls.

On ship he would have laughed at the idea that he might one day be ready to fight for the possession of a few milliliters of essential molecules. Then, he had always assumed such things could be replaced. Now, he knew that they could not be. And he wanted them badly enough to risk whatever he had thus far gained to get them. Openly defying the order to back away, he lunged again for the vials.

A snarl forming on her lips, Hli poised to strike him, but Anii had ordered that the Stranger was not to be slapped or disciplined in any way but verbally, unless he attempted to escape. And despite his impertinence, Hli did not think that this was what he was trying to do.

"Disobedient slave!" her angry words lashed at Padrec as he glanced up at her from his knees, the precious vials in his hands, "If it were for me to say, I would not allow you so much privilege!" Still filled with wrath, she swiped her spear at him, causing him to duck defensively, although there was no danger of her striking him. "Get up!" she ordered to regain her lost dominance. At least no warriors had been nearby to witness her failure to control the Stranger.

Aware that he had traded Hli's goodwill for the vials he had carefully tucked into his sash, Padrec gave the aging female no more trouble on the journey back, realizing all too well and too late that he had very likely jeopardized any possibility of future excursions outside the nom.

Immediately upon returning to the nom, Hli presented the problem to the Queen who anxiously awaited them. Hli was not gentle with her spite. "The male is insubordinate. He must be disciplined! I tell him "no," he does the thing! It is time to leave, he does not go! He is as stupid as a drone, to make such bother over a handful of pretty bottles!"

"What bottles?"

"Can you not see how bulky he is? He keeps them closely, in his sash."

Anii went to Padrec and did not wait for him to give them to her but went for them herself, dipping her hand into his sash. Though the anger rose into his cheeks, he did not bother to glare at Hli, well knowing it would have no effect, expect, perhaps, to infuriate her more. Anii studied the bottles in her hands, and those she had passed to Hli, before turning to Padrec.

"What is in these, that you have so angered Hli to gain possession of them?"

The language failed him. The Ibisian language had no words for such substances. But he tried, haltingly, to describe what they did. "They are stains, fixatives—they help me preserve the specimens, to determine the structure, the functioning—"

Anii's eyes widened. "Of plants?" she asked.

"Yes, of plants."

"These are important to you?" She held out the bottles in her hands, showing them to him.

"Yes."

"Then you shall have them." She put her cache into his hands and directed Hli to do the same. "But do not disobey Hli again, Pa-dric. I will not have you abuse my patience with you." With that, she turned from him and her coldness tore into him as deeply as the beetle's claws. One day, he knew, he would anger Anii too far—and on that day she would turn from him forever. And it would not be anything he as a man could stop himself from doing.

But that night when he came to her, Anii pulled him down and all coldness was forgotten. In the heat of their lovemaking he sensed again the fires of the nuptial phase reaching out for him, wanting him, all of him, every cell and every thought, seeking something he could never give, until at last he surrendered and Anii, knowing that her victory was not yet conquest, satisfied herself with that part of him that was hers. *The time will come*, she thought as she watched the sleeping Stranger in her bed, *when you will forget whatever it is that keeps you from me, when you will throw it away, and belong only to me*. But the waiting dragged at her and she sensed, somehow, that time was growing short. This nuptial phase she would mate as the nomari, and her pregnancy would drive him from her.

She turned to him, and he stirred and in that half-state stroked her in a way that made her quiver. Awake, he did not touch her so, as if he did not think she would allow it; and when she ordered him to do so, it was not the same. "Pa-dric," she said, and he responded sleepily. "There is a female of your kind. You will mate with her, and not with me, when the time comes. For I cannot bear to have you parted from me. And it is well, To-roya tells me, for you to do this."

"Toroya's an ass."

She did not know what he meant, for again, as often in his sleep, he spoke the language of his kind. And because he had not really been awake, he soon fell deeply back to sleep and did not wake again until morning.

But in the morning, after he had left for his own room, he found himself barred from the Queen's private chamber. The warrior-guards who normally deferred to him were respectful but firm and would not let him pass. At length Hli arrived to explain to him the sudden change in Anii's demeanor. "She entertains her mate. You have your bottles, Stranger; go play with them, until she sends for you."

"When will she send for me?" he wanted to know. "Tonight?" He worded the question in a way Hli could not take as disrespect.

"Perhaps."

And now, because he could not be with her, all he could think about was Anii. Beside himself, he went to the room beside the greenhouse. It was a new chamber, built onto existing rooms, which Anii had given him to house his bare-bones laboratory. With the instruments he had recovered the day before, it had begun to resemble what it was supposed to be. He had barely entered when he saw that he was not alone.

One of the women from the human colony stood there, nervously watching him with the wide, wary eyes of something caught in a trap. "Who are you?" The question sounded harsher than he had intended.

"Janelle. Janelle MacDonald. Bio-medics, remember?" A faint smile, that one shade too defiant to be timid, accompanied the answer.

"Yes." He finished entering the room, but kept the table between them. Now that the initial shock had passed he did remember her, a busy, efficient woman a few years older than himself. He had seen her sometimes, and taken note of her, but they had never really spoken. He eyed her warily. "Why are you here? I didn't ask for you."

Her eyes widened slightly, letting him know she thought that he had. "I was told to come here. In fact," she turned away from him, "I was quite simply *brought* here. You need help with this equipment, right?"

"From a bio-medic?"

She looked at him, and abruptly laughed, relaxing. "Well, I do have some basic skills. Bio-electronics and crystal circuitry might apply in these circumstances—and botany *is* a biological science, the principals should hold, if not the parameters." She picked up the microsynthesizer. "This looks intact."

"It is. It wasn't damaged. Look, Miss MacDonald," he said to her, "you don't have to stay. I can dismiss you. The warriors will take you back if I tell them to."

A hollow thunk, barely heard, filled the silence as the microsynthesizer was put back on the table. "You can do that?"

"What?"

"Command the warriors?"

"Within these chambers, and as regards my person and my contacts, yes."

Her hands lifted the spectrometer from the counter, but he could see that it did not really interest her. "And you did not ask them to bring me here?" she asked.

"No."

"Then Toroya and your Queen have been doing your dirty work for you." Her gray eyes, sharp and cool, met his with blunt contempt. "I met her the other day, your Anii. Toroya had me stand there beside him while they spoke a few words of Ibisian gibberish. I don't know what they said, but I suppose I must have met her approval. She told me I had been chosen to work with you."

Padrec looked away, unable to meet her eyes while he considered. He didn't know why the woman was ill-tempered and hostile—but maybe she had reason. Someone had maneuvered them both, of that he was sure. But to what end? That was easy enough to guess.

Janelle leaned toward him, her expression puzzled but still strangely guarded. "You didn't know about this, did you?" she sounded surprised. "They didn't tell you—does that bother you?"

"What do you think?"

"I think your Queen cares about you. And if you had wanted a woman, you could have chosen your own. You don't think that Toroya—?" Her gray eyes delved sharply into his.

"Don't you?"

With a sigh, she nodded, and pale waves of hair grown much longer than he remembered from the ship drifted down across her eyes. She swiped at it with an impatient hand. "He's been trying to get me paired off for several weeks now. He hasn't resorted to promoting rape yet, but I've let him know that's what it would take. So he sends me here—" she glanced about the small, cluttered but spacious room opening off of the glass-walled greenhouse, and gave a barking laugh. "—He sends me here, knowing I'd work with the devil himself just to get out of that compound! I could have just known he'd pull something like this!" She shook her head and her eyes came back to him, sharply questioning. "But you, Padrec Morrissey, are not at all what I expected."

Trying to appear casual, he asked, "What did you expect?"

She ducked her head. Would it serve any purpose to let him know that the humans in the compound thought him arrogant and indifferent, like Toroya, a man who approved of their captivity for purposes of his own? The Queen's human lover, who had forgotten he was human? When he visited the compound, he seldom stayed long and had few words for any of them—. *Or was it that we had no words for him*? True, Toroya had always insisted that Morrissey was being misjudged . . . he was not arrogant, but shy . . .

"I didn't expect to find someone I'd care to work with," she answered truthfully enough. Emboldened by his indecision, her voice bridged the distance between them. "May I? Work with you?"

Padrec hesitated. He hardly knew her; she had not exchanged two words with him before this and she had made it clear she only wanted to get out of the compound, if only for a few hours each day; working with him was just a handy excuse, nothing more. But remembering the crowded conditions under which the humans were being kept, he decided he could not blame her for seizing the opportunity. And why shouldn't he help her? It was little enough to ask of him. . . .

"Sure." He gave her a small smile, as resigned as it was friendly, and handed her a tray of smoke-damaged microscanner disks which she was to run through the scanner.

By the end of the day they had worked out a cautious rapport, businesslike on her part, receptive on his, colored by his unspoken pleasure in her company. Except for the dubious friendship of Toroya, Padrec had not had much contact with other humans, and none that could be called friendly. With Janelle MacDonald he experienced again interaction with another of his own race and culture, the naturalness of behavior, of language, an ease of communication which unfolded as they worked together. She even volunteered to take the miscroscanner back to the compound with her, to continue sorting the disks and to see if she could find someone who could manage an adjustment to the machine. Although protective of the device, now truly irreplaceable, he handed it over, taking the chance on trusting her.

When it came time for Janelle to leave, and the golden sun had begun to drop its last rays through the gleaming glass of the greenhouse windows, he parted from her reluctantly.

The next day Padrec went to the human compound to pick up the microscanner. Janelle, crisp and almost cold, handed it to him; only once, when he looked into her eyes as she related to him the sortings she had made, did he detect her latent friendliness.

"Most of them are ruined—I'm sorry," she said.

He nodded. He had not really expected to salvage very many, even though he had dared to hope for some sort of miracle. But his Terran soul was running out of faith in miracles.

"It really means something to you, doesn't it?" she asked then, surprising him. "To do this?"

"It's all I have left, of myself. She can't take *that* from me." But the way Janelle looked at him made him reluctant to say any more. He remembered the way she had spoken about Anii the day before. "Classifying the life here is important," he said, "Even if we never get off, we might as well know what we've found."

"As if it matters—about the plants, I mean."

"Maybe it will matter, someday."

She didn't bother to answer, the look in her eyes was answer enough. She couldn't believe he was that much of a fool. He could scarcely believe it himself. But he had learned that any purpose was better than none at all. He said good-bye to her and to the others in the room, and turned to leave, not even surprised when they did not respond. As he left the workchamber, Padrec found Samuro Toroya waiting outside, his orange garment a signal in the drab recesses of the passageway. Beyond him, Padrec's warriors guards stood by with their usual wary eye to his reactions, ready to defend him if needed.

"I see you picked up your microscanner," Toroya

said, indicating the device. "I envy you the luck to have found one."

"I knew where to look."

"I could use one. Don't get me wrong; I'm not asking for yours. But studying nonhuman physiology is next to impossible without scanners, or even one of those primitive lens microscopes our ancestors used a few hundred years ago. I've tried to put one together, but the lenses aren't working out—"

Padrec smiled, if only to himself. The passageway they stood in was narrow and the presence of the warriors made him conscious of speaking with another human being. "I thought you said lens-grinding was hardly a lost art—"

"It isn't. The knowledge is there, but the technology is a little hazy," Toroya admitted.

"Glass composition, polish, grinding techniques. . . ."

"Don't say 'I told you so.' "

"I didn't."

"No, you didn't." The man contemplated him for a moment, then said, "You never do."

"You'll get it right, in time."

"Yes, I suppose we will. There is so much to do, so much to relearn, and so little time. Our generation will have to reproduce skills our ancestors outgrew a long, long time ago—or lose them completely."

"The Ibisians are glass-makers," Padrec said helpfully, although he was sure that Toroya knew this. "Surely they have some degree of skill they could teach us?"

"Oh, yes. But it is mostly rote."

"I've noticed that," said Padrec. He had found ample opportunity in his close contact with the Ibisians to observe that workers, while they performed their functions diligently, seldom understood what they were doing, or even why they were doing it.

"Oh, they mix a little ground this with a little ground that, and fire it like this, and it comes out just so—" the xenologist's expression spoke plainly his mingled feelings of frustration, admiration and dismay.

"And there are other workers whose sole task in life is to *produce* the ground this and the ground that—and other workers who mine the this and that. You see, they just do it—they don't have any understanding of what they are doing. The workers have no capacity to understand, only to do."

"But glass-making is the function of a specialized warrior caste," Padrec countered, drawing on a growing and detailed knowledge of the nom that was second only to Toroya's. "They may not be raving geniuses, but they are more intelligent than workers and might be able to tell you something."

"No good, my friend—the pattern holds true not only in glass-making, but in every other facet of life in the nom. They do a thing in a certain way—because that is the way they are taught to do it. They don't know why it works, or how." He sighed, the social complexity that had initially fascinated him now thwarting his efforts. "The system works. It works because the function is bio-chemically transmitted from one generation of nomari to the next and encoded in their brains. The brain is receptive until a pattern is placed upon it by another worker, or warrior, in the function they are assigned. The skill isn't *learned*, Morrissey, it's programmed."

"Little biological computers, all in a row."

"Something like that. Except for the queens," he amended with a semblance of discovery. "The queens are genuinely intelligent."

He looked at Padrec, saw something that made him take notice, maybe the slight bruising about the mouth. "How is it with you and Anii?" he asked quietly, carefully. "She is coming on her nuptials now."

Padrec flinched, wishing there was some way he could get around Toroya's interest in that facet of his life. But what to him was secret and deeply intertwined with his very being, was to Toroya the scientific opportunity of a lifetime—such as it would be for them both. The warriors standing nearby, watching this meeting with cold yellow eyes, were all too powerful reminders of the changes that had overpowered them.

"Do you ask the other men the same thing?" he answered a bit tersely, "And do they also tell you it is none of your business?"

"Padrec," Toroya told him gently, taking him by the arm and leading him just a few more steps along the passageway, into yet another of the cramped and tiny rooms which made up the human compound. Padrec saw at once that it must be Toroya's private chamber; the drawings, and the primitive microscope on the low table told him that. "Padrec, listen. Believe it or not, I care. Not only about you, but about what happens to the others. But I know you better than I know them—I even prefer to think of you as my friend—and your situation is different from theirs. Anii is the Queen of this nom, and her nuptial phase is going to rule it. And you. The nomari are bound to the nom, and to every other aspect of their lives, by the dominant chemistry of the ruling Queen. You may also be bonded to her chemically—."

"I'm not nomari, in case you've forgotten, Toroya. I'm human."

"Human—and hers."

Padrec turned his back on him, paced to the other side of the room. His warrior guards, having decided that Toroya presented no threat to their Queen's interest in the Stranger, remained without.

"Padrec," Toroya said softly, "you don't know what this relationship might be doing to you. Her phase is going to boil in your blood; you are going to want her—" he grabbed Padrec's arm, his hard grasp holding him fast as he attempted to leave, "—you are going to want her. Her hormones are already priming you for it, and you don't have any biological or cultural safeguards—"

Suddenly, violently, Padrec resented the scientist's intrusion into his life. "Look, Sam, it's bad enough being a freak in this circus without you trying to turn me into a case study! I'm doing all right, I can handle

it—better than most, from what I can tell—and what
Anii and I do during her phase isn't something I care
to discuss! So just stay out of it! And don't try to give
me some song and dance about Janelle—" At the
other man's wary attention, he shrugged, then continued with rigid control, "She's onto you. Even if I
wanted her, it wouldn't work."

Toroya stiffened, but a smile flickered bitterly in
his cold dark eyes. "Janelle is paranoid; she sees me
working behind every man who so much as smiles at
her. Surely you don't think I'm as nefarious as all
that?"

"I don't know. Maybe you are. Maybe we all are, in
situations like this, when society's been shot out the
tubes."

"Is that what you think?"

"Tell me it hasn't been."

"All right. Maybe it has been. Almost certainly things
will never be the same again, for any of us, no matter
what happens now. What we have to do—what it is
our human duty to do for the others—is to devise
ways to deal with it. You, and I, are in unique positions to help them."

"I think we've had this discussion before," Padrec
said. He wandered idly across the room, taking in its
sparse appointments, so different from the refinements
of his own small room in the Queen's sumptuous chambers. But Toroya's official garment of orange cloth
reminded him that at least the scientist had power of
a minor sort, while he had none at all. Anii barely
consulted him, on the pretext that his loyalties must
not be divided. He wondered if she guessed just how
divided his loyalties really were.

Toroya did not have that conflict, he made no secret
of his goal to enculturate the humans to life in the
nom, and a glance at the low table that was the
room's only piece of real furniture provided evidence
that the man worked hard; his notes, written on dry
bits of Ibisian paper, were copious. Noting where his

guest had wandered, Toroya moved quietly forward, picked up the scattered papers.

"I am keeping records of the survivors," he explained, the sheets rustling as he gathered them together, "Backgrounds, attitudes, adaptive behavior . . . break-downs in physical and psychological adjustment. There is a lot of stress, a lot of depression—some of them aren't taking it very well."

"Did you really think they would?"

"I think they will, in time. Transculturation is a slow process."

A bit irked that Toroya had taken the notes before he could see if his name was among those in the stack, Padrec said, "Is my name there, with the rest of them?"

"Any reason why it shouldn't be?"

"No, not really—it's just that—"

"Do you really want to know what I have to say about you?"

He did, but it was probably better not to know. So he said that he didn't and dropped the subject. Toroya accepted that tacit understanding, his eyes following, seeking yet more answers. "I understand she lets you go outside the nom," he said simply.

"She knows I'll return."

"Why?"

"What?"

"Why do you return?"

Padrec found himself thinking, the answers coming out like a shrug. "Well, in the first place, where would I go? Provided, you understand, I could get away from my guards, cross the plain without being recaptured— And life, for me, at least, isn't so bad here. No worse, I suppose," he said archly, "than it is for you."

"And Anii?"

"As you said, her nuptials are coming on her."

"She'll be getting pregnant this time. Doesn't that bother you?"

Padrec frowned. "Of course it bothers me. It bothers me that she's Ibisian—but I'm not exactly in a position to do anything about it."

"It might relieve you to know she'll only be pregnant for about three months."

Toroya had a motive for leading the conversation in this direction, but Padrec was perplexed as to what he hoped to accomplish. Having this man take a personal interest in his sex life was, well, somehow distasteful, and distinctly offsetting, but he did not believe that interest was in any way voyeuristic, any more than it was aimed at him directly. It was the *fact*, that of a human male and an Ibisian queen, engaged in a continuing relationship, and the effects it would have, not only on them, but on the community at large. Having understood this, Padrec relaxed, trusting to Toroya's personal friendship to keep his interest purely technical.

"That's a rather short gestation for a large mammal, isn't it?" he said, attempting to force the conversation into a scientific bent. Toroya, too, relaxed into the rapport they had developed for each other after the crash, when they had worked together briefly, too briefly, devising new ways to survive.

"Yes. The human norm is nine to ten, and I've seen a few sub-species where it went to twelve. Longer is better in some environments, with physical limitations determining the finite length of gestation. But three months is a very short time; the embryo is barely a third of the way through its development."

"Then it isn't developed enough to live outside the womb," Padrec tried to recall everything he knew of human reproduction, "The lungs aren't developed yet; it can't feed—"

"No. And they don't. The embryos are transferred immediately to incubators and immersed in a nutrient jelly. Where they continue to grow at an amazing rate." Toroya smiled reflectively, glanced at the young man, who looked to him to provide more answers. Padrec knew him well enough by now to wait for his response. "I suspect it is an adaptive variation," the scientist explained. "A queen's gestation may consist of six to eight embryos—one or two of which may be sexed, the remaining neuter—and it would be impossible for her to carry so many embryos to term. Her body hasn't evolved for it—and even if it had, she would become very large and slow-moving within a few months, making her physically vulnerable, and restricting her ability to rule the nom."

"So instead she gives birth to very immature fetuses—"

"For which the society has evolved a satisfactory means of *in vitro* gestation."

"Wouldn't that require an advanced technology?"

"I would hazard to say that the prototype had one, and that it went off on a wild tangent when it developed the Ibisians."

"An experiment?"

"Maybe. We haven't stumbled across any reliable source of data on the prototype, or even a clear idea of what it *was*, except that it was almost certainly what we would call human." The xenologist's voice took on a conspiratorial intimacy. "Have you ever noticed, Morrissey, that there are no Ibisian children?"

He had noticed, but had not really considered it. And now he saw that Toroya had.

"They emerge from the pods full grown—or nearly so. Anii might have emerged only a year or two before she ever met you."

Like Venus rising from the sea . . . or Athena from the split skull of Jove, newborn and already at the height of her power and sex . . . All at once Padrec had a sickening thought. "This nutrient jelly," he prodded, "where do they get it from? It would have to be organic, sterile, complex—"

"Replete in every amino acid and element essential to the formation and maintenance of a human—or essentially human—body. The Ibisians are a very efficient society, Padrec, they make use of everything, even their dead queens and workers."

Padrec swallowed. "You mean—"

"That's what became of D'nia. Organic soup. Anii will produce the next generation of young queens using the bodily remains of her predecessor. Don't be squeamish, Padrec," Toroya said quite casually, noting the look on the young man's face. "To them it's perfectly natural. I am sure Anii fully expects the same to be done with her someday. It is a way of continuing. And besides, it isn't anything you haven't heard of before."

True, he thought, as the initial sickness subsided, although he had never heard of that particular method being used by human beings. Which meant the Ibisians were far less human than they had at first seemed. Emerging from pods full grown after cannibalizing their ancestors.

"They aren't planning to use us, I hope."

Toroya looked genuinely surprised that he could think of it. "Oh, I don't think so. As I said, they obey very strictly defined patterns of behavior, handed down through untold generations. They would no sooner use us to nourish their young than, say, a few moldering leaves."

A slow, brittle smile brushed Padrec's lips. "Or mate with us than, say, a beetle?"

Very slowly, Toroya's hand dropped the stack of papers he had been holding, raising a brief stir of dust on the table. In the stuffy air of this imperfectly ventilated corner of the nom, his sigh lingered heavily. "You're right, of course. An ordinary Ibisian, a warrior, or a worker, would never alter the pattern. They are incapable of it. But a queen, an intelligent, unprogrammed female, could. In your case, one did."

"So the queens aren't locked into patterns," said Padrec. "Do they create new ones?"

Those dark eyes, glinting, held his across the room. "She is creating a new one right now, with you."

Padrec jerked and turned away.

He didn't like to be reminded of it. He had not yet completely reconciled his feelings for Anii, although he had begun to recognize them. His alien princess—his Amazon Queen . . . his enslaver and his lover—the differences between him and her so great they constituted a gulf as wide as the space that once had divided them. And where did he stand, but somewhere between discovery and damnation—

But there were times. . . .

Sometimes he could stand back from himself, and look out upon the world he had found, and he could marvel at the fortune that had found him.

Except that he was not sure of it, of the solidness of the ground upon which he stood. What if one day it should fall away beneath him, and hurl him into that gulf he had not been able to cross?

And looking at Toroya, he saw that the other man was thinking the same thing.

By the time he left Toroya, and his questions, he was glad to seek the higher reaches of the nom, where he did not have to face the answers, or dwell upon knowledge tainted with the acrid taste of things he did not really want to know. But his spirits rose abruptly when informed upon reaching his room that the Queen had sent for him. He wondered if she had tired of her drone.

For all that Toroya had warned him of her plans and reassured him that Anii had no intention of dispensing with his company, the thought of her courting another, taking a mate, left Padrec cold. Although he must have known it from the first, the realization that he would never *have* her, in the way that humans have their mates, had come home like a boot to his gut. There was no partnership, and never would be. His body was something she owned, used, even took pleasure in, but it was nothing she needed, and in effect reduced him to an object. He could not even make her pregnant— And what good was his intelligence, trapped in this male body, where she would not look to find it, so long as he was intelligent enough to amuse her? His only advantage lay in her jealous love of owning him, the possessive nature which kept him closely held and by her side. He sensed in bed her knowledge that he had not given himself to her completely. It had become his only means of rebellion, his only element of control over his plundered life, to deny to her the one part of him she could not take.

Only in her nuptial phase, those long heated nights so many months ago, had she claimed him to the deepest core of his being, awakened in him the need to give his every breath, his every cell, to be nothing if not a part of her. And that phase was coming upon her again.

The silent workers took away his robe and after his bath he found to his surprise his Terran uniform laid out for him again. This time he hesitated. *What does she want now? Has she found some more captives for me to placate—?* But he put on the garments and, looking in the gold-plated mirror, saw a faintly attractive alien, a dark-haired young Stranger—and recognized that this was a member of a Terran field team, a captive, out of his element. He touched the PES patch on his left shoulder. *I am a Terran*, he reminded himself, *I was born on the dark fifth moon of the fourth planet of Ferro, but my father was born on the planet called Earth. If I have a son, I will tell him that. . . .*

When he had dressed, an attendant took him to the Queen's private chambers, but instead of taking him to the bedchamber the worker led him to the reception hall where she let him in and just as silently closed the door behind her. Padrec turned—and stared into a garden. What had she done? There were potted plants everywhere—even the four pillars at the far end, over-shadowing the raised dais, were towers of vines and greenery, as if she had moved the greenhouse into this room for one night. From the circular apertures in the conical ceiling overhead a golden glow of afternoon filtered down to gild the branches of small trees and lightly explore this sudden wilderness of densely shadowed thickets where flowers glimmered pearl-like through the leaves and twining vines hung down in luxurious tendrils of emerald green to brush the tops of trees. Even the carpets underfoot, rare and costly, jewel-colored with threads of scarlet and azure, in this strange new setting took on the softness of sodden earth, the silence of a forest floor ... Padrec looked for Anii but could not find her. She was not there. But why was he? *Does she want me to classify them, or what—?*

Was it possible, he wondered, that this was connected somehow to her nuptial phase? Last night he had sensed it ... yes, there was that tension in the air. He shivered without knowing why and hesitantly entered the room, making his way through the fantastic greenery to the hidden steps, now carpeted and soft, which led to the vine-covered dais. Those pillars he had seen from the portal rose with a suggestion of eerie green grandeur above his head, its golden canopy overhung with drifts of purple flowers hanging down like smoke ... just as that day in the forest. . . . Bound by wonder, a disquieting sense of having done this before, Padrec raised his hand—and found that those magnificent blossoms lingered just beyond his fingertips. Bracing himself, holding onto the vines running down one of the massive onyx pillars which held the canopy aloft, he reached for and took into his hand a single giant blossom and dropped back again to the floor. Once he had risked his life for one of these— Where had Anii found so many? A gentle rustle behind him made him spin around, startled, forgetting for the moment where he was. Anii stood there, clad only in wisps of frosty gossamer, and her eyes locked onto his with the knowing hunger of a predator who'd found her prey.

She walked to him, and her fingers, like his, stroked the soft petals and velvety throat of the flower. As he stood entranced and barely breathing, one of her fingers slowly dipped into the liquid tube at the base. Withdrawing her finger, she held it out to him, a drop of glowing liquid clinging to the tip. He parted his lips and took the nectar on his tongue: sweet, seductively sweet, as ethereal as the blossom which bore it. Anii's eyes shone as she left her finger to his mouth.

"It was you," his whisper barely pierced the heavy silence. He said no more, struck by understanding.

All this—to recreate that moment? It was a vast fantasy, the height of nuptial madness. . . . Confidently, in full nuptial phase and queenly power, her beauty at its height with her hormonal peak, Anii moved her hands to his garments and loosened the bindings in the front from throat to waist. The impact of her pheromones hit him full force as her lips touched his. "Be still, beloved," she said, drawing him to the floor and pressing him down, "Had we met that day, we would not have spoken."

The next morning when the drone was brought to her, Anii knew the time had come. Having Pa-dric to fill her arms had eased the tensions of waiting, but days spent in the pheromone-ruled presence of a maturing drone had accelerated her own hormones and increased the intensity of her phase until it was no longer possible to resist the urge to mate the one she had chosen. Just last night she had coupled with Pa-dric in a wild, sweet heat, and satisfied the urges of her body for the drone she must not take too soon. When she saw him, draped in the beauteous red garments of his privilege, attended by red-cloaked warrior-keepers who bowed away no sooner than they had entered, she knew that she had waited long enough, that he was ready for her. In his golden eyes wherein dwelt the sun of her desire, she saw the first bright rays of his new aggression, the shining light of his eagerness to mate, and upon his chest, broader now and only partially covered by the shimmering richness of his nuptial gown, there grew a golden sheen of fine young hair. But in his face all was still youth and sweet simplicity.

It should be night, she told herself, *with tall tallow lights and gold-painted shadows and the strident songs of the plains outside my windows rising to serenade my connubial night. In the most beloved tales the Queen always claims her mate in the hours of darkness.* She had only to wait a few hours more, wait for the sun to cover its bright face and darkness to fall upon the plain beneath a veil of stars and the light of three moons. Then long night would lie before her, waiting upon her pleasure. But what good was long night when the mating was short. . . .

In a chamber curtained with silken draperies of

dawn and golden light, she led the chosen one to her bed and there upon the red sheets of her desire he placed himself within the fateful arms of a pitiless destiny laid upon him by a goddess without mercy. In his childishness he had been precious, exquisite, enchanting—in his adulthood he was briefly magnificent, a creature so perfectly constructed for the purpose laid upon him that carnal lust burst forth like blossoms from the vines of need twining through her loins. Trembling, he knelt before her, his nakedness a glowing thing she worshipped. *Come into me, beloved, and place therein the precious gift of which you are but the worthless vessel.* He had been born for one end, his life fashioned for one glorious moment, generation after generation the torch that passed the flame; and she was the Keeper of that Flame, the Queen in whose womb the next generation slept until conceived. Her craving to be set afire burned more brightly than the piercing perfection of his beauty. Wanting him beyond reason, she felt her desire narrow to a single point of exquisite, all-consuming lust, Anii drew the golden youth into her embrace and lovingly clasped him to her as the point was pierced and she was complete, his maleness for that moment the pole about which her universe centered. *My children, my immortality—give me the gift and I shall see your beauty again in the offspring of our engendering. That alone has the goddess promised you. Oh, lovely one, feel the pleasure that you give me—*

A great wracking shudder passed through him as her pleasure in him reached its fullest and his in her had taken him to heights undreamed of—and then he gasped twice and collapsed in her arms, spent. She held his slack, departing beauty in her arms, cradling him as he weakly struggled and, the light dying from the questions in his betrayed eyes, gave up the life that was in him. *The Spark has passed to me,* she rejoiced, throwing back her head in victory. *Thus does the male create life, by sending life from his own being that other lives might take from it.*

She lay for many moments beneath him, treasuring his passing, the beauty that once again, in death, had the power to move her to tenderness. Her lips brushed his lovely throat. Poor stupid thing, you do not even know why this must be so. You perform for the pleasure and die for the need. Such is the way of the goddess with you.

As gently as she might stir herself from a sleeping lover's arms, Anii stole from the bed and summoned the attendants, who wrapped the body in the red silk sheets of his passing and bore it from the chamber. No unpleasantness was allowed to mar the Queen's connubial night or distress her unduly. Personal servants, as silent and attentive as her needs required, laid out her gown and served ambrosial drinks from trays of beaten copper laden with the most tempting delicacies as she wandered her chamber restlessly, her nuptial phase as yet unended. Her pregnancy would make itself known within hours, but until then her body must endure its now meaningless yearnings. No male must come near her, or surely she would succumb to passions not yet fully reconciled. Pa-dric, especially, must be kept from her tonight, for even to think of him drove her nearly mad with wanting to taste him and drink to the full of his heady blend of gentleness and strength, of resistance and yielding. But she could not afford him to dilute her pregnancy, or in any way imperil this first mating.

But I have provided him the warm arms of another, one To-roya assures me will not want to keep him.

During the nuptial phase of a ruling queen, nearly every individual in the nom was influenced by the pervasive chemistry of her courtship and mating, in the case of a young queen much more so than with an old one. D'nia's phases, at the end, had barely stirred the nom from its daily routines. Anii knew that her own was having far more effect. Other queens, their phases keyed to hers, had taken male Strangers from the compound with her persimmon and were using them with gratifying abandon, while warriors and workers kept close to the nom. If the phase ended suddenly, the nom would know of her success nearly as soon as she did.

But until then she would not see Pa-dric nor inquire what effect her nuptials had worked on him.

Padrec, however, could feel in his blood that Anii would be mating that day. Last night had wrought its changes, had brought him to that fevered state he now knew too well, only to be hurled into this interminable day, a day he spent in meaningless activity he did not even know his reasons for pursuing, except that it kept him occupied, kept him from thinking about *her*. But his mind could no longer focus on other pursuits, and often would leave Janelle to finish whatever he was supposed to be doing and he would flee to the quiet and solitude of the greenhouse, where the constantly recirculated air drew away the worst poisons of his strange fever. Anii's pheromones diffused through the air of this place, permeated the cushions and wall, filled him with urges he could neither define nor explore. He only knew that he had felt them before, and that they had left him enslaved to this alien world forever.

I want her. I want her and she has stopped wanting me. She wants to be pregnant, and she wants the stupid creature who can give that to her— What am I to that?

And like a fool I am burning for just the barest touch of her ... in a rut! he realized, almost wanting to laugh at discovering the source of his despair. *I'm in full-fledged rut! Just like some male animal around a female in heat. . . .*

A sound at the door barely punctured his self-absorption. Janelle, vaguely concerned and nondescript in one of the short gowns that the Terrans were made to wear when they came into the nom, pressed a shallow bowl of sweet Ibisian nectar into his hand. "Here," she said, her tone helpful, "I wish it was coffee."

He looked down into the dark depths, then drained

the bowl. It was too sweet and tasted awful. "So do I."
His hand shook slightly as he set it aside.

"It's not just you," she offered, trying to make him
feel better, "Everyone feels it. I guess, maybe for you,
it might be a little worse.

"Maybe just a little," he agreed, smiling up at her,
then looked away again. "I've been through it before,
of course, but then I was *with* her. Even last night,
she was there—I could—" he exhaled raggedly, having reached the limit of explanation. "I want her,
Janelle, and not just because of this. I don't know
whether she is Ibisian or human; I can't seem to tell
the difference anymore."

He felt her fingers upon his hand, a quiet touch,
gently reassuring. "Neither can she, I think."

"Oh, yes, she can. That's why she's with one of her
drones right now instead of me—"

"She'll come back to you. Everyone knows it; in the
compound, they talk, you know, and I listen. They say
she's mad about you." Taking both his hands into hers
and warming them, she smiled across at him with
faint wonder, "I used to ask myself, along with the
rest of them, what it was she saw in you. But now I
think I know. I understand her. You are really very
sweet, very gentle—it must be lovely having you."

"Janelle—"

"She's very lucky, you know. I could almost envy
her." Her eyes looked into his, trusting him with her
appraisal, warming as their glances met and lingered.
Her smile faded as she said, with telling sadness, "If
only you weren't hers, I might be tempted to find out
if I should—"

She felt it too, it was in them both . . . her touch on
his cheek was a summons, reminding him of other
times, other women . . . his brain reeling from the
pheromone-saturated air, Padrec bent to kiss her
trembling, openly inviting lips. How warm she was!
How real . . . Janelle MacDonald, crisp, efficient, always busy Janelle, who had never once looked his
way or had two words to spare for him on ship. . . .

Janelle leaned into the kiss, breathless, exploring the newness of it. Her mouth parted, open, seeking more. Only then did Padrec realize what was happening to them. But he found that he didn't care. As he had wanted Anii so many months ago, he wanted this woman now. Why had he ever wanted to keep them from this? She wanted him too, he could feel it in her body pressing up to his, her hand upon his thigh. . . .

Too late, Janelle awakened to what was really happening, the thing to which she was falling victim. She backed away, eyes wide with disbelief at what she was doing. "This is insane—I can't—not with you—" She pushed herself away from him and dashed from the room as he made a grab for her.

"Please, Janelle—"

He ran after her and caught her finally in one of the outer chambers, still within the quarters. There, in the stronger essence of nuptial pheromones that hung in the very air of the royal chambers, Janelle weakened. "No," she said, pleading against the burning need that was taking hold of her own being, leaving her moist, hot, wanting the man who pulled her into his arms, "Please, don't—"

But she let him carry her to the thickly carpeted floor where her struggles melted into surrender and she, too, responded to the alien stimuli, her arms, instead of fighting him, drawing him to her, pulling his mouth hard against hers . . . and tasted the sweetness that had enchanted an Ibisian queen, a depth of desire that plunged her into the core of her own being. . . . She wanted him, and her hips lifted to him as his body lowered onto hers, encountering thighs slack with lust, welcoming the tender passion with which he took her, the gentle, loving ride of two bodies entwined in an act of pure sex. There, upon the carpets of that alien chamber, they responded to the alien heat that had claimed them, immersed in the urgings of their two bodies, enjoying each other again and again as slowly the golden light outside the windows gave way to darkness. Only much later, sweat-drenched and drained, did they draw apart, embarrassed and deeply shamed to realize how fully they had succumbed to a thing outside themselves. The horror of it reached them almost instantly.

"Janelle, please—" Padrec tried to console the weeping woman. But her clothes, damp and stained, told the truth of what had happened. He did not want her to think he had planned on this outcome. "Janelle, I didn't want this, not this way. I think, maybe, Anii thought—oh, God, Janelle, don't be angry—"

With a mangled cry of humiliation and rage, Janelle struggled to her feet and fled from him, the chamber curtains flying in her wake. Padrec threw himself backward on the carpets and let his eyes be blinded by tears of pure misery at knowing that because of him another human being had been hurt, misused. She had not wanted him. In a pheromone-induced heat any man would have served, just as for him the only real need had been for a female body upon which to spend himself. The act in which they had engaged had been physically pleasurable, but it had lacked even the vestiges of emotional sharing and human warmth. And her new, painfully tender liking for him, the first fragile relationship he had built with another human being since his capture, was surely shattered beyond repair—he would have to be a hopeless idiot to think it could have survived.

Not since the day he had accepted Anii's ownershp had he felt so horribly used, like some dumb animal caught in a trap. A trap he should have known was lying there in wait. A haunting, lingering echo inside his skull recalled to him something Anii had said . . . *There is a female of your kind. You will mate with her when the time comes. . . . And it is well, To-roya tells me, for you to do this. . . .* When had she said that? He couldn't remember. But he had let Toroya reassure him, humor him like a child, while all the time the man had been playing games with his life, and with that of the woman as well . . . And what must Janelle be feeling, thinking he had taken advantage of her?

And maybe he had. He had known they were being manipulated, maneuvered, and he had done nothing to put a stop to it. Because he had wanted to be with her. Another human. He should have known that it was not to be.

I should have been stronger. I should not have allowed this to happen.

But he had.

I must go after her, find her. I must explain—

But when he tried to follow her the warriors would not let him leave the queen's chambers, not even to look for her, and when he tried to force his way past them, they wrestled him to his own dark, secluded room and stood guard outside until, emotionally drained and physically exhausted, he slept. That night was forever a haze of condemnation and renewed doubts. Anii had betrayed him. That she had taken a drone of her own race for reproduction he could accept, he *must* accept, for that act was as necessary and natural to her as life on this planet. He could not keep her from being what she was. But what was he? To which world did he belong—? He twisted in his bed, tortured by horrid dreams in which he envisioned himself bound by ropes so thick and heavy he could not move beneath the weight of them; they drove him to his knees and he was not able to rise, for every time he tried his bonds dragged him down ... and Janelle, her face unseen, running, screaming, from the Ibisians in the forest ... Anii turning her back on him, and another queen, smiling as she led him away, a metal collar being placed around his neck, choking off more than tears. ...

Each time he awoke, his heart clotted in his chest until he recognized the quiet darkness surrounding him, the fragile reality of his own room. Only then would he lay back again, grateful for the damp softness of the flat pillow beneath his tear-stained cheek as he sought to escape from the horrors of his dreams, and wishing that reality could be so easily wished away.

"You had no right!"

Neither Toroya nor Anii frightened him. His disgust for both of them had left Padrec immune to any feelings for them at all. So obvious was his distaste that neither of them dared approach him.

"It was for your own good, Padrec," Toroya told him calmly. "During a queen's connubial, the pheromones of the drone are added to those of the queen. The effect on you must have been devastating. Your state of arousal might well have become toxic, maybe even dangerous."

"And you threw that poor woman into it? Didn't you think what it might do to her? What I might do—" Barely controlling the emotions threatening to shred his composure completely, Padrec clenched his hands and stared at the floor. "I raped her. I forced her to the floor and then I raped her."

Toroya bowed his head. "I'm sorry, Padrec. For your sake, I wish there had been a better way. But she was willing, surely you know that. The pheromones affect females, too."

"And that makes it all right? It makes it all right to put her in that situation? Just because a man is suicidal doesn't mean you should put him on a ledge and shout 'Jump!' Can't you see that you are raping me, her, the whole god-forsaken human race? You're so screwed up you wouldn't recognize a moral choice if it hit you in the face." He gave up on Terran, and said to Anii in formal Ibisian for the sake of those watching, "Take him away, please. Please, get him out of here. I cannot endure the sight of him."

Anii ordered her attending warriors to lead the pale, visibly shaken Stranger away. Not once did she remove her eyes from Pa-dric. His rejection of To-roya, whose visits he had previously welcomed, and his emotional denouncement of his mating with the female, puzzled her. He acted hurt, distraught, as though somehow he had been violated—and so far she did not understand the reasons for it.

I should learn their language. I wonder if I could. Then I would know what they say to each other.

With Hli watching each tiny movement for indications of possible violence, Anii approached Padrec until she stood but a handspan before him. But he refused to look up at her, and continued to sit despondently on the edge of his bed.

"This mating was needed. To-roya but did what I told him to do."

"But you were wrong. Can you not see that? You were wrong to ask him. You were wrong to do it."

Considering herself affronted, Anii glared down at him. Behind her, Hli snorted and muttered at such impertinence.

But Anii felt more strongly her need to know what had brought her gentle lover to such a violent pass. "How was it wrong?" she demanded. "The female's assigned function was to ease you."

"You cannot assign her to that." He at last looked up at her. "She did not choose me. I did not choose her. It was—" But if there was a word in the Ibisian language for rape, he had not yet learned it, so he finished by explaining as best he could. "A female of our kind does not mate with a man she does not want. And the man must not force himself upon her."

Anii stared at him, stunned at what he was trying to tell her. She had not thought of the Strangers in terms of cultural sensibilities. Far less had she assumed them to have this, too, in common with the nomari. Only queens, among the nomari, retained the right of choice. And in phase, a queen wanted to mate. Willing or not, if at the height of her phase a drone was readied and presented to her—yes, she would mate. But it was seldom done, usually at the hands of hostiles who held their new queen captive all her life, until a younger, nom-born queen was raised to replace her. But always the male remained oblivious, incapable of choice.

Not so among the Strangers. The female possessed few sexual enticements, and none like those of the nomari; the male therefore had to be willing to perform his function. She had no means of forcing him. Conversely, if the male was willing, but the female was not, and he could overpower her ... yes, it was possible among Strangers for the male to force her to mate. And that was the taboo. The taboo Pa-dric now thought he had broken. That the male could force a mating was alien to her, that he should feel remorse for an act that was natural to him, more so, and yet ... his sensitivity to the female's violation told her just how deeply he felt about this matter of choice. She also saw how difficult it would be to reconcile him to the fact that his choice had been taken from him. More than that, she felt a growing anger that To-roya had not foreseen this consequence. She had taken too much care with Pa-dric for too long, to allow another's carelessness to harm him.

"Toroya will speak with the one you mated," she said to him, "She will know that it was not of your doing. No more than it was your doing when first you mated me. Your kind cannot punish you for what you did not do."

"Oh, Anii—" She didn't know. She was alien, not human. She didn't know ... Padrec sensed that she would never, quite, understand what he was feeling. Many Terrans would never be able to grasp the strictness of his beliefs, pounded into every fiber of his being by a mother who had practiced an archaic religion and had named her son for an ancient Terran saint. His punishment would always to be know that he was, ultimately, responsible for the act.

"What must I do to console you?" she asked. "It will not happen again. I knew my phase would stir you and I but wanted to provide for your need."

Gazing into her eyes, he answered in all truth. "It was not her I needed, but you."

"Beloved—" He had relented. Anii reached out her hand, touched her fingers to his hair. "I, too, need you. I but wish it might have been." She put her other hand to her pelvis and announced abruptly, "I have conceived."

To the triumphant gleam of her eyes, he said, "I see." But every muscle in his body drew tense at the alienness of her knowing so soon, so certainly . . .

She took his hands and clasped them, five-fingered within hers, asking him to share with her this moment of joy and warmth in her achievement. Had he not helped her to it? "None will challenge my queenship, now that my fertility is proven. The warriors will not abandon a queen during her breeding. My dominance will be uncontested." She stopped. Pa-dric's smile was too wan to be the response she had wanted. Did he fear for his own place, now that she did not need him? Turning his hands in hers, Anii kissed each thumb, wondering as ever that such large hands should be so gentle. "Oh, Pa-dric, beloved, I will not abandon you. In the hands of another, what secrets could you tell? But my needs for you have changed, and you will no longer be required to share my couch."

Padrec nodded that he understood. No sex. Just as well, he thought, he would hardly be any good for it. His new and abundant burden of guilt had all but obliterated his desire for sexual contact. Anii's removing it from the realm of possibility only left him feeling inordinate relief.

Anii noted Pa-dric's response with relief of her own. She had feared he would protest being deprived. "You do not mind?"

"No," he said. "It will free me for other things."

"Your work with the plants," she said, seeing a way in which his energies and intelligence might be put to good use. "You will pursue this interest?"

"I suppose so."

"It seems to me that you should. The nom might

prosper from your interest." He glanced up at her then, with childlike curiosity. She knew then that she had judged him correctly. "You have seen, from afar, the fields where the nomari reap the grains which feed us. These grains are plants. And you may possess knowledge that would be of use to the growing of them."

"Yes," Padrec said. Despite himself, his mind raced with excitement at the opportunity to actually practice his profession. He had experience, however small, in agronomics. He might even be able to use the talents of one of the geologists for an initial soil breakdown and analysis. . . . "Yes, I think maybe I could increase the amount of grain the nomari can grow."

His rapid grasp of her plan startled her. She had expected him to accept, but not to engage in establishing a goal for his work. *This is not simply an intelligent drone,* she reminded herself. *Pa-dric is something else again, something not nomari. How easy it is to forget it!*

"Yes," she said, "You will go out into the fields, and study our agriculture. The plants we grow and the way we grow them. Then you will tell me the ways a Stranger would improve these things." She looked across the room to where Hli leaned upon her spear, her orange eyes slitted with her intense pondering of the young Stranger. "You may be very valuable to me after all, Pa-dric, if you can profit the nom."

Outside the nom the season changed, the days grew shorter and the climate cooled as the winds shifted and moisture from the sea swept inland to drench the plains. While Ibis had no true winter, the plain followed a seasonal pattern of rains and dry spells. Padrec watched the winter grain crop being brought in and insect herds slaughtered, their carcasses harvested and ground into a protein powder which, mixed with the grain, formed the staple product of the Ibisian diet. Only the queens, and sometimes warriors on the eve of battle, ate medallions of fresh roasted flesh, or dined on the soft sweet larvae raised in vast subterranean caverns. Giant aphids, their abdomens swollen with milky fluid, were brought in from secret forest ranges and attached to the underground walls, to be fed enough to allow them to survive and their juices milked throughout the dormant season. The nom continued its perpetual order, a strangely human race dominating a world not evolved for humans.

Anii, her queenship secure with her pregnancy, had resumed her interest in Padrec. Wanting to be sure of him, to recoup whatever she had lost through her neglect, she indulged his pastimes and allowed him his studies, delighting when he solved the problem of a blight which had damaged part of the harvest or proposed new hybrids to increase production of vital grains, taking pleasure in his growing collections and knowledge of local plants and especially of the drawings he made, several of which she had bound into a book to be used in educating the young. She treated him with gifts of oddities gathered in far places, and long nights spent on shared glances and private conversations that reaffirmed his place with her, as well as a physical possession that erased all doubts as to the nature of her conquest. She would have no intercourse with him on account of her pregnancy, but having seen him agonize over the events surrounding his mating with the female Stranger and his anger at having been entrapped, she did not press him to take a human lover. Secretly, she was pleased that he had found no lasting pleasure in the female's company. Less pleasing, and of more consequence, was Pa-dric's opposition to To-roya.

"You have no place in this," she reminded him. "To-roya has the leadership of the Strangers. You do not. Your only place is here with me."

"They did not choose him to lead them."

"It is not for them to choose. Nor for you. To-roya will see that they learn to live among the nomari, as you have learned to do."

With a sigh he tried to explain. "My place is privileged. And I live by your side willingly. It is easy for me to be content where I am well-treated."

"Then be content, and forget this foolishness," she said to him, "Your people must accept their slavery before they can be allowed to live among us. And they are few; their numbers must be increased. To-roya has promised to see to this."

"Oh, I'll bet he has." Again he spoke with alien words. She had come to know that he expressed harsh or painful thoughts in his own language. By the look on his face, she could see that her arguments did not satisfy him. There was no time to humor him, however, for the discussion was interrupted by Hli, announcing the arrival of one of the older queens who had been an important supporter of Anii and whose courtesy visit she had been expecting.

"Enough, Pa-dric," she said, drifting away from him to signal that this conversation was ended, that other business more pressing now demanded her attention.

Upon the raised dais of red marble which graced the formal reception chamber, Anii awaited the entrance of her visitor. The older queen, Bhi'hia, arrived per-

fectly groomed and arrogant of her station, her golden
beauty barely faded and enhanced by veils of brilliant
color; she bowed deeply to the ruler of her nom, her
presentation dignified and subtly aggressive. Such a
deferring of subservience was common in older queens
who, as they left their reproductive years behind, often compensated for the loss of importance by becoming otherwise bold and outspoken. Such queens made
excellent subordinates since, unlike younger queens,
they lacked sufficient fertility to aspire to the nom.
When Anii had accepted the ritual greeting, the visitor rose again to her feet, tall and confident. Almost
too boldly her eyes touched upon Padrec where he
stood to one side.

"Truly, Anii," she said in the rich voice of approval,
"you have kept the prize of the Strangers for yourself.
How lovely he is—and he stands there so docilely! I
still cannot believe you do not bind him in some way."

Anii did not appreciate the direction of her conversation, although it was true that she displayed Pa-dric
at her side for just that reason. It was her intention
that other queens should envy how her Stranger stayed
by her, how obedient he was. She had even taken to
letting him outside the nom again, short expeditions
to the plain to gather plants. Always, and without the
least hint of trouble, he had returned. . . . "If I would
need to bind Pa-dric as you do yours," she said pointedly, "I would not keep him."

Taking cue from the way Anii's eyes looked past the
visitor, Padrec saw that someone else had come into
the room, unnoticed in the wake of the queen's entry,
an attractive, golden-haired young human, ill at ease,
standing just inside the guarded doors. An elaborate
harness bound his hands with short chains to a girdle
at his waist.

The older queen indicated the young man, her eyes
shining with obvious pride, and said, "My beautiful
Es-dan still needs his reminders. But he expressed a
desire to speak with another of his kind. And I thought
that he could do worse than to learn from your Pa-

dric. Of course," she bowed again, "it is for you to say
if such may be allowed, Great Queen."

Not taking his eyes from the other man, unable to
look away from the raw hope written there, Padrec
nodded his consent to the silent question Anii directed
his way. "I will take him to the greenhouse, show him
my work—we will not disturb you."

"It pleases you to see him?" She was giving him an
out if he wanted it.

"Yes."

"Go then."

The other queen watched, gratified, her eyes burning, as Padrec led the other from the room. He heard
Bhi'hia say, "So, he is as well-spoken as he is beautiful."

When they had left the queens and were alone in
the quiet passageway leading to the greenhouse, the
other man put a hand on Padrec's arm. "I have to talk
to you."

Something in the way he said it, his lack of hesitation, indicated that he had come on more than an
impulse. Stan Scoriusci and he had been friends once,
of a casual sort. They had gone through PES training
together, learning shipboard procedure and routine,
the challenge of living and working in close quarters,
and when they had made call at some obscure outpost
in the Rigel system, Stan had taken him under his
wing and together they had made the most of his first
leave. It pained him to see Stan now, much changed,
his blond good looks pale and strained, those clear
green eyes robbed of youth, wretchedly desperate.

"Please, Padrec, don't turn away from me."

"What makes you think I would? God, Stan, it's
good to see you!" He took the other man in his arms
and hugged him, full of joy at seeing him again. When
the gesture was not returned, he looked down at the
girdle restricting the man's movements by lengths of
short chain linking his wrists to his waist. "Stan," he
whispered, grasping the chains, "This is monstrous!"

"I've seen worse. At least she's stopped using the
collar on me. It got to the point even she couldn't

stand the sores on my neck." With an abrupt jerk
Stan pulled away, but the action was found by urgency, not as a rebuff. "Padrec, look, I don't know how
much time they'll give us. This was the only way to
reach you—you don't come to the compound anymore—"

"What are you talking about?"

"Rubinsky wants to talk to you. When Bhi'hia announced that she would be visiting the Queen, I told
him I might be able to get you the message." He
flashed a pained, faintly triumphant smile. "I had to
flatter the old bitch to get her to bring me; I was so
willing to please that I thought she couldn't help but
see through it. I told her you and I were friends—"

"It's the truth, Stan."

"Are we? It's changed. In the compound they say
you've gone over to them. When I said I'd try to talk
to you, there were plenty who said I shouldn't even
try."

Padrec moved away from him, the hurt carving like
a knife into his heart. That people who did not know
him might think so, he could almost understand. But
Stan was his friend.

"You don't know what it's like, Padrec. I don't know
what you've done, or what happened to you, but you
haven't gone through what the rest of us have. Everyone knows it. You haven't worn chains around your
neck, so tight you could barely breathe or swallow, or
shackles hammered about your wrists while you
screamed because you'd seen what they would do to
you—" Stan closed his eyes rather than look at the
gleaming bronze bands gripping his own wrists. They
were lined with pads of soft cottony fiber, but others,
perhaps, less prized for their beauty, were treated
with less care. Swallowing, he continued. "You haven't
been beaten until you were unconscious; you haven't
been starved, or locked in a dark room because you
won't eat the filthy food they give you, or drink the
dirty water; you haven't been made to sleep naked on
some cold floor because some damned Ibisian doesn't
think you are human." With a muffled cry, he slumped

to the stone steps leading down to the greenhouse and, as Padrec took him gently by the shoulders, broke out in soft sobs. "She did it to me. I didn't know what she wanted. The shuttles sent us to look for Rubinsky. I was captured and before I knew what was happening, I was in her bed."

"I know," Padrec said, barely more than a whisper, staring with horror into the distance above Stan's trembling head. "Really I do."

"Every time I don't understand her, she punishes me, and her subservients are just as bad, some of them are worse. Some days I don't even move. She lets me go to the compound because it gets me out of her way. It's at night that she wants me—" He gave a strangled laugh and a groan of despair. His eyes stared defiantly into Padrec's. "Wally Ebert's dead, you know. He killed himself. Took something sharp and cut his throat. That bitch he slept with threw him out on the garbage heap; we looked at him for days. Toroya finally got permission to go out and bury him. Sometimes we wonder who's next."

"I won't let it go on," Padrec promised him. "I'll talk to Anii—" But he knew, even as he said it, that even if he did, it would do no good. Anii would not presume to tell her queens how to treat their bed-partners.

Stan, too, shook his head. "No. *You* have to help us, Padrec. You're the only one who can."

"I wish I could. Lord knows how I've tried, how I want to—" He pressed his hands hard into those of his weeping friend, "But what can I do, Stan? I'm as helpless as you."

A rustle of curtains at the far end of the passage alerted them to Hli. The subservient came to stand over them, barely acknowledging Padrec as she delivered her command. "The queen Bhi'hia's audience is over. This one must go." With rough brusqueness, she ordered Stan to his feet and, taking hold of the chains binding his wrists, forced him to follow her retreat along the passageway. Twisting for one last look behind him, Stan cast a plaintive plea back at the man who had been his friend, "Rubinsky—Padrec, please, talk to Rubinsky—!"

It was easy the next day to get permission to go to the compound. He had not planned to go. Now that he knew what his fellow crew members were thinking of him . . . he did not want to have to confront them, look into their eyes as they condemned him in silence. But the memory of Stan's tormented, despairing face would not allow him to forget that final plea, the words that came back to haunt him. Rubinsky wanted to see him. Why? *I should go, find out. Stan risked the anger of his queen to come to me, even when other people told him not to bother—* Again the pain of that rejection clutched at him, but he shrugged it off. *Is that what it is? Are they so desperate that they are willing to try anything, even me?*

But had he ever really given them the chance? He had found it easier to keep that distance between them, to avoid having to face them, having to explain. How could he expect them to condone his happiness, or accept that he was in love?

They would condemn him for it. They already had, without ever knowing him.

But they were his people, and they were reaching out to him. He knew, whatever the reasons against it, that he would go to them.

After a morning clouded by the shadows of such thoughts, Padrec at last sought audience with Anii. He was admitted to her private reception chamber without question, her attendants having long since learned that his requests for access were always granted. Anii was standing beside the window when he entered, her tall body, still slender, awash in golden light, the bare swell of her abdomen the only sign of her advancing pregnancy. In her shimmering rose-pink garments she wore a glow of femaleness and motherhood more powerful than her former virginal state, and he found himself drawn despite his misgivings about the changes taking over her body. About him, Anii had no such ambivalence.

"Beloved," she said, her eyes warming at the sight of him, taking in the color and cut of his garments, "you do not always dress to please me."

It was the oldest strategem in the world, the universe—women throughout the ages had used it to sway their men—and Padrec felt a rush of chagrin at having been caught in an act of manipulative behavior. He blushed, but yielded to his embarrassment. "I wanted to please you that you might grant my request."

"You please me just by being. What do you desire?" Extending her hand, she bade him stand beside her at the window. There, far above the dusty plain with its vista of grasses gone to seed and the last, brilliantly yellow gasps of late season flowers, he made his request.

"I want to go to the compound of my people, and spend some time with them."

She pondered him, newly curious. "Why? They want nothing to do with you. It has been long since you went there."

"Not because I have ceased to care about them. The man who came here yesterday was once a friend of mine. Being with him reminded me of others I have not seen in a long time, and—" he drew a breath before gazing into her eyes with genuine concern "—I would like to see to them."

Troubled, her fingers caressed his cheek, softly, with concern of her own. "My beauty. They are not worthy of your care—they cause you pain—"

"Only because I do care. It is more pain to think of them, and not to know."

"To-roya would tell you of them."

Stubbornly, he looked away.

"So you will not talk to him, and must see them for yourself," she said, knowing better than to press so sore a point, "You use silence against him as others would use a knife. And you know that this day he is to have an audience with me, and that if you go to seek the Strangers you need not see him."

"Yes." What else could he do but admit it? Being able to avoid Toroya had played a part in his decision to visit the compound that afternoon, and not in the next day or two. "Will you let me go?"

"I should say no," she said, her mouth turning over in a tiny frown of displeasure tempered by just the right amount of indulgence. "You will be unhappy if you go. And you will be unhappy if I refuse you. Therefore go, if that is what moves you. But this thing with To-roya must end. See, he comes." Her look had gone across the room.

Turning, Padrec saw Toroya enter, escorted by Hli. The xenologist had dressed for his audience in the Ibisian style, an orange robe elegantly sashed with golden cords, trimmed and hemmed with black barbs denoting minor rank, soft sandals as were used within the nom, his finger- and toenails buffed and polished to a golden sheen. He looked like what he was, a man of some importance. Upon seeing that Anii was not alone, that Padrec stood with her, Toroya paused in the doorway, hesitant, uncertain.

"Come, To-roya," Anii addressed the man she had chosen as her liaison with the Strangers. "He will not bite you."

"Of course not, my Queen." Toroya regained his composure, bowed deferentially, "Our differences are not so deep as all that."

"Pa-dric will speak with you, if he wishes to visit the other Strangers."

"Does he wish to visit them?"

"Yes," Padrec said, keeping his voice toneless, "I want to see how they are doing."

"It's been a long time."

"You may take the credit for it, if you wish. After what happened—"

"And what did happen, Morrissey?" Toroya asked quietly. "What would you have done if Janelle had not been there for you?"

"I would have lived through it. I would have gone through hell on my own terms, not yours—I would have been as frustrated as hell, but I would not have dragged some poor woman down into it with me—"

"Janelle understands that what took place was not of your doing."

"Wasn't it? It's my damn fault they're all here to begin with, isn't it? If I had managed to get killed with the others, you would still be a curious freak and the rest of them might still be free—"

"Good God!" Toroya stared at him, understanding at last most of what stood between them, "Is that what this is all about? You feel responsible for that?"

Anii turned on them with a taut flare of her rose-pink garments. "Speak as the nomari," she directed crossly. Only then did they realize they had been speaking Terran Standard.

Toroya's dark eyes dropped before the golden, demanding gaze of the Ibisian Queen. "If it may please my Queen," he said, "I think it would be well for Padrec to visit the others. He has been too long separated from his kind. His worries about them are genuine and cause him real concern. These things are best set to rest by confronting them."

"He has already been granted my permission to do this. It pleases me that he should also have yours." Her fingers touched her consort's hair, a casual tenderness and gesture of departure. "Go now, and satisfy your misgivings. Hli will direct the warriors to see to your safety. I do not wholly trust these others."

Anii remained silent until Pa-dric had left. For some reason, she found his refreshed interest in his own kind unsettling. It took away from her a part of him she had hoped to claim as her own. He belonged to them still, more than he belonged to her. She regarded To-roya as he knelt on the tiled floor several steps below, in the center of her receiving chamber.

"You take Pa-dric's part quite freely," she observed pointedly, descending by a few steps to lessen the distance between them. Her regal gown of rose silk swept the milky tiles with the softness of a kiss.

To-roya bowed his aged head. "I am fond of him. He has gone through much—and come so far. But I fear his adjustment is delicate."

"Of late he has been content," she said, brushing her fingertips upon her gown, reflecting. "His work pleases him. I do not like this wish of his to visit the others. Always he returns to me moody and unhappy, as if the cut between him and them is new and filled with pain."

"I should say that he is filled with pain. I have told you before the reasons for it."

"He feels responsible—"

He nodded. "He must see them. You cannot separate him from what he is—and he must learn to cope with it."

"That is your wisdom. My better judgment says to keep him from them, and in time he will forget."

"You give him too little credit for remembering."

"You give him too little credit—but for him I would have little tolerance for your insolence." She frowned. "As for you, his anger has not lessened."

"I regret the ill-feeling between us. Padrec is one of the few men whose regard I would have."

"It was foolish of you to trick him into mating, if you knew he did not wish it."

Toroya looked up, met the golden smoothness of her eyes. "I sought to protect him. The mating served to provide release at a time of acute, possibly harmful, arousal. We do not yet know the complete effects on our males of prolonged states of arousal due to pheromone intoxication. Perhaps abstinence is not damaging; perhaps it is. If nothing else, it is violently uncomfortable—" He smiled painfully. "I can speak for that."

"You had access to a female?"

"No, Great Queen. I fear I did not. The experience, however, proved—enlightening. Poor Morrissey—he never did have a chance."

Distinctly amused by the thought of an aroused To-roya, Anii said, greatly curious, "So what did you do?"

He told her.

"So Pa-dric did have recourse?"

"A poor substitute at best. It profits no one."

"Even so, I can understand his anger. One time I allowed you this use of him. Do not presume again: I will not allow him to be used as a breeder, To-roya."

With great deference, the man bowed, his face to the floor. "I must inform you—the woman, Janelle, has conceived. Padrec will know that the child she carries is his."

"This is the child of his mating?"

"Yes. I will not hide that I am pleased with this."

"You are pleased, but what of Pa-dric?" Anii wanted to know, marking To-roya's reservations, "He did not wish to mate, or participate in increasing the Strangers. Are you telling me he will be displeased?"

"It may—unsettle him. Among our kind, males also feel a responsibility toward their offspring. He will want to see to its welfare."

It was a fascinating concept. Among the nomari the male had no role to play beyond that of fertilization and never saw his offspring. Anii asked To-roya to explain further the Stranger attitude toward their young. This he did at length, until her curiosity was satisfied. It amazed and disturbed her to think that Pa-dric would know and care for his offspring, even as she would know and care for her own.

"And he will want to protect his young?"

"Oh, yes. Our society, you see, has no workers, no warriors, no asexual castes to safeguard our females as they bear and raise their young. Survival in the past often depended on the male's ability—and willingness—to protect and feed his mate and the young she bore him. In this way he could provide that his own offspring, at least, would survive. This willingness became part of our pattern of social interaction, and remnants of that behavior live on even now when we do not need it."

Anii pondered this information. Queens protected their young—and their mates—to the death. Had she given Pa-dric over to an instinct stronger than her hold on him? A dull seed of anger took root against To-roya for advocating this thing that threatened to take from her the mate she so fiercely and passionately fought to possess. She could not give him offspring—and the pale-haired female of the Strangers could. She felt the vague stir of her own young within her and wondered if ever he had felt the same. . . .

"This female," she asked coldly, "will she make demands on him?"

"Janelle?" To-roya smiled without amusement. "I think not. She barely knows him—and does not want him. I suppose she will give him his due as the father, but—"

"She does not wish him as a mate?"

"No."

Relieved that the other female would present no obstacle, Anii descended the last few steps. "This is disturbing," she informed To-roya, standing over him. "I welcome Pa-dric's child, because it is his and it suits me for your kind to have many offspring, but I do not want him to wish to protect it. We must see that he does not have to. You shall provide for the needs of the female J'nel. I do not wish Pa-dric to be concerned about her or the well-being of his young one. Perhaps the child will be male, with the look of him, and can be raised as a mate for my daughters." That thought softened the lines of her lips with pleasure, and brought a new warmth to the moods of her eyes as they dwelt on the man kneeling at her feet. To-roya alone of the Strangers had shown himself so readily subservient. "You see, To-roya," she said, turning from him to seek the comfort of her cushions, "He will have no reason to complain."

But Toroya, though he was silent, looked doubtful.

Padrec took care with his appearance before going to the human compound. Not wanting to look any more like an Ibisian favorite than he was already assumed to be, he wore a plain robe of fawn-colored cotton unembellished by embroidery or barbs. Only the medallion around his neck, which he wore whenever he left the royal apartments, set him apart as belonging to the Queen. That, and the several bronze-skinned warriors who accompanied him, their hard protective footwear rapping out a staccato warning of their approach. He made his way quickly through the wide upper corridors of the nom, ignoring curious pauses by wandering subservients, the glowing stares of an occasional young queen, before at last he could hurry downward through the narrow lower levels to reach the jutting, recently added place where the Strangers were kept. He could see at once that it was an improvement over the old place. For one thing, it was less cramped. The guards at the entrance bowed at the sight of the Queen's warriors and let them, and him, pass. Inside, several humans working in the open-air courtyard glanced up from their work to stare at him.

Padrec stood there, feeling conspicuous, noting the snickers that a few men exchanged before returning to the tasks they had stopped upon his entrance. A few others continued to watch him, trying not to appear obvious. A stiffly formal subservient in the orange garb of a minor official appeared and bowed before him. "Honored One," she said as he cringed at the designation, the public notice of his place. Her look, however, was respectful.

"I have come to visit," he said simply. "Where is the one called Rubinsky? I was told that he was here."

"Rub'ek-si?" From her face, he could tell she had not heard of him. He scoured his brain for Rubinsky's first name. He had heard it. . . .

"Martin," he said. "He may be called Martin."

"Mar-ten. Yes, we have such a one. His hair is the color of my robe, and he has a hairy face—"

"Yes. Mar-ten."

"Come, I will take you to him."

She led the way across a courtyard of staring faces to a passageway which led to a large room with walls roughly fashioned from brick, its conical ceiling high and yet unplastered, still, apparently, under construction. A number of men and a few women were seated on crude wooden benches, working on a few disembowled pieces of Terran equipment. All work stopped as soon as he entered.

"Mar-ten," the subservient ordered the bearded, red-haired man who rose to his feet at the far end of the room. "This one has asked to speak with you. Treat him with the proper deference . . . or need I remind you of your place?"

"No," Rubinsky said stiffly. "I know who he is."

"Very well." She turned back to Padrec, and said, indicatng the warriors who accompanied him, "Shall I leave you? I see you are well guarded."

"Yes, leave us." When the subservient had left, he turned to the chief among his warriors. "Tsennu, leave us also."

Fierce eyes gleaming like shards of yellow glass scanned the roomful of humans, then settled on Rubinsky. "That one, I do not trust him," Tsennu stated flatly. "The other time, he threatened you. The royal one ordered that you must not be endangered."

"I will not be endangered, Tsennu. Leave me with them."

Reluctantly, Tsennu backed away, leading the rest of the warriors from the room, but she placed her spare body just outside the portal, her sharp eyes marking every movement within. Lifting his chin, aware that every human eye was upon him, Padrec approached Rubinsky.

"You wanted to talk to me?"

A bitter frown twisted the man's mouth as he nodded. "Nice trick," he said, indicating the warriors, "I didn't think you would come."

"Why not? Because I'm not welcome?"

A single indrawn breath, from where, he could not be sure, answered him. All else was silence. Then Rubinsky granted him a sharp, grudging laugh. "Should you be?" After a meaningful silence, he said, "Wally Ebert is dead. He killed himself."

"I know. Stan told me."

"You don't sound surprised."

Fighting back against the rejection, the accusation, behind that statement Padrec said simply, "I'm not. I saw him once—he was being abused. I could see that he was unhappy."

"And you're not?"

"What does it matter to you if I am?" he said. "You never thought to ask me about it."

"I guess we deserve that," Rubinsky said after a moment's pause. "Maybe we deserve that and more." He stopped, flicked his fingers in the direction of the door. "Can you get rid of them?"

"The guards?" Padrec did not need to look back to know what he meant. Despite himself, a slight smile formed on his lips. "Sorry. But you heard what Tsennu said. She saw you attack me once and, well, it's common knowledge that I am not popular among you— Anii gave orders. The warriors won't leave. But they don't know any Terran. We can speak freely."

"We need your help."

"What kind of help? I think I should tell you right now that I don't have the influence you might think I have." Before they had even told him what it was, he was looking for a way to refuse them—or was it simply that he did not want to promise them too much? But Rubinsky shook his head.

"No, Morrissey, it's not that. We know you don't

have that much say. Hell, half of us have been through
it, and while you may have gotten off better than
most, we know there's no power in it. You're as much
a prisoner as we are, and that is why we think that,
well, just maybe you might be willing to help us. We
want to escape."

Padrec found himself gripped by an overwhelming
sense that he should have known what they would
ask of him. What else would they be thinking to do?
Hadn't he considered escape as the very first of his
options? This group was larger, not one man looking
after his sole skin, but two, three score of human lives
to be set free—not a task easily engineered, and far
less easily undertaken. Only now were they getting
around to it. "Do you know how difficult that would
be?" he asked nonetheless.

Rubinsky's blue eyes narrowed at him under their
lowered lids. "You're not saying we shouldn't," he
observed.

"Hell, no." Padrec smiled thinly, remembering his
own attempts. "I tried it myself, at first. As you can
see, I didn't get anywhere." He shook his head. "But I
was one man, and I was alone, and I thought I had
nothing to lose. I didn't know there was another human alive on this planet. You have a lot of people to
think about. How many of you are there? Fifty?
Sixty?—If only a few escape, those left behind will be
clapped in chains and forced into a far darker form of
slavery than what they now think unbearable. I can
all but promise it."

"We know that better than you ever will," the other
man said grimly. "And we won't leave behind anyone
who can possibly make good on it. We've got a way
out. What we need is your help doing it."

Padrec wondered if he should even listen to this
man's crazy scheme. Even if it was a good one, with a
chance of success, did he want to be involved in something that could just as easily prove a failure, a terrible mistake for which he and too many others would
pay too high a price? If he chose to side with them . . .

he did not want to think of that, of what it would mean to him personally if ever Anii should find out. . . . His safety, his security, all that he now had—how could he throw it away? Through the walls, coming from chambers he could not see, he heard the trailing sounds of human music, sweet notes and sweeter voices, singing words he could not quite bring to mind but which filled an emptiness within him he had not even known was there. . . .

Seeing the hesitation in the young man's face, Rubinsky's expression lost its distance and became brutally raw with emotion. "For God's sake, man, what is there to think about? Haven't you seen what they're doing to us? Don't you care?"

"Martin, no! Don't you know what you're asking of him? We've never given him the time of day, and now we're asking him for this—" A woman's voice broke from among the several humans standing behind him and Janelle MacDonald stepped out from the obscuring shadows of the others. Padrec found himself suddenly wanting to run away, as though he had been caught in a shameful act he now had to face, sure that every man—and every woman—in the room must be thinking of how he had forced himself on her, how he had not even inquired after her since. . . . But Janelle came forward quietly, without condemnation. Her voice, however, was hesitant, desperately pleading. "We're not asking this just for ourselves, Padrec," she said. "But what about our children? What of them? Some of us are—" She drew a deeper breath before going on. Her halting gray gaze met his directly and, though her lips trembled slightly, her voice was firm. "I'm pregnant," she announced bluntly.

As Padrec tore his startled glance away from hers, not yet able to cope with the painful, meaningful, implications of what she was trying to tell him—his? —Janelle continued. "Most of us are. The women. Somehow our cycles have become keyed to those of—of the Queen—" she said tactfully, "And when she went into her phase, those of us who weren't already—"

Impatiently thrusting himself to the fore, but keeping his movements non-threatening, aware of the warriors just outside the door, Rubinsky said in a vicious undertone, "Well, how about it, Morrissey? Do you want your son to be dragged off to serve in some queen's bed as soon as he shows signs of puberty? Hell, who knows, maybe he'll be marked out at birth. I mean, his dad was such hot stuff—"

"Martin, please," Janelle begged, her eyes filling with tears, whether of anger or concern, or pure humiliation, Padrec could not tell.

"No." Rubinsky cut off her protests. "He has to think of it. We all have to consider what it means if we don't."

My son, Padrec thought as Rubinsky had known he would. *Janelle's pregnant with my child!* He had never thought to hope for such a thing—or fear it. It occurred to him to think that the child might not be a boy—he could as easily have fathered a daughter as a son—but what if it was? What if it was and things remained as they were now? Would he want his child—any human child—beaten down as Stan had been? Chained? With the unerring vision of a guilt he still allowed to torment him, Padrec saw again the doomed, hopeless eyes of Wally Ebert, leashed to his mistress, a man so brutalized that he had finally committed suicide. . . . What if his own situation with Anii was unique, never to be repeated . . . ?

"Yes," he said at last. "I'll do what I can. But—" he forestalled the glint in Rubinsky's eye. "—it had better be good."

"It is. It is—here, sit down, and I'll explain it to you." He cleared a space on one of the benches, sat Padrec on it and himself before him, the others crowding near, prompting the warrior standing guard at the door to step forward in warning. "Stand back," Rubinsky ordered. "Let the damn thing see him." When Tsennu had eased back into position, he continued, stating the fact bluntly. "We have the sleds."

"Where?" The shuttle sleds, operational, intact—yes, of course! How else had they come here?

The geo-team's commanding officer smiled grimly, acknowledging the growing realization in his listener's eyes, and began to outline the history of a rescue attempt that had failed in every way but one, their last remaining gasp of hope. "When we came to look for the ship," Rubinsky explained "high-magnification recognizance showed that the vessel had been breached by external attack, something primitive but effective, and nothing we wanted to run into. So when we landed to look for survivors, we left the sled, hidden, some distance from the ship and went in on foot. What we found were Ibisians, and they found us, took us by surprise, but they didn't get the sled. It's still out there."

"And the second team's sled, was that captured?"

"No. We relayed a message before we set out, saying that we were leaving our sled, and why. When we didn't come back, they knew something was wrong—and when they came after us, they left their sled in the same hiding place where we hid ours. They found it by tracer."

"So you have two sleds—"

The big man nodded. "And they're the big ones. Utility sleds, not field scutters. In this gravity each one can carry approximately four metric tons, maybe sixty people—"

"Even at that, we're pushing it," one of the other men, a land-systems mechanic, warned quietly.

"We have no choice!" Rubinsky snapped. "It's the only shot we've got." His large, powerful hands clenched with restraint as he forced control into his voice, "Morrissey, the sleds are out there, but we can't get to them. Maybe Toroya could, he's been pressing to find out where they are—I think he wants to set traps using the tracers—but he knows we're holding out on him—"

Padrec swallowed, nodding he understood, and said, "You want me to get the sled."

"You're the only one who can. Everyone knows that golden girl keeps you on a long leash, that you can get around. You can even leave this goddamned hive; she knows you'll come back." A brief flicker in the man's otherwise cold eyes alerted Padrec to at least one reason for such deep resentment against him. They envied him his freedom. Rubinsky blinked, driving aside the hostile influences. "If you could get her to let you go back to the ship—"

Padrec shook his head, interrupting. "I wish it were that easy. Anii is very possessive. She doesn't let me off on my own. Everywhere I go there are guards to look after me. And when I leave the nom she sends along her subservient and *twice* as many of those—" he jerked his thumb at the warriors standing outside the door. "I'd have a hell of a time trying to sneak off to look for your sled, much less get it back to you!"

"Padrec, please." Janelle took the place beside him as Rubinsky made room for her. Somehow her hand found its way to his knee, but when he looked at her he saw only the woman scientist who had helped him set up his lab. "There must be a way," she pleaded. "We just have to think of it."

"I'm a botantist, not a strategist—"

"Can't you just club them over the head or something? Or carry a knife and cut their throats?" the sled mechanic said, glancing at the warriors and trying not to draw their notice. But the warriors did not know enough about Terran humans to be suspicious.

"You could make a run for it," said Rubinsky. "Get hold of the spare blasters in the sled—"

Even though he understood the sentiment which led to such statements, Padrec felt his gorge rise at the thought. "No," he quickly put both suggestions where they belonged, "No blasters! I won't be part of any killing—"

"Not even of them?" Rubinsky demanded.

"Especially not of them. They killed us out of ignorance and fear, but that's stopped. They aren't killing us anymore. And they won't, unless we start killing them. And I won't be responsible for that."

"He's right," said Janelle, supporting him. "If he

sets a pattern by killing them, and then he doesn't make it, or the plan doesn't succeed—it might as well be a death sentence for all of us."

"All right, all right, I see his point," Rubinsky conceded. "We don't want to risk that. We want to save people, not get them killed if we don't pull it off. The eastern colony needs us, if we're ever to survive on this planet."

"Is that where you're going?" asked Padrec. He had guessed as much but thought he might as well confirm the plan.

After a moment, the redheaded leader nodded. "I left a hundred and forty people behind. A hundred and twenty are still there. By now the colony must be self-sufficient. We were well on the way to it before—" he sighed, his expression reflecting his wish to be with the men and women he had left behind. He had not found his wife among the survivors of the main ship, and now all that remained of his life was back there. He was determined to return, and to take the remnants of his human race with him. "You have a lab," he said, turning back to Padrec.

Padrec considered. His reagents, the microsynthesizer—yes, there were possibilities along that line. . . .

"I could make a gas, knock them out, maybe," he said.

"That would work." Janelle's gray eyes glowed, almost pretty with excitement. "The Ibisians are similar enough to the essential human type so that we can predict the probable reaction to certain substances. What works on us would probably work on them. I know that the microsynthesizer is in working order—"

"It would have to be a simple gas, something easily manufactured from available molecules," one of the chemists from the main ship put in.

"Chloroform?" someone suggested.

"Ether," Janelle pronounced more firmly. Her biomedic training gave her some insight into the requirements of molecular synthesis. "It is easily made from available sources—and the effect is longer lasting. Chloroform acts faster, but the subjects would only be out for fifteen minutes—maybe less. We don't know much about their metabolisms. But they do get drunk, and ethers are a related group. And the effects of ether are longer lasting—"

"Diethyl ether is simple to make," the biochemist confirmed. "Sulfuric acid and ethanol. The microsynthesizer can make up the necessary dehydration catalysts, and distillation is relatively easy—"

Padrec gave them a hesitant glance, then nodded. "I can do that. The reagents in my lab provide ready sources of ions."

"You'll do it?" Rubinsky asked.

He could feel their eyes on him, their doubts. To them he was still the Queen's lover, not entirely to be trusted, except, perhaps, with their desperation. Things hadn't changed, only the surface; it was no longer ice, but the water was still freezing, and he knew he was not being invited to jump in. They wanted his help, not his agreement. It would be so easy to say no, to walk away and pretend he was doing the right thing by all of them, himself included. If only he did not feel in his very bones that it might work—

If only it was all wrong, I could turn them down; in my mind at least I could say I was protecting them. But the plan is good, it can work—

"Yes, I'll do it."

Rubinsky hurried, barely giving Padrec a second glance. "The sleds are two ridges east-northeast of the ship, skirting the forest. It's a twin formation ridge; we found a blind cleft with an overhang. The thing's covered with a shield net, so you can't see it until you're close. You won't need ident, just press the activation key. You know how to drive the damn things, don't you?"

"I usually take the smaller units, but yes, I think I can handle a utility."

"Drive units are the same. Acceleration is less, but max altitude is greater, and that's what we need here, because you'll have to get it up to this level, right up against the wall of this hive, for us to pile in. Can you do that?"

"Have you checked it out?"

Grimly, Rubinsky nodded. "Should make it. The walls here are a good sixty meters. I wouldn't want to jump it, but the utility shouldn't have any trouble."

"Even with sixty people aboard?"

"Max load. I thought of that." He was a born officer, the kind to take command. Padrec felt no hesitation in following him—any questions were simply for his own understanding—and Rubinsky accepted that need with the ease of natural leadership. The queen who had tried to bring him to heel had been unsuccessful, eventually rejecting him as unmanageable and, in her eyes, too ugly to keep. In doing so, she had thrown him right back where he could do the most harm—or good. "I don't think there will be sixty people," he said bluntly. "Some won't make it to the jump-off point, they'll be detained or get stopped somewhere along the way. And some just simply won't want to go. But anyone who wants to go, we'll take."

"And you'll take off into the sunrise and never come back—"

"You're damn right, we'll never come back. We never wanted to be here in the first place."

Anii met Padrec upon his return to the royal chambers. Before he could even say anything, she put her arms around him and pulled his lips to hers, kissing him gently, a delicate savoring as of some rare nectar she wished to keep in her cup.

Even her voice stroked him lightly, a subdued entrance into their conversation. "I have been told about the female, J'nel, that she carries your child."

"Anii, please—" It was too much. He had not even had time to think of that himself. . . .

She pulled away from him, troubled by some note of distress in his voice. "Does this displease you?"

He could not turn aside from her eyes as they burned into his, seeking the truth. "No," he was forced to admit. "A child could never displease me." Then why was he unhappy? What did it matter that he barely knew the mother, had never wanted to make love to her, had done so in a pheromone-intoxicated heat alien to everything he was or ever had been? A child conceived under such circumstances could barely be real to him.

"You worry," Anii said, drawing him with her to the cushions of her private chamber. She poured for him a bowl of the sweetest nectar and pressed it into his hand. "To-roya has told me how the males of your kind have concern for their offspring. Do you think I cannot understand this? Or that your young ones would not be precious to me? I shall see to the mother, Padric, she shall have her own apartment and attendants to see to her needs. And should your child be male, I shall see to it when the time comes that he is given to one who will be gentle with him. You need never fear that any offspring of yours shall be treated cruelly."

"You can't promise that, Anii. I know you want to, but you can't."

But I can. I can give him, or her, its freedom.

To mask what he was thinking he raised the nectar to his lips and drank, noting as he did how his hand was trembling. Only then did he appreciate the magnitude, and consequences, of what he was planning to do. *I am going to defy her—she has shown me nothing but love and kindness, and I am going to throw it all away on a heritage that offers nothing in return—no love, no future, no joy. . . . And for what?*

I am doing this for them, not me.

Anii touched his hair, her favorite gesture of late. "My beautiful Pa-dric. Why are you so unhappy?" Her voice, the lingering gentleness of her touch, her restraint with him, indicated genuine concern. He sensed her underlying fear.

Taking her hand, he kissed her fingertips. "I cannot explain. It is something deep within me."

"Something you cannot tell me?"

When he did not answer, she waited patiently, then pressed gently. "O Pa-dric, if you would but tell me the source of your troubles! I love you too well to see you in pain."

The words were drawn from his heart before he could think of what speaking them could mean. "Then let them go, Anii," he implored, turning to her and harshly clutching her lovely six-fingered hands which stroked his with gentle entreaty, making the plea he had made so many times before, knowing it futile and knowing that he had to try one more time before he did an irrevocable thing. "They don't belong here. They are being beaten in body and spirit, without even a ray of hope to lighten this burden upon them, and they cannot bear it without breaking. They are suffering, Anii, and I want to help them. It's not natural to keep men in chains, it drags them down, it leads them to death. I cannot simply stand by and watch them die—"

She did not ask whom he meant. As before, he

spoke of all his kind. But in a frightening new way, just under his words, she could hear him speaking of himself. Fear touched her love for him. She drew away, never knowing how the movement tore into his heart, or how near he was to revealing himself. "Oh, Pa-dric, you ask me for what I cannot give. Don't you understand, your Strangers belong now to the nomari? As slaves they are useful and valuable; free, they would be too dangerous for us to long tolerate them. The nomari will keep them." Then she turned back to him, and her eyes were golden flames within her face, an incandescence born of something far more powerful than her anger. "But you, dearest, are mine alone. And I will keep you from all manner of hurt. If to see them makes you so mierable, then I will make it so that you need not see them—"

"Anii, no!"

"No, beloved, I am decided. I will not lose you to their misery, Pa-dric," she said. "Nothing, be it of my making or theirs, shall be allowed to make you so unhappy that you would die."

Suddenly he understood. Ebert's death had led her to think that he, too, if he were sufficiently unhappy, would choose to take his life. She cared . . . she cared that much for him. . . .

"Oh, Anii," he said, though the admission plunged him again into despair. To know how much he had, and how much he had to lose. . . . "That could never happen. I wouldn't take my life; nothing you could do would ever make me that unhappy."

"Then prove to me that you are mine. Deny your kind and be wholly my beloved—"

Her kiss bore all the passionate knowledge she had gleaned through so many months of knowing him, that what stood between them was there forever, a line that he must cross and maybe never would. She could never take him from his people. He would have to leave them. How could she love him so, this dark-haired Stranger from beyond the stars? Padrec tasted her love on her lips, felt it in her hands, the tender pressure of her body against his, and knew that if he loved her now, he would be bound to her completely. *Love me, Anii, love me,* that aching emptiness cried out inside him. *Love me so that I won't be able to leave you.*

Her body answered to her need to hold him, to keep him, knowing with the deep insight of love's possessive longing that he was struggling for a way to leave her. He filled her arms with an inarticulate ache, beautiful, precious, his sadness a deep pool from which she drank the sweetest pleasures of his body. Later, lulled by his warmth, his body tamed by its own spent passion lying beside hers, Anii spoke the thoughts that had led her to take him despite the restrictions of her pregnancy. "Oh, beloved, is there no end to my wish to spare you unhappiness?"

"Anii, believe me, whatever happens—" Holding back on the tears, Padrec whispered his promise to the shining waves of her golden hair beneath his cheek. "I have never been happier than I am tonight. I could never leave you. Just don't make me go—please, don't make me go."

But he knew then, beyond all knowing, that Anii, by her refusal to release his people, had sealed him to a choice carved out of his very heart.

Two days later he got her permission to go to the ship. It had taken very little in the way of explanation: his work in Ibisian agriculture, so promising, already showing impressive results, provided that. Even Hli, now that he respected her dominance, had taken to approving his outings. "Let him go," the subservient had said. "The season grows cold and soon enough the rains will come." Indeed, a great roaring storm swept down out of the mountains that night, buffeting the nom and flooding the plain with water. Padrec stood at the windows, watching a spectacle seldom seen by men who spent their lives in space stations and research ships, or stranded on planets of more temperate climate. Great yellow slashes ripped blue holes in a tumultuous sky, hurling rain against the glass-sheathed windows, where it ran down, glistening trails just beyond his fingertips. That morning he had prepared the ether, depleting his reagents to make the chemicals needed to purify the vapor, render it a safe anesthetic. Looking at Hli, he wondered if she would appreciate the steps he was taking on her behalf.

Anii, true to her words of that night, would not let him visit the compound, but she had allowed Janelle to be brought to him, to run checks on his equipment. Though Anii had remained in the room with them at all times, he had managed to slip in a few words of Terran with the message that he would make his attempt the next day and that it was up to Rubinsky and the others to gather the humans in one place. As she tuned a transducer Janelle whispered the remaining plans. "We'll hang something over the wall, a red sash—"

The plain outside the nom was damp with rain from the night before, water filling the normally dry stream beds they crossed on their way to the farthest hills at the foot of which the ship lay in what was now certain to be its grave. Padrec knew what to do. Hours spent in thought had led him to a plan, crude perhaps, but simple enough to have a realistic chance of succeeding. The core facilities had suffered the least structural damage and most of the chambers remained intact—steel-walled, polymer-sealed, airtight—easily sterilized in the event of contamination due to chemical spills—even gutted of their equipment they perfectly suited his needs. Hli followed him through the catacomb-like chambers, less his jailer than a watchful shadow, her orange eyes scanning the last remnants of a mission that had failed. "You say this nom traveled the stars?"

"Yes."

"It does not look like something that could."

"It was damaged before it ever came here," he told her. "We would not have landed if we had not been damaged."

"You would have stayed—up there?" She gestured

vaguely toward the ceiling where the heavens would be, the frown on her mouth filled with doubts.

"Yes." In one of the technical sections he found what he was looking for: a small room which could be secured from without, with a huge piece of equipment in it. It hardly mattered what the equipment was—it looked like a centrifuge—what mattered was that he could call in the warriors for help in moving it. And the chamber which held it was buried deep in the ship, far enough from the periphery where the rest of the warriors would be standing guard, that any noise at first would go undetected. After checking out the room's airtight features, Padrec called Hli's attention to the metallic monster bolted to the floor. "There is a storage room underneath this item," he said. "I want it to be moved."

"This thing? It will take much to move it. Look elsewhere for what you need."

"It is *stored* down *there*." It was a lie, a blatant lie; a Terran elementary teacher would have known as much. But Hli saw no reason to doubt him. In the nom's lower levels there were many such caches. And items from this strange place had several times proven to be of great value to the nom. The large crystals, especially, were prized as ornaments. Grumbling because they had brought no workers with them this trip, she hailed the warriors who waited within sound of her call and directed them to move the hulking piece of alien machinery. The warriors laid down their spears and strained at the corners of the thing. It budged but did not move, and Padrec felt confident in asking Hli for more help. Grudgingly, Hli agreed to summon two other warriors. "But if they cannot move the thing, we will cease to attempt it," she told him. Ten, out of the twelve warriors who had accompanied them. As the Ibisians worked on moving the immovable object, Padrec stealthily retrieved two large bottles he had carefully stowed in his pack and unwrapped them. Closing his eyes, he offered a small prayer that this was going to work, that no one would be hurt, or killed. Even old Hli, in her way—well, Anii was fond of her, and she had never done him any real harm. As the Ibisians all bent their backs to the task of moving something he had never really intended they should move, Padrec drew a deep breath and held it. Then, opening the stoppers on his bottles, he dashed them to the floor, splashing the volatile liquid across the room, and ran out the door, reaching the manual controls and turning the emergency lock before any of the stunned, coughing Ibisians could move to stop him. He then leaned against the door on the other side, alone in an outer chamber, listening to the Ibisians pound and scream mutely for help, biting his lip against the sound of fear in their voices, almost able to feel the noxious vapor stinging delicate mucous membranes in nose and lung and eyes. They did not know that it would only render them unconscious for a while, in a while. Why did it take so long to work? If only he had had the means to concoct something stronger, faster acting. . . .

It will be a few minutes, just a few minutes . . . then they will have breathed in enough of it to put them under, make them quiet . . . then I can leave them. They won't get out. . . .

Only then did the reality of what he had done sink in. He had succeeded in putting all but two of his guards out of action. He had also committed himself to this reckless plan which had drawn him from a life he had never thought to find or wanted to have, to the very edge of an abyss he dared not contemplate. It is set in stone now, no matter what I do.

He might as well make it work.

The dead ship opened before him, cavernous and desolate, emptier than it ever had been as he crept along its abandoned passageways, past patches of light from the gaping holes in its skin, tattered now, battered and destined to become part of this place where it had landed with such suddenness and violence. Somewhere, just outside the ship, Padrec would find the other guards. He doubted Tsennu and the other warrior would suspect him of treachery: for months now their only concern had been for his well-being, his safety, not that he might attempt to escape. Pausing at the huge hole in the hull that had twice now served as his entry into the downed vessel, Padrec fingered the small vial in his pocket. He had synthesized a little chloroform as well, knowing that he would never get all of the warriors into one place, that guards were always posted. Taking a pad of cotton cloth, he wetted it and shouted to Tsennu, gesturing as if in urgency and, as the warrior whistled to her companion and followed him within, he clapped the damp cloth over her face. Very quickly, knowing these twisted passageways too well, he dragged the warrior's body to the area where the others were entrapped and deposited it just outside the door. He had barely concealed himself around a corner when he heard the other coming, probably following by smell. As it came into the passageway, he grabbed it by the neck and forced the chloroformed rag over mouth and nose holding it there until that warrior too went limp in his arms. Then, with the sash from his robe, he bound the Ibisians hand and foot, back to back, each to the other. It wouldn't hold, not for long, but it might buy him a few minutes of time before they could free themselves and release the others.

Outside the ship again Padrec clambered onto the lateral vane that ran the length of the ship, searching the land around the fallen vessel. The great scar of that landing, now healing with grasses and erosion, lay in thrown folds of earth, stretching to the horizon, a grim and dying reminder of something already fading, being absorbed into the planet. The hills he wanted were far away, an hour's walk or more, with no time to waste. When the warriors came to, they would quickly come after him. The price of their carelessness would be high, perhaps even their lives, if they returned without the Queen's prized Stranger. Grimly, blinking back all thoughts of what his own recapture would mean, Padrec set out, running, then

walking, his mind more consumed by feelings of lone-
liness than freedom, and what should have been ela-
tion was closer to despair. He had to succeed. Failure
would mean that everything—his sacrifice, his an-
guished indecision, his hopes, even, for the child he
had unwittingly fathered—would in the end amount
to nothing but another brief rebellion and a final, this
time unalterable, defeat. If he could pull it off, at least
he would have something.

But not Anii. And not slavery. All he would have
gained would be the freedom to choose.

Between an alien's love and the wasteland of his
own shattered culture and emotions. . . . The great
molten bowl of Ibis carved temples of light onto the
face of the dry eastern hills by the time he reached
them, great clefts of shadow plunging between blazing
crests. Which cleft? he wondered, which cleft would
have drawn them? The western face of the hills showed
several. Frantically searching, he followed one to a
blind end, found nothing, skirted the ridge to another,
looking for some deep passageway, some sign of the
clue he sought. An overhang, Rubinsky had mentioned
an overhang . . . a flash of golden light reached into a
darkly shadowed cleft, touched a ridge of red earth, a
crumbling facade . . . Padrec stopped on the threshold
to catch his breath. Damn, he was out of condition.
His heart was pounding in his chest as he groped his
way into the wide gap some long diverted stream had
cut from the small canyon. Behind a shield net and a
screen of dense thorny shrubs he found the sled.

He trembled uncontrollably as he touched it, cold
metal, silent and inert, waiting. Clawing at the shrubs
which covered it, he cleared the vehicle, a huge thing,
metallic and ugly and beautiful—the big blue PES
lettering on its sides achingly familiar, reminiscent of
those times not so long past when a vehicle such as
this meant returning to ship or shuttle, safety and
security and home. Tears stung his eyes through his
joy and newly heartened resolve. *Look at it, it's real!*
Someone had very carefully backed it into its hollowed-

out hiding place, leaving the control consoles readily accessible. He changed his shapeless Ibisian robe for the snug comfort of his regulation uniform, seeing it as a statement he must make, an affirmation which somehow made sense of what he was doing. Only when he had changed did Padrec climb the sturdy metal frame and check out the huge open cargo bay, removing several small crates of supplies as being superfluous. They would be coming back if all went as planned; if not, none of this would be of any use. On impulse, fearing that others would forget or simply ignore his order not to kill, he searched the vehicle for blasters, finding several, which he discarded over the side along with two boxes of sounding grenades—useful geological tools but potent weapons when employed as such—before he went forward and sat before the panels. He had never driven a big utility sled before, he had always taken the smaller ones, but some things remained basic. The start key was one, the accelerator another. He hit the green key, activating all systems, and felt again the force of long experience operating a complex piece of advanced technology by nothing more than seat of habit—the key, the drive systems, a gentle forward thrust on the hand-governed controls. Once clear of the hills, it was almost second nature to gun the vehicle to full speed, skimming the blurring plain beneath a full-bellied golden sun turning to amber, passing far to the east of the glinting carcass of what had once been a starship. Crossing the plain in his general direction, bypassed in a rush of wind, he saw a party of Ibisian warriors and surmised that they were his guard from the ship, recovered and hot on his trail, too late.

Within minutes he reached the nom.

It loomed at him across the plain, a massive hand thrusting itself in his path, vast and nonthreatening—a sight grown familiar to him. He never hesitated on his approach. The nom had no defenses against the type of attack he was mounting. No missiles, no cannons, no anti-aircraft ability—it would take the Ibisians several minutes, even under optimal conditions, to turn the catapults or to move archers to the upper levels where they were not normally needed. And by then he would be long gone. Even now the Ibisians working outside the nom were staring and milling in confusion at the sight of the flying machine.

Rubinsky, true to plan, had hung a length of scarlet cloth over the side of the wall of the human compound, marking the place where he should bring the sled. Although he had never been a skillful handler, Padrec angled the sled so that it hugged the side of the nom, and eased it upward until it was level with the top of the gritty, formidable wall. He had no sooner pulled up than two men leaped onto the sled, followed by a steady stream of escapees.

"By God!" Rubinsky shouted, glaring at him as he settled into the co-pilot's chair, "we'd about given up on you—! Stan! Terrance—check the side bays!" He rummaged for something in the pilot's compartment in front of Padrec's knee. "What the hell!" he sputtered.

Padrec knew what he was looking for. "I took out the blasters, Rubinsky. I told you—no killing, remember?"

"You goddamned blasted—"

"I got the sled, didn't I?" The sled rocked, and Padrec automatically compensated for the slight sinking as more people piled into the back. Out of the corner of his eye he saw warriors gathering on the terraces behind and above them, heard rather than saw a spear striking at the sled. "Forget the blasters! Get them in!" Rubinsky shouted to his followers within as cries of alarm broke out from the cowering humans in the sled. "Everyone get in so that we can get out of here!"

An Ibisian spear tip shattered in a spray of glittering shards against the windshield right in front of Padrec's eyes and he instinctively ducked, the inadvertent motion causing the sled to dip dangerously. Janelle crept along the floor of the sled to wedge her body between him and Rubinsky. "Steady it!" she snapped. "There are only a few more." Padrec glanced back. He saw two men straddling the ledge, helping one of the women into the sled. The cargo bay was packed with people. But there was one face he looked for that he did not see. "Where's Toroya?" he asked.

Someone screamed, and Padrec had a horrible glimpse of a woman falling from the sled, landing in the midst of a crowd of Ibisians on the ground far below, where she twisted briefly before being beset, an arrow lodged in her chest. Other screams broke out from the rear as arrows rained up at them and at least one of them snagged Padrec's hair as it buried its deadly tip beside his ear. Archers spreading out on the ground and the adjacent terraces were now in a position to take shots. Stan and another man who had stayed behind to help the others tumbled in and Rubinsky cried, "Go! Go!"

To throw off aim and because the sled might not take more altitude, Padrec let the vehicle drop suddenly beneath his control, sprays of rock and sand erupting from the wall where only moments before a cowering mass of people had been. Giving the machine full draw on its fuel cells, he cut a line away from the nom as fast as he could, too frightened to even look back. But to his dying day he never forgot the burst of cheering that was blown away by the winds of their passage as they burst into freedom over the reddish plain beneath the hot gold sun of Ibis, or the way Janelle MacDonald threw her arms around him and Rubinsky both, laughing and crying with joy.

They made the twin ridges ahead of twilight, outrunning the last rays of that blood-amber sun, well ahead of a search party of Ibisians treking single file across the plain toward them. Hli's party from the ship had picked up his trail and was following it. "We'll be gone before they get here," Rubinsky told him, slapping his shoulder and turning to direct the reloading of the supplies Padrec had discarded. Most of the men gladly, and ominously, armed themselves with blasters.

But Padrec stared out at the plain, feeling the call of it, its scents teasing his nostrils. The eastern subcontinent was tropical, steamy, insect-infested—. Somehow, for him this wide plain which spread forth from the forested edge of the mountains had become *home*.

I am an Ibisian now, he recognized something he should have known much sooner. *Toroya knew—he marked it the first day we talked about it.* That day at the ship . . . had there ever been a ship? When he saw it, he knew that there had been, but that part of his life no longer seemed real, as if it had faded, or dropped from him like a dream upon waking. Or the world upon dreaming. . . .

"Morrissey! Are you with us?" Rubinsky was scowling at him. The red-bearded captain and a few others approached from the fully loaded sleds, the second one having been brought around and parked at the base of the rocky cliff which sheltered the first. "Get in. We're leaving. The instrumentation may be programmed in such a way that it can find its way across a sunless moon, but I like to see where I'm going—."

"I'm not going."

"What, man—are you crazy?" Rubinsky looked sure of it.

"No. I'm going back." Not until he said it did Padrec realize it was what he had always intended.

"Do you know what you're saying? Those people—those things!—aren't going to welcome you with open arms! In fact, you'll be damned lucky if they *kill* you!"

Janelle put her hand on his arm. "Come with us."

Padrec shook his head, then looked toward the plain. "My life is back there, what's left of it. Anii loves me—at least she *did*—and whatever she may choose to do with me, I don't think she will kill me. But she can make it worse for the others if I don't go back—the ones we left behind."

Not every human who had wanted to escape had made it—some had been detained, forced to labor elsewhere, kept closely by possessive queens—others, like Toroya, had not been told, since no one wanted to take the chance of those people warning the Ibisians of their plans. Padrec knew without needing to remind them of it that had he not been needed to bring the sled, he would have been among those not told.

"You have to do what you think is right—but you're welcome to stay with us," Rubinsky said, "And I'm not just saying that. We could use you at the settlement— we are mostly geological and marine teams and don't have a trained terrestrial botanist. And I'll damn Toroya until the day he dies, but his breeding plan is a good idea, something we have to consider for the next few generations. You're valuable, Morrissey. I'd hate to lose you, and especially to them."

He meant it. Padrec could sense his sincerity, a strong gust of clean air filtering through the cracks of the wall between them. But the wall remained, and so did his resolve. Standing among the others he saw the slender blond figure of Stan Scoriusci, rubbing his arms where the bonds had been struck from his wrists, his face blank with disbelief. Padrec gave him a weak smile. "You don't need me, not anymore. But those people back there will. They are the ones who will be alone now, trapped in an alien society with no way out. I can't offer them a way out, but maybe I can help them learn to live with it. Maybe I can help the Ibisians learn to live with us. The Ibisians aren't going to stop wanting human men for their lovers. Someday our two races will meet again. I would like it to be different next time."

"There's more to it, I can see that in your eyes. It's her. Get your head together, man! It's not like you're married to the thing!"

"I might as well be. I don't think I will ever want a human woman again. I don't think I *can*. You've been there, Rubinsky—you know what I'm talking about."

For a moment the man's eyes fell, his face revealed a naked, clawing need. "Yes. No man could ever forget. Ibisian women are gorgeous, heart-stopping, it's their nature to take a man from his maker. Hell, I want them still. But don't you see, they're not meant for human beings—they're all chemistry, and a man can't take it."

"Maybe not. But I'm not going to give you half of myself. That wouldn't be fair—and it wouldn't work. I couldn't stay with Anii because you stood in between. Now that you are gone, and free—I know that I want to be with her. And only her. Don't force me to come with you; I won't stay."

"By God, Morrissey, you're more man than I ever hope to find again on this god-forsaken planet. But I wonder if you know what you're doing. It's tempting, but I won't force you to come—that'd be fine thanks for what you've done. We have few enough means at our disposal to thank you properly."

Padrec hesitated, wondering if he dared ask, then said quietly, "Look after Janelle, and the baby."

Rubinsky's mouth firmed, accepting that responsibility, and his response was a vow sealed in a friendship that had never come to pass—and now never would. "Like my own, Morrissey. I'll see to it."

"Martin," Janelle said, wildly pleading, "you can't just let him go back. That's murder! Make him come."

But Rubinsky shook his head. "I won't take any man against his will—or hold him prisoner at the colony for any reason but that he wants to be three. He's a big boy—I can't make him come if he doesn't want to."

Eager to be on their way, the other men mutely wished him well and ran off to the sleds. Janelle looked about to plead with him, but then, her eyes filled with tears, she merely reached her hand to his face and very gently kissed him. "When I think—" she bit her lip then said quickly, "Even though I hardly know you, I'm glad it's your child. I thought you should know that." She turned and walked as fast as she could in the direction of the sleds.

Rubinsky seemed, too, to want to say something more, but he simply gripped Padrec by the arm and said, "Good-bye, man—" and walked away. Moments later the sleds lifted with the slow, easy grace of countless centuries of human dreams and, barely looking on the shattered memories of this one, sped off to the east, bearing his past farther from him with every breath and moment.

They're gone. He watched them until he could see them no more. They were gone. Dully, still dressed in his regulation grays, daring to savor these last few minutes of freedom, he climbed to the top of the rise, heading unerringly west to where Hli and her party of Ibisian warriors marched toward him, the dust raised by their passage forming a swirling, ruddy haze about their slender silhouettes.

Padrec met the Ibisians at the foot of the hills, their long shadows first touching his feet and then his legs, the rest of him. No sooner had he looked at Hli's face, trying to determine what his reception might be, than the angry subservient heeled back her hand and struck him with a stinging blow across the face. "Fool of a Stranger! What have you done? I saw the flying metal machine—"

He told her, and she slapped him again, this time so hard she drove him to his knees and his lip broke, blood trickling down his jaw. "I am done with you!" Hli's orange eyes erupted in pure rage. "I should slit your throat—or cut off that part she so enjoys that she would cease to see a need for you—and then might we all be rid of your stupidity! Soon you will scream to have gone with the others—" Tsennu lashed the cords tightly, binding his arms behind his back, her normally impassive bronzed face harshly satisfied at having recaptured him. In a kind of red haze, Padrec remembered that a warrior's only alliegiance was to its Queen. In Tsennu's warriors eyes he was not an individual, not a being, not distinct from his function; living or dead, he was Anii's, nothing more. . . .

If she will have me.

It was midday the next day when they reached the nom. A small army of nomari warriors, led by Bhi'hia, had met them half way and, convinced by Hli of the impossibility of pursuing the others, had returned with them. Bhi'hia's temper had been fouled by Stan's escape. "Anii's beautiful Pa-dric," she said, her voice viciously mocking. "What a shame those lovely eyes are to be food for the beetles. At the least I can have a taste of you first—" But Hli and Tsennu had crossed their spears before him, forestalling her intent. "I

have not heard Anii give him to you," the aged subservient said darkly. "This one is hers, until I am told
otherwise." Though Bhi'hia withdrew proudly, those
cruel eyes of golden glass did not withdraw at once
but lingered, letting him know there were worse pun-
ishments than death or torture, that his future might
be that very life he had spared the others from living
. . . a life gutted of hope and pride and gentleness,
without meaning . . . without her. . . .

Through a crowd of hostile warriors all armed and
garbed in the red cloaks of war, their bright eyes
flashing as fiercely as their bronze-tipped spears which
followed him, Padrec was dragged into the Great Hall
of Eshunn, Hli and Bhi'hia forcing a path to where
Anii and the other queens waited in golden congrega-
tion. With a kind of slow twisting horror, as though
through glass, he saw several human males standing
helplessly among the queens, kept there by chains,
those men who had been unable or unwilling to escape. A few women stood nearby, unbound but no less
captive. He saw himself in their eyes, already becoming legend: a captive not yet a slave, the man who had
defied the queens of Ibis to free his people, and won.
But in their pale, frightened faces he recognized what
they also knew: that the harsh order of Ibisian society
must break him, force him back into the grooves by
which it lived, or it must kill him, and with him the
threat of more and possibly greater harm at his hands.
Disobedience to a queen never went unpunished. . . .
As he came before the throne he looked up—and saw
Anii in her crimson robes, her splendid warrior-queen
crown of golden scarab horn again upon her brow, his
fate coldly staring back at him from the harsh knowledge of betrayal in her eyes. Had he really expected
Anii to forgive him? To pardon him because, of all
foolish things, he loved her? He had thought to throw
himself upon the mercy of a love that blinded him to
his own death, that would endure whatever punishment was handed him, if only he could seek to arouse
it from the warm ashes of something not yet wholly

gone—only to see now, in her alien eyes, that it was. Toroya stood at her side, the only man in the room not bound, his face stricken and suddenly old, all but saying aloud what Padrec feared most. When he came to the foot of the steps leading up to the throne, the warriors hurled him to the ground and, unable to catch himself, Padrec landed like a prize trophy on the floor at her feet. Above his head Hli's voice broke across the silence like stones flung against glass.

"Here is the unworthy one, Great Queen. He had the effrontery to return. The others are gone. He tells us they are far from here."

Steeling herself, Anii glared down at the man she had loved so far as to allow him the freedom with which he had done a deed that had sliced policy and heart alike to shreds. When she had heard . . . even now that pain tore at her like a living thing, its hateful claws still gripping heart and throat, choking the life from something once beautiful . . . Pa-dric had fled her, had probably slain Hli at that thing he called the ship, had taken the female and his young one and stolen the precious Strangers from nom and queen and vanished with them in one of his machines. She had herself seen him from afar, his dark head among the others; To-roya had told her Pa-dric had controlled the thing. His words of submission, his words of happiness with her—lies, all lies! Her screams of rage and betrayal had left To-roya cowering on the floor, his face horribly pale, as she had sent her warriors after them, east, to where, again, To-roya had said they would certainly flee. In the hours that followed she had wept, none daring to leave her, none daring to come near—the nom had been impotent with her rage . . . And now, seeing him enter, and Hli with him safe and alive, her heart throbbed again within her breast, the feelings there too deep to ever be gone. She had thought him gone, gone forever . . . why had he returned? Hli had sent a message: Pa-dric had come back willingly. He walked into her hall in the garments of his kind and laid his deed before her like an offering upon the field of victory. An offering and a hostage—the deed, and himself. He was hers, if she wanted him. But the deed was forever his, like the very stars in the sky, beyond her reach.

This is your moment, she granted him. *I cannot take it from you—nor do I want to, if only that I might remember that look in your eyes! That look of a race which has traveled the stars. Live this moment forever, beloved—the price you pay will be your pride! For I will draw the sweetness from your triumph, blacken it and turn it to dust.*

You will show them the price of defiance.

The warriors roughly thrust him to the ground below her chair, and the great hall fell into silence. From her side, a flurry of orange robes descended to kneel on the steps before her. To-roya lifted his eyes, his arms in supplication.

"Be merciful, O Queen, spare him," the aging Stranger pleaded, "He did but what he had to do."

"You dare defend him, To-roya? He was disobedient—and betraying of the trust put in him."

"He could not do otherwise. Great Queen, I beg you to hear me—put to the choice, he could not choose against his kind. Once, I know, I told you this."

Yes, he had. She remembered that day, that early conversation, when To-roya had told her that Pa-dric could not accept his people's slavery ... but the old one's warnings had not kept her from this moment. "Your counsel did not keep Pa-dric from rebellion, To-roya. The Strangers are proud and rebellious. Your leniency has already lost me too much."

To-roya trembled. "Great One, it is human nature to rebel against domination. We Strangers are ourselves a dominant species."

"You are dominant no longer. If it is not your nature to be submissive, perhaps lessons can reinforce that behavior in you."

This, indeed, lay at the heart of any decision. Pa-dric's rebellion must not inspire other disobedience. Her plans lay in ruins, her queens angry and, now, potentially rebellious, herself humiliated. Redress was only possible in punishing the traitor who had brought this upon her—punishment such as he would bear with him always, even unto the pyre.

Must I kill you, beloved? Even the thought brought tears to her eyes of golden ice. *Am I to be like the goddess and kill all those I love? Who then would warm my lips, give me release from the heat of my nuptial bed? Am I to spill your red, red blood upon this floor and ever after hold but memories in my arms?*

Who then would be punished? The dead did not suffer, but the emptiness in her being would endure forever. There were other ways to make Pa-dric see the folly of his rebellion, others who were more expendable.

"Great Queen," To-roya persisted in entreating despite her determination and displeasure, "I take his part for love of you. I know your feeling for him and that it is deep. We Strangers understand this. We, too, are creatures of emotion, of intelligence. I can promise you, on my knowledge of him, that he will never leave you. Few seek their slavery willingly. Give him his life and he will be yours. Among our kind men like him take but one mate all their lives."

Mine. The possessive desire to keep what she had blossomed as To-roya's words sank into her being like nectar. To have but one mate all his life . . . yes, there was the essence of it. With a bare turn of her head, she spoke to the orange-garbed Stranger. "You wish his life more than he does." Pa-dric moved to speak, but the warrior guarding him pressed its spear to his throat, stopping the words. Captives awaiting justice awaited only that. "Is he of so much value, To-roya, that you risk your own?"

That aged head, so strangely balding, bowed before her. "He is my friend. And I know that you love him. I would not poison you against us with his death. And he is young, and there are few of us . . . I would spare any of my people if I could."

"How fitting, then, that I bow again to your wishes. You shall have Pa-dric's life," she said. Relief flooded To-roya's lined face at her words. Pa-dric, his face tinged with hope, glanced up from the floor, but she would not meet his eyes. Dispassionately, she extended her hand, signaling her warriors, pointing to the one she had just gifted. "His life and also his punishment. Such is your fate as counselor; as you give poor advice, you have made a poor bargain."

Padrec gave a mangled cry as the warriors turned to where Anii pointed, to Toroya. The startled xenologist, stumbling back from her in disbelief, tumbled down the few remaining steps in a heap of orange robes. "No, Anii—no!" Padrec cried, beseeching her. "It was me—punish me! Not him!"

But To-roya had ceased to be of use to her now that the Strangers, but for a few, were gone. As Padrec struggled against his bonds and the warriors holding him, begging Anii to spare the other man, several warriors bore down upon Toroya with their spears, pinning him to the floor and severing his throat, cutting off his mortal scream in a spray of blood. True to the Queen's directions, they killed him quickly.

Padrec heard his own cries of anguish resounding from the walls as, awash with a pain too great to bear, he was forced to his knees in the spreading, still warm pool of Toroya's blood. Feeling that blood, spilled only to punish him, as it soaked into his clothes, was more than he could stand, and Padrec broke down uncontrollably, begging them not to kill any more, to kill him instead . . . that he was the one they should punish. Only then, sobbing, did he see that that was exactly what she was doing. She was cutting him to pieces . . . Samuro Toroya alone of anyone had wanted to be his friend, in the end had wanted to save him . . . had wanted to stay on Ibis. He had survived crash and slaughter, had tried to understand their captors—and now they had killed him. Had killed him for no other reason than to terrorize a man for an act which, had he known of it, he would have stopped him from doing ... *and now he's dead, he's dead because he couldn't keep me from this ...*

Anii gestured to Hli. "Chain him," she said.

She watched, cold-faced, as Padrec's hands were freed and placed before him on blocks brought in for that purpose and bands of metal hammered about his wrists. Around the room, the onlooking humans watched in horror and bleak sympathy, knowing that now indeed the Queen's favorite was feeling the pain they had always known, that for him it was just beginning ... Numb, Padrec did not fight the bonds as they were fastened to his wrists; he was too empty of sense to feel them, as if that part of him had died and was not able to experience the horror of what was happening to him. He still had not grasped it all, the blood soaking his knees, his hands, the memory forever burned into his mind of Toroya's horror and disbelief as the subjects of his scientific obsession plunged their spears into his chest and shoulders, holding him still to cut his throat.

He said Ibis was all he had ever hoped to find, except, dear God, it found us first.

But the pain of shackles biting into his wrists forced him to focus on reality and, drained even of hope, he gazed up at Anii in mute despair, unable to plead for himself, knowing she would not hear him if he did. He had forgotten that she was not a woman, that she did not love as women loved. She was nomari, a queen, and beautiful ... and this was his punishment, to be reminded of it with all the savagery of which she was capable.

"For rebellion against the nomari, the punishment is death," she told him, her words cutting into the dull haze of his reason. "Since it pleases me that you should live, I have taken in your stead the life of another of your kind. This leaves only your other crime—that of disobedience to me. For that, and for betraying my trust in you, you have ceased to deserve my kindness. You are a slave and shall be beaten as a slave, that others may see the price of rebellion. One life and half of another. No Stranger shall ever again want to taste the justice of the nomari. Hli—" She turned from him to her subservient. "Take him to the common ground and place him there for all to see. He is to be whipped. Two thousand lashes."

Padrec tried to hold himself steady but he felt the blood drain to his knees. Two thousand lashes! He doubted he could stand two hundred . . .

Even Hli hesitated. "It is too harsh. It will kill him!"

"I want to be certain he feels it. Do what I say."

Two workers, their fingers like many-banded cuffs of living metal on his arms, dragged him away, not even allowing him the dignity of walking. Such was his fear, he doubted that he could. Whipped—. Terrans had long since abolished corporal punishment, did not permit any human being to deliberately harm or mutilate another . . . his own mother had never laid a hand on him . . . *This can't be happening to me. I'm a human being, not an animal . . . I love her . . .* On the sunlit platform of the common place Padrec stumbled as he was shoved against a massive column of stone and his chained hands bound to rings on either side. The workers roughly peeled his Terran garments from his body, leaving him in his single undergarment, his back bare to the hot sun as murmurs rose from the Ibisian audience. Always before, except in the privacy of a queen's chamber, the Strangers had been kept covered. The rough pillar, hewn from a single block of flinty black stone, dug its sharp edges into his cheek, burned his face as he clung to it, eyes closed, wanting only to have it over, one way or another. *Where is she?* he wondered. *Is she watching this?* He had seen, as he had been dragged onto the platform, several queens seated within a covered enclosure at his back, looking on with eager anticipation. Of what? Of torture, of blood? Did they wonder what a Stranger sounded like when he screamed? Was that what she wanted from him? To hear him beg for mercy, throw himself at her feet so that she could pick him up again? The warrior chosen for the task un-coiled a length of supple reed, slapped it several times upon the platform and then, suddenly, without warn-ing, brought it down upon his back. That first lash licked his skin with a tongue of searing agony more hellish than any he had ever thought to feel. The second was worse. Each lash after that was a tendril of fire that wrapped around his ribs and crushed the breath from his lungs, pain that clawed at his throat, screams he desperately strangled, determined that no one, not them, not *her*, should have the pleasure of hearing him cry out. In the silence, the voice of the lash laid bare the muscle over backbone and ribs with rhythmic violence, challenged only by the rasp of his chains on the stone as his hands, knotted with pain, twisted in the grip of sharp-edged metal cuffs and he allowed the force of the blows to crush his body to the stone, trying without success, to become stone him-self. The pain made his legs buckle, only his chains holding him upright. *The flesh and blood of another world—what does it matter? She doesn't care if she kills me . . . she doesn't care that I came back, that I love her. All she wants is to hear me beg. . . .*

After the forty-eighth lash, he did not care. He had never been particularly brave, had never had to be . . . he did not have the fortitude, the training, to endure much pain. He was alone, tortured . . . his fate to be decided by a woman who would do this to him until he relented, gave in, owned that his life was no longer his, but hers. . . . The sound that broke from his throat cried out surrender as much as agony, for he called out her name as they shattered his spirit as well as his body, breaking him in the only way they understood it. He barely heard his own scream of agony and despair—for him it was drowned out by the sounds of the whip and blood rushing into his skull, and his descent into that world beyond pain and breath where he could not know or care that the lashings were stopped and his bindings released, allowing him to fall to the platform. Even as he slid from his chains, the world turned black.

Hli turned to Anii, who had watched each blow from the shadows, her dispassion chilling to all who saw her gold-crowned, crimson-clad figure at the back of the others, her eyes fixed on the platform where the Stranger was being punished. Only Hli, who knew her best, could see the tears unspilled in her regal eyes, and when the Stranger had called her name, she was not surprised when Anii had ordered the lashing stopped, in her own heart unable to bear more. "He will live, royal one," Hli said from where she knelt at Padrec's side. "It was but the pain which caused it—"

Pain. Anii tried not to remember the times she had promised never to cause Pa-dric pain. And now . . . she had ordered this pain, only to have him call on her with the last conscious breath that was in him. How had he stood so much? Gentle Pa-dric, who knew not hardship nor pain . . . Even now those who watched looked to see if she would order him revived and the punishment continued. Looking at him, his wrists cruelly chained and bleeding, his body bloodied by the lash of her royal anger, she knew that he had been punished enough. That cry, filled with all the anguish of his loss, had moved her at last, purging all wish to hurt him more. She understood what he had done. He had given the Strangers their freedom, given them their lives and that of his young one to be raised among them and then . . . *You sent them from you, that you might be with me. That is why you returned.* She had seen it in his eyes, the manner of his returning, this gift of his victory: that his people no longer stood between them. Pa-dric loved her, loved her enough to depart his own kind, the female who bore his young, and return to her, surely knowing he must face her anger, maybe even this . . . only a few days before, possessed by a passion she had not understood, moved by the warring needs within him, he had pleaded with her to free the Strangers, knowing that if she did not, it would fall upon him to do this—that he would be forced to choose between them. She had refused, and he had chosen to drive that spear into her heart.

Well, she had given it back to him. It was enough.

"He has learned his lesson. Take him to my chambers and tend him there," she told Hli tautly. "The Strangers are soft, and cannot bear much punishment."

"He deserves more, for having stolen our Strangers from us," Bhi'hia argued. "Shall he suffer no change of station? The slave defied you. Give him to another?"

"Why, if it pleases me to keep him?" Anii faced her subordinates smoothly, her confidence unshaken. She had expected such a demand before all was done. "He will be much chastened, and obedient enough. I will not sacrifice my ease to replace your loss. Pa-dric has been punished for his deed. He need not pay again because your cruelty caused your Es-dan not to want to stay with you, as Ranlii's Ro-len did, or Iria's Andru. And Pa-dric himself chose to return to me. No, if you could not keep your own Stranger, you shall not then ask for mine. Or do you forget that I am Queen of this nom?"

And no Queen ever allowed others to take or possess her drones. Or her Stranger. Sexual possessiveness by natural extension included any male she claimed as a mate. Sweeter yet was the fact she wished it so. Bhi'hia and the other queens understood her motive and did not challenge her decision. No touch of weakness must mar her cold façade, nor diminish her sway over their lives. All in the nom, nomari and Strangers alike, had seen her power and now they had seen the consequences of opposing it. Pa-dric's suffering had served its purpose. As she turned to leave, the nomari bowed deeply as they parted to let her pass, and the eyes of the Strangers followed her like those of trapped beasts, of slaves who did not recognize the mercy behind the terrible punishment they had witnessed.

But as the great sun set and splashed its ruddy amber light across her chamber, Anii allowed a deep and secret joy to come and fill her hollow vessel to the rim again. Her Stranger—*hers*—had returned to her! To-roya's last words had given her the key: she had lost the Strangers as slaves, but she had gained Pa-dric's willing heart. He had told her the price—and he had paid it. Her heart throbbed with the pain of knowing what it had cost him to make that gift. *I have hurt you—because you hurt me. . . .* She glanced up from her thoughts when the heavy silk curtains across the entrance to her private chamber were brushed aside, and Hli entered, fresh from tending Pa-dric's wounds. "The Strangers are delicate," the subservient complained straight away. "His skin cuts as easily as the skin that forms on milk!"

Anii felt her own skin pale. "Is it so bad then?"

Hli scowled, but not unkindly. "Worse than it should be. But he shall not scar so badly; the salve will see to that—and you were wise to have him whipped *as'falna*." She used the proper phrase for the practice of beating disobedient queens with whips not having barbs which left deep gouges in the skin. Once her initial anger had cooled, Hli had recognized that the Stranger had planned to spare her life and those of the warriors, and her stance toward him had softened such that she did not wish to see him ruined, deeming that his actions bespoke of more intelligence than she had given him credit for. "But he will not stay abed. He waits outside to speak with you."

"He dares that?"

"And more. What worse can you do to him but kill him? And that he does not fear."

Turning proudly, still courting her anger, Anii said, "Let him enter. If he does not fear the lash, then let him fear my tongue." But she watched the curtain with an intensity akin to fear, wondering what her reaction would be to this first sight of him. How brave he was, or foolish, to tempt her royal anger! And yet her heart ached to see again the gentle beauty she had cherished—and to know that she could still cause in him something more than suffering.

*   *   *

Pa-dric entered between the arms of his guards, who forced him to his knees before her and departed, dismissed by Hli. "Speak," Hli said. "She waits."

He spoke slowly, not raising his eyes, picking his words from a mind numbed by too many horrors but struggling for a purpose that would keep him from sinking into despair. "I wish to claim Toroya's body. I want to bury him."

Anii studied her lover for a long time in silence. His looks had suffered; he looked strained and pale, physically sick, probably from the pain of his lashing, the still oozing marks of which showed through the fabric covering his back. The shapeless slave's garment which hid the worst of her abuses did not hide his chains, however, or the ugly sores where the metal had rubbed his skin raw at the wrists. He was broken, yes, in body . . . and yet he dared to request her permission to perform a ritual of his race, knowing it might provoke her to punish him again. He feared her, and yet he feared his own conscience more. And it was that conscience which would bind him to her now, and forever, if only she could find it in her heart to forgive him.

How lovely he is, even now. Slave's rags cannot hide the beauty of his spirit, nor can whips drive from him this freedom he gives himself to choose. Keep him—and find pleasure in his choice.

"To-roya served me better than you served him," she said, not wanting him to know so soon that her anger melted with each moment his presence reminded her of what she had yet to gain. "He died as the other Strangers died, and you shall bury him as you buried the others, in bare ground, with your hands. And then you shall return to me."

He looked up at her then, daring the fragile hope of a man with nothing left to lose except his last reason for living. She crossed to him and her hand drifted soft as a lover's touch to his cheek. "Go," she said. "Do this thing. Then we will see what happens."

By torchlight and in darkness Padrec buried Samuro

Toroya. Hli found for him a place where the ground, still damp with the last rain, was soft and there in the shadow of the nom he used his bare and fettered hands to scrape a mean hole in the earth to hold the body of his friend. Enough warriors surrounded him to hold ten times his number safely captive, but not one moved to help him. Anii had decreed that he was to do whatever his ritual required—so long as he did it alone. The scabs forming on his back broke and bloodstains spotted the light robe he wore, the pain there still raw, hindering his every movement; but worse was the pain in his hands, the blood which, oozing from beneath the manacles he wore, had begun to run down the lengths of chain which bound him. He only wished he could mind, could make it matter. But in his mind even the worst agonies could be but penance for a life caught on the crosshairs of his choices. Toroya's fate had been bound up with his from the time Anii had captured him, fixed in orbit around the lovers like a satellite which, daring to come too near, had been consumed. Inexorable as that fate had been, Padrec wept for knowing that Toroya's death had sealed all their fates.

My friend. His last chance at human friendship, shattered along with the rest of his dream, ripped out of his hands before he could touch it ... the others would look to him, he would guide them, comfort them, offer himself to their pain—but they would not be able to share his, or ease the burden of being assimilated into an alien culture. Sam would have been able to do that.

Briefly he thought of Rubinsky, the sleds speeding east under three moons, seeking a new life beyond the noms. They were free. Rubinsky, Stan, Janelle and the child he would never see—a double gift to them. He had provided them an opportunity to fashion their own lives, their own future, and then he had chosen for himself. In freeing them he had freed himself, had set the human wheel to spinning. All choices led in a circle. In the end they were all doomed to become part of Ibis. Tears from his eyes fell onto Samuro Toroya's still, dead face.

Oh, Sam—I never knew you . . . but you were dazzled by Anii, blinded by her love for me—and mine for her. You forgot your own humanity in thinking that it could be like that for the others. . . .

And not for the first time he wondered if it would ever be like that again for himself.

His eyes drifted up to the shadowy tower of the nom, light pocked and crowned with sentinel torches, beckoning to him to enter. And when he did, he knew, he would never leave again. He would live out his life in that maze of loathsome pits and luxurious prisons, the hovels of human slavery and the forbidden sensuality of silk-lined nuptial chambers where the golden queens of Ibis would claim their human mates. For there would be others, new captives and those born to their fates, the men who even now pleasured their mistresses in some hidden chamber high in that light-crowned tower. Tearing himself from the sight, he met Hli's torchlit eyes and saw reflected back at him the knowledge that he recognized his fate. Be content, Stranger, she seemed to be saying, for you there will be a second chance—.

And in that knowledge he shoveled with his chained and bleeding hands the dirt onto Samuro Toroya's grave, the final resting place of the man who had wanted to stay on Ibis.

Anii moved from the window where she had been standing for hours, her eyes fixed on the torches gathered on the plain below, their flames guttering in the building winds of another storm. Down there, in the midst of her warriors, with Hli standing guard, Padric would bury his dead and, with that sacred ritual, she hoped, the last remnants of the world he would never see again. She would see to it that he did not. Nothing would remain to remind him, except the stars. They would always remind him, and her, of where he had come from. Perhaps, in time, she would understand it. But the strange devices in which she had indulged him and which had contributed so greatly to his disobedience had been or were being destroyed, as was every other piece of the Strangers' alien machinery that had cost her so much. His garment, though she would always cherish the memory of the way he wore it, she had ordered burned. Only the drawings he had made did she leave him—she found she could not bear to destroy anything he had created. And the delicate drawings were of the flowers of Mi, and the plants that grew in the fields surrounding the nom . . . and though he would sketch others, they would be of plants her warriors brought to him, for she would not let him travel again outside the nom.

Beset by weariness, feeling now the sleepless night, she rubbed her back, easing the ache of pregnancy. Already the young stirred within her, the next generation of nomari rulers and warriors, soon to be born tiny but complete. To-roya had said that female Strangers bore their single young for nearly a full turn—. She sighed, seeing the imprudence of having had the old one killed. He had been intelligent, and useful in his way. There was so much she did not know about

220

Strangers ... ah, but she had been angry, for it had
been To-roya who had persuaded her that Pa-dric must
mate, must be allowed to visit his kind, and that
counsel had cost her dearly. To-roya had served his
own ends before hers. She would give Pa-dric nothing
by which to hold on to the old ways, none to turn to
but herself ...

*You are the male, and the male must serve. I forgot
and this is the price I pay for it, that I must force upon
you these reminders. Tonight, beloved, none stand between us but memories—and in time those too will
fade. I accept the gift. Soon, when all have seen that
you are chastened, I will have you freed from your cruel
chains ... but you will wear the bracelets forever, so
that you and all will remember that you are mine.*

For she was determined that the Strangers who
remained in the nom, and those who would yet be
brought to live there, must have no doubt as to their
place in the order. The queens of the nomari would
channel their nuptial madness with human mates—
only the gathering would now be more difficult. But
wherever the Strangers had fled to, in time the nomari
would find them. Already there were rumors of captives in the eastern noms.

She turned again to the dark veil of night outside
her chamber window. Below, winding across the flat
dark land, she could see a line of glowing torches
filing back into the nom, returning.

DAW

The really great fantasy books are
published by DAW:

Andre Norton

LORE OF THE WITCH WORLD	UE2012—$3.50
HORN CROWN	UE2051—$3.50
PERILOUS DREAMS	UE1749—$2.50

C.J. Cherryh

THE DREAMSTONE	UE2013—$3.50
THE TREE OF SWORDS AND JEWELS	UE1850—$2.95

Lin Carter

DOWN TO A SUNLESS SEA	UE1937—$2.50
DRAGONROUGE	UE1982—$2.50

M.A.R. Barker

THE MAN OF GOLD	UE1940—$3.95

Michael Shea

NIFFT THE LEAN	UE1783—$2.95
THE COLOR OUT OF TIME	UE1954—$2.50

B.W. Clough

THE CRYSTAL CROWN	UE1922—$2.75

NEW AMERICAN LIBRARY
P.O. Box 999, Bergenfield, New Jersey 07621

Please send me the DAW Books I have checked above. I am enclosing
$_____ (check or money order—no currency or C.O.D.'s).
Please include the list price plus $1.00 per order to cover handling
costs.

Name _____

Address _____

City _____ State _____ Zip Code _____
Please allow at least 4 weeks for delivery

DAW

Unforgettable science fiction
by DAW's own stars!

M. A. FOSTER

☐ THE WARRIORS OF DAWN   UE1994—$3.25
☐ THE GAMEPLAYERS OF ZAN   UE1993—$3.95
☐ THE MORPHODITE   UE2017—$2.95
☐ THE DAY OF THE KLESH   UE2016—$2.95

C. J. CHERRYH

☐ 40,000 IN GEHENNA   UE1952—$3.50
☐ DOWNBELOW STATION   UE1987—$3.50
☐ VOYAGER IN NIGHT   UE1920—$2.95
☐ WAVE WITHOUT A SHORE   UE1957—$2.50

JOHN BRUNNER

☐ TIMESCOOP   UE1966—$2.50
☐ THE JAGGED ORBIT   UE1917—$2.95

ROBERT TREBOR

☐ AN XT CALLED STANLEY   UE1865—$2.50

JOHN STEAKLEY

☐ ARMOR   UE1979—$3.95

JO CLAYTON

☐ THE SNARES OF IBEX   UE1974—$2.75

DAVID J. LAKE

☐ THE RING OF TRUTH   UE1935—$2.95

NEW AMERICAN LIBRARY
P.O. Box 999, Bergenfield, New Jersey 07621

Please send me the DAW Books I have checked above. I am enclosing
$_____ (check or money order—no currency or C.O.D.'s).
Please include the list price plus $1.00 per order to cover handling
costs.

Name _____

Address _____

City _____ State _____ Zip Code _____
Allow 4-6 weeks for delivery.

DAW

A. E. VAN VOGT
in DAW Editions:

DAW BOOKS are represented by the publishers of Signet and Mentor Books, THE NEW AMERICAN LIBRARY, INC.

NEW AMERICAN LIBRARY
P.O. Box 999, Bergenfield, New Jersey 07621

Please send me the DAW Books I have checked above. I am enclosing
$_____ (check or money order—no currency or C.O.D.'s).
Please include the list price plus $1.00 per order to cover handling
costs.

Name _____

Address _____

City _____ State _____ Zip Code _____

Please allow at least 4 weeks for delivery